Katahdin Drowning

A Killdeer Farm Mystery

Janet Morgan

Goose River Press
Waldoboro, Maine

Library of Congress Card Number: 2013936857

ISBN: 978-1-59713-139-1

First Printing, 2013

Published by
Goose River Press
3400 Friendship Road
Waldoboro ME 04572
e-mail: gooseriverpress@roadrunner.com
www.gooseriverpress.com

Acknowledgements

Several people are to be thanked for their assistance with my book. Ken Gilman traveled to Baxter State Park and to Millinocket's park information center on more than one occasion for me to confirm my facts about the park.

Special thanks to Susan Connelly, Christine Poitras, and Marjorie Pooler for their editorial and proofreading skills.

Wiscasset Public Library Director Pamela Dunning provided my photograph.

The Wiscasset Public Library Writing Group encouraged me to write and helped me along the way to deciding where to take this book. Group member Jackie Lowell was especially helpful in being the first one to read and give suggestions on how to make *Katahdin Drowning* a success.

1

What sights of ugly death within my eyes!
—Richard III, 1.4.23

A peaceful country road loomed ahead in an inky darkness that descends only after the sun has set and before the moon rises. The woman stood motionless in an attempt to get her bearings, but before she could acclimate herself to the pitch black, a set of headlights materialized. She was blinded as a vehicle burst straight towards her.

She had no time to react before the car sliced through her body, leaving her intact, yet cold, very cold. Her whole body ached with icy intensity—inside and out—as she realized she was still standing. She scarcely had time to wonder if she was still among the living before gravel bit into her bare feet, bringing a moment of clarity.

In the short second when the headlights had bounced off the nearby trees, she'd seen something terrifying. The image had made no sense, for it was dark within the car, yet she had seen the face of pure evil behind the driver's wheel. The maniacal face of Alfonse Sweetzer sneered back at her. The eyes glowing through the windshield of the big blue Cadillac plunged into the very core of her being.

Chilling though all this was, her mind quickly flew to what she had seen before the car had finished its pass through her body. That vision had been worse, much worse: a long, deep dent in the hood ascended to a cracked windshield. Encrusted in the cracks, blood—so much blood—

smeared its way across the top of the car.

She had no idea how long she stood frozen to the spot. Her body turned to stone as the moon finally lifted into the sky, illuminating the tree tops and creating a tranquility that slowly thawed her arctic body. It was then that her mind began to function once more. *I must do something,* she thought, as she propelled her feet forward. She staggered on, all the while wondering what the man had hit. Could it have been a deer? It had to have been something big, for whatever it was had been rolled over the hood, onto the windshield, and over the top of the large car. It wasn't long before she found out. On the side of that serene-appearing country road was a mangled motorcycle. A blue and gold helmet—cracked and scraped raw—still spun on its top just yards from where the motorcycle had come to rest.

A blinding hail of memories suddenly invaded her soul. Her throat closed. She could not breathe. She knew what would come next. She knew the ragged heap of clothing in the ditch held her husband's body, shrouded in death. She dare not look. She had to escape. As she turned to run, she screamed.

2

It was the owl that shrieked, the fatal bellman,
Which gives the stern'st good night.
—Macbeth, 2.2.3-4

Jessie Tyler gripped her face with ice-cold hands. It was too much to bear. Wild, uncontrollable sobs wracked her body as ugly thoughts thundered through her overtaxed mind. Would the horror never end? Would the man in the car never stop torturing her? After all, he was now dead and true justice had been meted out when Hades—in the form of a library statue—had struck Alfonse Sweetzer over the head. And yet he still haunted her.

The night's silence was cut by a horrific screech. Startled, Jessie attempted to fly from her bed, but she couldn't move. She was trapped! She struggled until she realized she was wrapped in a sleeping bag.

"What's going on?" Dara Kane's sleep-filled voice asked from nearby.

"What was that?" Jessie was breathless from exertion.

"You're the librarian. Haven't you ever heard a screech owl? Go back to sleep and stop wiggling around." Dara lifted her arm and noted the time on her glow-in-the-dark watch; it was only two-thirty. "We'll be getting up before you know it. You'd better get some rest," she whispered.

Jessie Tyler and her friend Dara Kane had motored up to Baxter State Park in northern Maine yesterday morning. In another day, they would be climbing Katahdin to stand atop Baxter Peak, the highest point in Maine.

Jessie tried to take her friend's advice, but she couldn't

get back to sleep after her recurring nightmare. She was afraid she would just slip back into the awful dream that frequently visited her ever since her husband's death.

In an attempt to relax, Jessie thought back on their arrival less than twenty-four hours earlier. This was Dara's first trip north. It was funny how this was her friend's first venture into the interior of the state. But, then again, maybe it wasn't as unusual as Jessie thought. So many visitors believed that the state ended in Maine's largest city of Portland. Little did they know that they had barely touched the surface of what the state had to offer. Even most Mainers rarely ventured inland, presumably because the largest part of the state's population had settled near the coast. Yes, Maine's coast was beautiful, but its interior held much charm as well.

Jessie rolled over and pulled her sleeping bag closer as she thought about how she, with Dara as her passenger, had driven her Jeep north towards the park with her son, Jonathan, following in his truck. His passengers had been Gina Day and Willa Royce. The group had long-standing reservations for three lean-tos at Katahdin Stream Campground at the base of the Hunt Trail—also known as the final leg of the Appalachian Trail.

Dara had been hyped during the whole trip north. She had fairly bounced in her seat when they exited Interstate 95 in Newport in order to take a less-traveled route to the park. "Wow! Look at that!" she said every time she saw something new. And it was a scenic way to travel, which is why they preferred to travel northeast through the small towns of Corinna, Dexter, Dover-Foxcroft, Milo, and Brownville before arriving in Millinocket. There they connected up with the Golden Road, which led to the park.

Soon afterwards, they were waiting to produce their passes at the park's southern entrance. Togue Pond Gate had always held a special thrill for Jessie. It signaled the entry into the realm of another world, nestled into the interior of one of Maine's most spectacular regions. One would think that the scenery would become repetitive after a while, but this was not the case. All two hundred thousand plus acres embraced nature at its best. The diversity of the land spoke for it. With forty-eight mountains, sixty-four ponds and streams, and a plethora of wildlife, no true nature lover ever tired of Baxter State Park.

Various trails led to the interior and made it possible to ascend many of the park's mountains. Jessie wondered what it had been like to be one of the first to discover this beautiful part of her home state. American Indians had undoubtedly been the first to traverse the waterways in bateaus. Jessie reflected on how thrilling that must have been.

Yesterday, however, she'd been content to see the late morning sun shine on the bright green leaves of countless trees and the various shades of blue glistening from ponds and streams as they passed sight after beautiful sight on their way down the tote road towards Katahdin Stream Campground. In her mind's eye, Jessie recalled her joy when they had finally arrived at the campground.

After Jessie had parked her car, she gazed around, noting how little it had changed since her last visit with her two Jonathans. That visit had been the fall before Alfonse Sweetzer had run down her husband. But she wouldn't let that spoil this visit for her companions; she was determined to focus on more pleasant things. Shade trees hung down here and there, some over the shelters that campers would make their home during their stay. It was truly beautiful here. Jessie never tired of looking at it, and she knew her thoughts had been mirrored when she'd heard Dara exclaim, "Wow, this is great!"

Jessie couldn't share Dara's enthusiasm when she saw 'Tyler & Son' written on the side of her son's blue work truck when it pulled in beside her. The logo always reminded Jessie that her two Jonathans had been denied their dream to always work together in their carpentry business.

She had taken her best shot at putting on a happy face as the newcomers voiced their appreciation. Once they had settled down to begin unpacking, Jessie had tried to shake away the pain as she headed for the ranger station to register with the park ranger. As she strode over Katahdin Stream's narrow footbridge, she noted that the water was higher than usual. Crystal clear mountain run-off slithered past the bridge on its path south. Small ripples rushed past on small caps that pooled around the rocks rising out of the water.

Once the business of checking in had been completed, the group inspected their lean-tos. Jessie and Dara had one. Gina and Willa, the two oldest daughters of Jessie's neighbor and friend Cassie, would share the second. The third one was for Jonathan. Jessie had been thrilled to discover that their lean-tos backed upon the stream. She vowed to enjoy this trip.

The memory of husband Jonathan's handsome face came back to her. A smile touched her heart, for she knew her husband would be with her in so many ways. The whisper of the stream relaxed Jessie into dozing off. She felt his arms around her as she slept the remainder of the night without incident.

Morning came all too soon, however, as it frequently does when camping. Jessie sighed with disappointment when she realized that her husband's arms no longer enveloped her. It was Dara who shared her lean-to. Dara, who was more than ten years her junior, groaned.

Jessie had to laugh, but she ignored Dara's comment on how uncomfortable their overnight shelter was; she just smiled. She smelled coffee brewing. Any day with coffee held promise. "So, okay, maybe I'm a bit stiff, too." She groaned as she rubbed her lower back. "I'm getting too old for this stuff. What's your excuse?"

Dara's laughed response was bit off when a howl of anger wailed across Katahdin Stream Campground.

3

The screech-owl, screeching loud,
Puts the wretch that lies in woe
In remembrance of a shroud.
　　　　　　—A Midsummer Night's Dream,
　　　　　　　　　　5.1.376-378

"Eeek!" A shrill squeal resonated throughout the campground just before a petite blonde woman erupted from a lean-to. "This is unacceptable!"

Across the stream, Jessie and Dara turned from their campfire to see what the commotion was all about. They sipped steaming coffee and watched in fascination as people came running from all directions in response to the loud outburst.

Jonathan, Gina, and Willa were among those who dashed forward from nearby. After setting a pot of coffee on the campfire to brew, Jonathan had taken the girls on a short excursion to show them some of the flora they shouldn't trample on during their upcoming hike. "What's up, Mom?" Jonathan asked over the din of the woman's continued screams.

Before Jessie could think up a response—for she truly had no idea what the problem was—the park ranger strode forward on reluctant feet.

"You!" The woman stalked over to the ranger and stretched her slight form up towards his face. "What kind of place is this? There are dirty, stinking varmints in my shelter. You get them out, and I mean now! And," she said as she gasped for breath, "I want my shelter scoured while I'm gone. Do something useful around here. Must I do everything? That bathroom is a disgrace. I had to tack my own curtains

7

to the walls to make it fit to use. Thank goodness I was smart enough to bring them. I can't believe you people don't have better facilities."

"You did *what?*" the ranger asked.

"Are you deaf? I said that I made my bathroom halfway fit for human habitation, you dolt. And by the way, I put a lock on it. Other people were trying to use it. Of all the nerve!" Veronica Verne stomped her feet with impatience.

"But, but you can't do that," the young park employee said. "Everyone shares the outhouses here. You can't keep others from using what few facilities we have to offer."

Jessie looked towards the two outhouses standing nearby and sure enough, the woman had adorned one of them with a padlock. She wondered what the ranger was thinking when she saw him sigh. She could tell that there would be no harmony in his campground as long as this woman was present.

During the altercation, Jessie tried to recall if she had seen this tiny blonde when they had arrived the day before. She was sure she had not, but there was something familiar about her. She was truly beautiful, but right now her anger blotted out the stunning features of her face.

As the woman continued to scream, the ranger shook his head and walked towards the lean-to that had been abandoned with a vengeance. Everyone stood around watching with bated breath—all but the screaming one—as the lean young ranger crawled into the recently vacated lean-to. And then the funniest thing happened: from within the three-sided enclosure, the ranger began to laugh.

Oh, Jessie cringed. *This is not going to end well.* As soon as the blonde heard unabated laughter coming from her overnight shelter, she began to shake with fury.

The ranger backed out from the three-sided enclosure, off the wooden platform of the lean-to, and turned to face the angry woman. The ranger stood struggling to control his emotions as he held two field mice by their tails. The mice dangling from between the ranger's fingers began to twitch in an attempt to get away. Granted, many women were afraid of rodents, but this isn't the type of wildlife that most people familiar with the camping world feared.

Jessie began to wonder what this woman would have done had it been a larger, more dangerous creature. A baby bear, for instance, would have been something to dread, since it would undoubtedly have meant a very large and very angry mother could be nearby.

Jessie turned towards Dara to share the moment, but her friend was gone. Looking around, she saw Dara inside the lean-to, rearranging their already straightened bedding. Jessie had no time to wonder at this uncharacteristic action when she heard the snickers of less circumspect campers. *The stranger doesn't like this,* Jessie noted, when she saw the woman's frame tense with renewed anger. Before the small, yet fit younger woman could snap out her displeasure, however, the ranger's face settled into a serious expression as he began to explain how many woodland creatures frequented the campground.

"Nothing," the woman said through gritted teeth, "I want to hear nothing from you, young man!" She spun around and glared at the others before turning back to the ranger. "I paid good money to come here, and I expect quality service. Someone with my reputation deserves the utmost respect." She took a deep breath and said, "Don't you ever clean these buildings? I bet there's a whole nest of those dirty varmints in there. You go back in and get the rest of them, and do not try to tell me there were only two in there."

Just who is she? Jessie pondered exactly what everyone within hearing distance must also be wondering. Well, almost everyone, for when she once more gazed into her lean-to, she saw a flicker of recognition cross Dara's face before Jessie's friend turned away in an attempt to hide a smirk of satisfaction.

4

If you prick us, do we not bleed?
If you tickle us, do we not laugh?
If you poison us, do we not die?
And if you wrong us, shall we not revenge?
　　　　　　—The Merchant of Venice,
　　　　　　　　　　　3.1.64-67

Instinct had told the ranger that this woman would be trouble. From the first moment Ranger Jerome Goodroe had set eyes on her, he'd known. Veronica Verne had sashayed into the park as though she owned the place. She had not impressed him. He had, of course, dealt with people like this before, but this woman had pushed him to the limit.

Goodroe had been a ranger in Maine's largest state park ever since he'd graduated from college. He began his training at the more remote site of Russell Pond. After months of training, he had won his first post at Nesowadnehunk Field Campground. His hard work there during the next five years had been appreciated. He had been in line for a promotion when the ranger assigned to Katahdin Stream had retired. Goodroe had applied for and received the position. In the process, the twenty-eight year old had secured one of the most desirable ranger posts in Maine. The only drawback to working as a ranger at Baxter State Park was that few people worked here during the winter months. His was a seasonal job, but he was single and his needs were few.

He didn't mind that he'd been sent dashing from his cabin to see why that horrible woman was screaming like a banshee. He couldn't help but smirk inwardly, however, when he had seen what all the fuss had been about. Field mice! Imagine screaming over a couple of field mice in the great wilds of the northern Maine woods. *It's just plain stu-*

pid, he thought. He had to admit, though, that he'd seen many people go ballistic over other wild creatures. Snakes, for example, were not popular. A snake slithering across the grass with its body winding back and forth frequently elicited quite a stir.

The ranger shook his head and pondered on how the woman had threatened to get him fired just because he'd been unable to swallow that initial beam of amusement. The young man knew little about the unpleasant woman, but she acted as though she might have enough pull to get him fired. It could become a test of wills, should it come down to a battle between a television personality and a mere state employee. He'd been told who she was and that she might have special needs, but he didn't realize the danger he faced—at least not yet.

Veronica Verne was annoyed by more than a nest of rodents. Upon her arrival at the campground, she'd been irritated to discover that she had not been assigned a bunkhouse. Her television director had made an initial venture to the park to check out logistics of filming the star in a natural setting. He, in his infinite wisdom, had decided that the sight of her emerging from a lean-to each morning would be much more picturesque on film. *Well, at least they hadn't assigned her to a stupid tent,* she snorted.

That director would be fired once she returned to Boston. She didn't think much of his marvelous ideas. He wasn't the one sleeping with wild and dangerous creatures. She was used to being pampered. Naturally the sight of those terrible rodents staring into her face as she had awoken was more than anyone should have to endure. Those people in the park were dimwitted idiots. Let them wake up—as she had done— to see four beady red orbs staring into her face. As those frightful eyes had dissolved into two faces, naturally she had screamed.

Janet Morgan

She was a well-known television personality who had the hottest exercise show on a nationally syndicated network. She had arrived at stardom after only a few years of scratching her way to the top. She would let no one tell her that she wasn't in shape. She was in her prime, even though she ignored the fact that she had passed her thirtieth birthday more than two years ago.

She was young and men were always falling over one another in their desire to get closer to her. That schmuck of a husband she was married to didn't deserve her, which is why she was at Baxter State Park. Once she had climbed this stupid mountain, she would post on her blog how she had done it in record time. And it was a bonus that this was the final leg of the Appalachian Trail.

Her no-good husband had only been sucking off her popularity during the two interminable years of their marriage. She was ready to dump him, television producer or not. His turn would come as soon as she left this horrible place. She grinned snidely as she recalled how she had already set her plan in motion.

But for now, she had to be careful with these bumpkins in rural Maine. Why, oh, why hadn't they found an easier stretch of the Appalachian Trail to film! Because the director of her show had said that this was the most prestigious part, that's why. And because the top of Katahdin—Baxter Peak— had the most beautiful sights she would ever see, he had assured her. Veronica had relented when she thought about how she would be queen of the universe when she was filmed standing at the top of the world. They would give her that promotion and her husband would be out on his ear.

And who cared if she planned to have a fling with this stupid cameraman! He must have thought himself clever when he'd rejected her advances last night, but just wait until tonight. She had plans. They would have a celebratory drink, and maybe she would put something in it, something to make him more amenable.

Katahdin Drowning

Just who did he think he was? Granted, he was handsome, but he was only a cameraman, for goodness sake. She'd crushed better men. She'd already put the first steps of her revenge into action. He could just say good-bye to his career.

5

*I'll be revenged on the
whole pack of you.*
—Twelfth Night, 5.1.37

Veronica Verne fumed. When she saw all the campers walk away as though dismissing her misfortune, she knew they were snickering behind her back. She would get even with them all, she vowed. She would show them, but first she would hike that stupid mountain. After the film was broadcast next week, they would be sorry they hadn't been nicer to her. As an added bonus, she would make sure her stupid cameraman filmed each and every one of them in an unflattering way.

She'd been advised to get an early start, but she hadn't planned to rush. After that pack of wild rodents had infested her lean-to, however, she decided she might as well get going, even though it was still early by her standards. That young ranger would be sorry, too, if he didn't have her sleeping place all cleaned out by the time she returned.

As she looked around, she spied her cameraman sitting on a rock drinking coffee and cooking his own breakfast. He hadn't even *tried* to help her in her moment of peril. Too bad she couldn't send him packing right now, but she needed him. She'd leave him here to be devoured by those rodents, but she needed him. But in a couple of days they would be back at the studio and he'd be history.

"You!" She barked out orders. "Coffee! Now! Stop being so lazy and get my hiking stuff. We can't laze around here all day, you slug. I pay you good money to do what I want, so

14

snap to it." When the cameraman held out a breakfast sandwich, Verne shoved it away.

"Just give me that," Verne said as she grabbed the mug of black coffee he had extended towards her other hand. While she sipped her coffee, she rebuffed another attempt to give her the sandwich.

"But you need this for energy," he tried to explain.

She whacked his arm away once more and the rejected sandwich spiraled out and landed in the dirt. After last evening's insult, she would *not* have him telling her what to do. She watched with disgust as two red squirrels fought over the discarded food.

By the time the squirrels had divided up the spoils, the cameraman had gulped down his own meal and left Verne to her liquid breakfast. She watched as he crawled into his lean-to, where all their gear had been stored. He retrieved Veronica's bag of clothing and pristine new hiking boots. He slung two new backpacks over his shoulders and returned to her campsite.

"I trust you're planning to carry one of those over each shoulder." She sneered when she spied the two backpacks.

"I can carry most of our supplies in one bag," he said, "but I also have my camera to cope with. Whether you like it or not, you'll have to carry the backpack filled with your bad weather gear."

"What! Me carry a bag? Ridiculous; besides, it's a nice day. I don't need all that stuff, and I will *not* be filmed with a foolish bag strapped to my back." She flicked aside the backpack, but grabbed her duffel bag, which she opened to remove a tank top and matching powder blue shorts. While she'd never been timid about showing off her beautiful body, she supposed she couldn't dress in public. These campers looked like absolute prudes to her, she decided, as she stepped over to her crude bathroom.

Moments later, she returned outside and began lacing up her new hiking boots. Once she was dressed to perfection, she looked around in a futile attempt to find a mirror. She shrugged. She knew the outfit accentuated her glowing tan skin. After adjusting her scrunchy socks on her perfectly formed legs, she crossed the short bridge separating her side of the campground from the others and strode towards the trail. She beamed with pleasure when she saw, but ignored, many people staring in her wake.

Just as she marched onto the path, she heard, "*Bertha?* Is that *you*, Bertha?" She flinched, but didn't miss a beat as she picked up the pace to leave all those unimportant people behind.

6

Ambition should be made of sterner stuff.
—Julius Caesar, 3.2.92

Evan Kinderhook did a double-take. Veronica Verne's cameraman was sure that the mousy man near the trailhead had been calling out to Verne. Could he *really* have been talking to *her?* Since miss high and mighty hadn't even slowed down, Kinderhook figured the man had been wrong. He shrugged, hitched his pack onto his back, and scooped up his camera. He was off and running. It took him some time to catch up to the careless fitness star because he had to stop and sign in for them both. She certainly hadn't bothered.

He quickened his pace once more, for he had to place himself ahead of Verne in order to get the shots she required for her television program. He was short of breath and puffing by the time he passed her, but he couldn't let up. He ran ahead, bent over to catch his breath, and then raised the camera. For almost three miles he kept up the stop, film, and dash off again routine.

It irked him to see her smile, but he had a job to do. He bet she loved keeping him hopping. He was sure she didn't care that he had to hike backwards much of the time. She never slowed down until they had reached a ledge where they must scale the face of a ten-foot ridge in order to reach the next part of the trail.

"Take a picture of me stretching up towards those bars," Veronica said, "then go up there." She pointed to the top of

17

the ledge. "Get some shots looking down at me." When he hadn't budged from the spot, she said, "Go on! Get up there now!" She rattled off the orders like a drill sergeant.

He complied. After he had finally accomplished all her demands, Verne said, "Now turn off that stupid camera and get back down here so you can lift me up. I certainly can't climb up there all by my self. I may be strong, but those bars are too high for me to reach." Because the cameraman—whose name Veronica still hadn't bothered to remember—didn't comply quickly enough, she yelled again. "Get to it, now!"

Luckily for Kinderhook, a couple of young men had seen and admired Ms. Verne. They flirted while they climbed up beyond her. Once on the top of the ridge, they pulled her up from above while Kinderhook shoved from below. She hadn't even attempted to use her feet to brace herself until she looked down and saw another man admiring her. Kinderhook gritted his teeth when he saw her preen as she pretended to climb. With one last boost, that part of the ordeal was over. Kinderhook climbed up to join her. By the time he stood atop the crest, Verne's two admirers were practically falling over themselves trying to impress her.

Once they had moved on, however, Veronica Verne, star of network television's exercise scene, had dropped all pretense of being pleasant. She pulled off her hiking boots and rubbed her sore feet. "Hey, you, make yourself useful. Massage my feet," she said to Kinderhook.

When she looked up towards where the other guys had gone, Kinderhook saw a frightened look cross her face. Before he could decide how to handle this new demand, she grabbed her boots. She quickly pulled them back on and laced them hurriedly before turning her back on the great mound of boulders they would soon have to climb. She shoved past him and scampered back down the rock face faster than anyone would have thought possible.

"Ms. Verne, where are you going?" Kinderhook called

down to her. Wondering if something had spooked her, he looked towards the mountaintop. There stood a tall man with hatred glowing in his eyes; he held up and shook a sheaf of papers in her direction. *This man must know her,* Kinderhook thought. No one else he had ever met had elicited such strong emotions as Veronica Verne.

She had apparently descended on her own, for he now heard her yelling from below. "Hey, you," she said as he pondered on what had made her change her mind about climbing Katahdin. "I'm talking to you." Hands on hips, she glowered up into his down-turned face.

"What?" He was puzzled. *Was their hike over?*

"Get up that mountain and film all the way to the top. I'll be expecting you back at camp soon. I don't have to do this stuff. I'm a star!" And that was the last time anyone admitted to seeing Veronica Verne alive again.

7

They will steal anything.

—Henry V, 3.2.41

Once the unreasonable woman had made her grand exit, everyone at the campground could relax again. Still, the celebrity had caused quite a stir.

"Well, that was something," Dara said. She shook her head with glee as she settled down in front of the campfire with her coffee. She already had her nose in a book when the next ruckus erupted.

"Will you look at this? My food's all scattered around." A man across the stream groaned. He had ignored the earlier goings on, but when he'd finally popped his head out from between his tent flaps, it was to a mess. Unfortunately for him, he hadn't read the park rules, so he had left all his food out of doors. At the sight of his cooler tipped upside down, he scampered outside to find most of its contents were missing. But there among the melting ice was the one thing he most despised: turkey bacon. "That stuff tastes nasty," he said to anyone who would listen. "But would my wife listen? And now we're stuck with it for breakfast, lunch, *and* supper."

"What are you yelling about?" the man's wife asked as she crawled from the tent.

"Well, dear, your turkey bacon's the only thing to survive the ravages of a vicious animal attack." His wife just smiled.

"What's so funny, Mom?" Jonathan asked when he heard his mother chuckling.

"Some people never learn," she said. "Those people over

there lost most of their food from the great wild bandits, but I guess even raccoons have good taste."

"Why do you say that?" Gina asked.

"Because their turkey bacon was the only thing left behind," Jessie said before she burst into laughter. "Jonathan, do you remember what happened to our cooler the first time we brought you here?"

Even though he had been a youngster at the time, he'd never forgotten. He shook his head in amazement to think that his mother could even imagine him failing to recall such an event. He hadn't been *that* young. "Yes, I remember. I guess most people don't realize why they're told to keep all food inside their vehicles overnight."

"What happened?" Willa was inquisitive about all her neighbors' past adventures, but right how she would settle for this one. She'd seen Jonathan put all their food—including that in coolers—inside the back of his capped truck before they'd gone to bed last night.

"We had a similar experience during our first visit here," Jessie said. "I guess most people think storing food away is overkill, but we know better." Jessie shook her head before she went on to explain how she and her two Jonathans had awoken to loud thrashing noises, which had alerted them to an intruder in camp. She went on to tell them how her son had just stood there in amazement as he pointed his flashlight at a retreating cooler.

"I still remember shouting 'Holy cow, where's our cooler going?' For a second I thought it had grown legs. Well, it had, sort of." Jonathan smiled at the memory. "And then Mom started yelling for him to drop it. That startled the raccoon. It stopped dragging our cooler, but it didn't just run off." Mother and son broke out in gales of laughter as Jonathan attempted to finish the tale. "It stuck its head into the cooler and grabbed all our chocolate. Mom had brought a large pack of Hershey's chocolate bars to make us s'mores, but that never happened."

"Nope," Jessie said. "He dashed off into the night with his bounty."

While everyone else laughed, Gina missed the point. "But I love turkey bacon," she said.

Willa pulled a long face and walked away in disgust as this proclamation effectively brought a close to the conversation.

8

He reads much,
He is a great observer, and he looks
Quite through the deeds of men.
—Julius Caesar, 1.2.201-203

When Jessie saw Dara sitting in her own little world wrapped up with a book, she was incredulous. "And just *what* are you reading?" Jessie was so surprised that she forgot to ask Dara what she knew about the unpleasant woman. "After all *you* had to say about this being a time for exercise you bring a book into the park."

Dara just laughed. She knew she'd been busted, but the book had been too good to leave behind. What else could she do? She hadn't had time to finish it before leaving home. "Oh, Jessie, but I just *had* to find out who did it!"

"It's a mystery?" That was just too much. Jessie was an incorrigible mystery reader herself, and she had stayed up late the night before their departure just to finish the one she'd been reading. Besides, Dara was a professor of European literature. She didn't read mysteries. *Well, I guess she does,* Jessie decided as she grabbed up the book to see if it was anything she wanted to read.

"Hey, give that back to me. You can read it when I'm done," Dara tried to make up for her faux pas. "It's really good!" She dug the hole deeper.

Jessie laughed and handed it back when she saw that it was a Leslie Meier mystery. *Chocolate Covered Murder* was the same book she had just finished at home. She recalled how much fun it had been to try to guess who the killer was.

"Oh, you'll love the ending," Jessie threw out the offhanded comment. She walked away from the campfire with satisfaction etched on her face. Had she looked back, she would have seen astonishment written on Dara's.

Jessie had to be content with the one book she had packed. As she opened the guidebook to Baxter State Park, she recalled the mysteries she had finished reading a few weeks ago. When she was younger she'd read all Georgette Heyer's Regency romance novels, but had ignored the author's mysteries. She had rectified that omission over the summer.

Jessie loved British mysteries. Heyer invoked a feeling of simpler times, undoubtedly because she was a writer from the early part of the twentieth century. The woman *could* create a vivid scene. Her *Death in the Stocks* had a unique backdrop for her stabbing victim: the stocks in the town square of a country village.

Earlier this summer, her hometown of Wyleyville had been the scene of two murders: the first one had been the man responsible for her husband's death. Jessie would have loved to have seen *him* in stocks.

Thinking about Sweetzer, however, reminded her of last night's recurring nightmare. She had to wonder if that scene resembled the real 'accident' scene. She had never visited the place where her husband's body had been found. It had seemed too gruesome to ever visit that country road Jonathan had been riding on when Sweetzer had mowed him down.

"Are you really that upset with Dara for bringing a book out here?" Jonathan's interruption came as a welcome relief.

"Of course not," Jessie said. "I was thinking about something else."

"I know," Jonathan said. "Come with me, Mom." The two walked off arm in arm to reminisce on the last time they had been here as a whole family. Once they were out of sight of the other campers, her son asked, "What's wrong?"

"Oh, Jonny," Jessie said before she burst into tears and

melted into her tall son's lean frame. "Sorry." She mumbled her unhappiness against his chest. "I keep forgetting to call you Jonathan, and that's just the problem."

Surprisingly enough, Jonathan understood. "Mom, I should have guessed. You miss Dad." He tightened his arms around her and just held on until the storm of tears had subsided. "This was too much, wasn't it? I should have known that coming here would be rough on you."

Before Jessie could object, he said, "Hey, I feel it, too." Tears formed as he held her to him. "I'm sorry. I try to be strong for you, but I miss him so much. And right now he would want us to walk it off. Let's go a little further before we return to camp."

Jessie pulled herself together before she stumbled from his arms. "Yes, let's do that. I need to tell you something. Something I haven't told you since...well, for a long time."

"Is something else wrong?" Jonathan asked as he wiped away his own tears. "Look, there's a grassy spot over there. Let's sit."

After settling down, Jessie told him about her nightmare. "It was ghastly, Jon...oh, it is so hard to call you Jonathan. It means you are the only."

"No, I'm the second, and it means that another, better person, came first."

"Not better, just another. You remind me of your father in many ways, but you're your own person and you deserve to carry his name."

Jonathan smiled. "Well, now that we have that settled. Be honest, Mom, have you had this dream before?"

"You're so smart. Yes, Jonathan, I've been having various versions of it ever since your father died. I just can't shake it. In my dreams I always come by too late to save him."

"It's probably as much as you can handle, Mom. I don't know how to help you stop having the nightmares." Then he had a thought. "But maybe I can, at least there's something that worked for me. Remember when I used to wake up screaming and saying that bears were chasing me around inside the house?"

Jessie did remember. He'd only been seven when nightmares had plagued him. "Oh, Jonathan, I told you to change the outcome while still awake. Remember how I said to shove one of them into an oven as it chased you?" To her son's nod, Jessie said, "So what do you suggest? That I shove Alfonse Sweetzer into an oven?"

"Well, something like. Maybe before you go to sleep, you should think of doing something bad to him; you could shove the guy off a cliff, or something."

Jessie perked up at the thought. "I'll do it. Now let's go back for the others. We all need to do some hiking to get ready for tomorrow's more serious challenge."

"Agreed." Jonathan laughed as they walked back to the campground. This was one of his favorite spots in the whole world. He sure hoped nothing bad would happen, but one never knew when his mother was around. She seemed to be a trouble magnet.

While Jonathan had his own thoughts, Jessie recalled how an owl had awakened her early that morning. An owl was frequently a harbinger of death in Shakespeare plays. She certainly hoped the implications were wrong this time.

9

Nature's own sweet and cunning hand laid on.
                    —Twelfth Night, 1.5.240

Jonathan rounded everyone up to map out the day's plan. "I thought we'd hike over to Grassy Pond this morning." When Gina groaned, Jonathan sighed. It wasn't as though he'd just thought up the idea. "Hey, it's a nice, easy hike. It's only just over a mile, and there's a chance we'll see some wildlife, maybe even a moose." That made Gina smile.

The only other grumbles came when Jonathan suggested that everyone carry a backpack with the necessities of the next day's hike: water, snacks, and cold weather gear.

"But why?" Gina's voice quavered.

"Because that's what we'll be carrying tomorrow." Jonathan was patient with her as he handed her a brown baseball cap. She accepted it with a smile because it made her feel like she was part of a team.

Each hiker, decked out in matching ball caps, carried a happy smile in expectation of seeing a moose as they headed for the Grassy Pond Trail. Months ago—after Jessie had confirmed how many were hiking—she had purchased the hats at a convenience store in Sherman.

Everyone, including Gina, found the hike fairly effortless as they neared the spot where Katahdin Stream met up with Grassy Pond before it meandered on through their campground and beyond. Trees swaying gently on a cool breeze made hiking more pleasant than usual for a sunny morning in late August. The humidity was down and Gina hoped it would stay that way for the following day's trip up the mountain.

When they turned a corner and caught their first sight of Grassy Pond, they all suddenly ground to a halt. A baby moose stood squarely in their path. "Oh, look!" Gina said. "It's so cute, and it's a baby!" As she pushed past Jonathan, she extended a hand. "Oooo, can we pat it?"

"No." Jonathan whispered as he pulled Gina back to safety just before the head of another moose rose up from beneath the water. It was the baby's mother, who had been feeding for succulent plants on the bottom of the pond. "Never go near wild creatures, no matter how harmless they look," Jonathan said in a low voice. He knew Gina had never been big on traipsing through the wilderness, but really, she should have known better. None of the others had tried to walk up to a moose.

The young moose stood looking at them for only a few seconds before it slowly turned and walked towards the pond. Jonathan knew that while the baby might have welcomed Gina's touch, the mother would have been another story. Mothers in the wild were much like all mothers in that respect: instinct made them protective of their young.

An upset Jonathan contemplated the diversity of this group. He and his mother had traversed these trails several times, but this was a first-time experience for the others.

Willa was the group's next most experienced hiker. She'd never been to Baxter, but she had spent countless hours traversing lesser mountains and trails in Maine, most recently with her father. Joe Royce had just moved back to Maine after leaving a prestigious Boston law firm to settle in Portland so he could spend more time with his only daughter. Willa had taken advantage of that move by talking him into mini-vacations at such places as Acadia State Park and the Bigelow Mountain Range.

Dara might seem to be the novice, but she had taken up a strenuous regimen of walking months ago in anticipation of this trip. She had also hiked over countless trails during the last month.

Gina was the odd man out, so to speak. She really was turning into a city girl. She was about to begin her senior year at the University of Southern Maine. Next year, she had told Jonathan, she was going to go on to get her masters degree in the state's largest city. Once Gina graduated, Jonathan feared that they might never see her back in Wyleyville, other than for holidays. He suspected that Gina had gotten most of her workouts in at the exercise room at USM. He wondered if this was Gina's last ditch effort to impress him.

As the hikers walked on, Jessie became caught up in the beauty of the hike. On either side of the trail a diversity of trees sported iridescent green leaves of varying shades. The sun shone through some, unveiling a vein system that held each leaf stiffly erect.

Soon the Grassy Pond Viewpoint sprung up in front of them and the pond's deep green water was visible once again. Everyone was momentarily rooted to the spot as they stood looking down at the beauty of it all.

"Oh, look over there." Dara broke the silence. She dropped her backpack and pointed towards the far side of the pond. A bull moose stood majestically with long strands of grass dripping from his large antlers.

The party of five found a comfortable spot to sit and watch the show. The women snapped away with their digital cameras while Jonathan was content to observe. The mother and baby moose were again visible in the distance, but the male moose ignored them as he fished for underwater plants. From time to time, the mother moose looked in their direction and kept a wary eye on them. After several minutes, she ushered her baby from the water and into the woods, where the twosome slowly disappeared.

By this time, the bull-moose had wandered from their sight as well, so the hikers decided it was time to return to camp. They retraced their steps rather than complete the longer Grassy Pond Loop. Jessie knew that Jonathan had other plans for the afternoon and he didn't want to wear anyone out. The walk had been invigorating and interesting. The scenery was dazzling and the wildlife had done their part in making everyone happy.

As they reentered camp, Jessie wondered what new adventures awaited them that afternoon. They were all eager to be bound for Katahdin Stream Falls, but Willa seemed to be super-charged with excitement. Jessie, too, hoped something thrilling would happen, disregarding the old adage: be careful what you wish for.

10

He is drowned in the brook;
look but in, and you shall see him.
                    —As You Like It, 3.2.287-288

Katahdin Stream Falls was the Wyleyville group's final destination of the day. Because the falls was located on the north side of the Hunt Trail, they would be passing it again on the following day during their journey to the summit of Katahdin. Today, however, they would go there to just enjoy the scenic view. Dara was especially receptive to this idea in the hopes that it would keep them away from the campground during *that woman's* grand return.

Dara prayed that the woman who had stepped out of her past would be leaving on the heels of her successful climb. *Oh,* she thought, *why did she have to come here and spoil my very first trip to the park! Maybe she'd fall off the mountain or something.* Dara knew she was being uncharitable, but she couldn't help it.

Dara sighed. She wished she could confide in her friend, but she didn't want to lay that burden on Jessie. She watched her friend heat the homemade chicken and vegetable soup Jessie had made for the trip. Everyone ate in silence before they all retreated to their lean-tos for a rest. Dara did not sleep well, not until exhaustion finally took her away from her worries for a short time.

When Jessie crawled from her lean-to, she saw that her son was already up. She smiled as she silently watched him making ham and cheese sandwiches for the hike. "Hey, let me help," she said, and took over packing the sandwiches into Jonathan's backpack. By the time she was finished, everyone was up and ready to begin their excursion onto the first part of the Hunt Trail, also known as the final leg of the Appalachian Trail.

Jessie pulled her shoulder-length red hair into a ponytail before shoving it into the back of her brown baseball cap. Taking up the rear, she observed a cheery mood running though the group as they hiked more quickly than they had that morning. Jessie noticed that Willa was especially chipper. Ever since she'd begun working for the local newspaper back in Wyleyville, Willa had been obsessed with writing and photographing human interest articles for them. Jessie could see the gears grinding as the teenager mentally planned a nature piece, complete with pictures.

"Wow, this is spectacular!" Willa's voice sizzled with pleasure as they walked along beside Katahdin Stream.

They made the steady climb that soon led to a bridge crossing the stream. Gina glowed with excitement as she stepped onto it. "From up here you can see the rocks below the glistening water. It's so beautiful."

Jessie watched her son smile with contentment. While they all seemed to be having fun, Jessie knew he worried about Gina. She seemed more interested in him lately and Jessie wondered if their roles had become reversed. She knew Jonathan had always had a crush on her, even as children when they had begun school together. Jessie noticed how Gina had changed in the last year.

Gina seemed to be more interested in Jonathan lately. Jessie silently observed their interaction: how he'd been especially nice to her, but in a brotherly way. Gina's reaction to that change had been furtive. Now she was acting bubbly for the first time. Jonathan suddenly dashed onto the bridge to help her as, in her excitement, she was being careless. "Whoa, Gina; you almost dropped your camera." He snagged it as it began to slip from her fingers.

"Oh, Jonny, what would I do without you," she said without thinking.

"I'll always be there for you. We've been friends forever, and always will be," Jonathan said.

Ouch! Jessie thought as she saw a flash of pain cross Gina's face. Jessie was glad that it wasn't far now to the falls, as she wondered why her son was distancing himself from Gina in more ways than one.

Jessie continued to watch Gina as the falls appeared in front of them. It was a sight to see. Each, without exception, was enthralled at the sheer beauty of the water cascading downward as it hit first one outcropping of rocks, then another. Willa was the first to raise her camera and start snapping off shot after shot. The others followed as she moved down the path to get a closer view of the water's eighty-foot drop to the stream below. When the base of the falls came into view, Willa froze.

"Jonathan," Willa said. "There's a body down there. It looks like that woman from the campground, the one who was yelling this morning."

"How can you tell?" Jonathan asked as he moved to her side. As Jessie came up to stand beside her son, she could see someone stretched out, half in and half out of the water. Long, blonde hair fanned out from around her head.

"I know it's her. See how tiny she is? She was wearing light blue clothing when she left." Willa's hand shook as she pointed. A blue outfit hugging the small body consisted of a tank top, shorts, and matching socks. That's what the woman had been wearing, Jessie noted, as she looked down towards the stream to one side of the waterfall. The ground nearby was littered with footprints.

Jessie resisted when her son attempted to draw her back from the perilously steep slope. "Willa's right. That is the unpleasant woman from the campground." She breathed quietly, as though by keeping her voice down, she would pro-

Janet Morgan

tect the others from the horrific vision laid out below.

"What's wrong? Gina asked as she stepped forward.

Through Gina's gasps of horror, Jessie calmly observed that the skin visible on the back of the woman's arms and legs was almost as blue as her outfit. The head was face-down and it wasn't moving, save the lapping of water gently pushing against her bobbing head. Jessie took a deep breath to calm her nerves. There was nothing they could do. The woman was undoubtedly dead.

Steady now, Jessie helped Jonathan usher the others back to the safety of the trail and settled them down on the grass. Each hiker looked at one another in shock, but it was Jessie who spoke first. "Jonathan, run back to camp and get the park ranger. We'll wait here."

Jonathan started to disagree, until he realized that his mother was right. He could get to the campground—and back—faster if he went alone. "Okay. I'll do it, but no one should move until I get back with the ranger."

All four silently nodded in agreement as Jonathan dashed off down the Hunt Trail. When Jessie turned around to see if everyone was okay, she saw Dara gaze back in the direction of the dead woman. Jessie saw a sense of fascination etched on her friend's face before she carefully changed it to concern. *What gives?* Jessie wondered. Dara had seemed happy at this awful sight.

11

Sad hours seem long.
　　　　　　—Romeo and Juliet, 1.1.161

Time passed at a snail's pace while Jessie waited for her son to return with the ranger. It was the quietest time she had ever spent with the others as they huddled together in silence. An eternity seemed to have passed since Jonathan had left, but Jessie knew he would be back as soon as possible. She hoped it would be soon as she noted that the others weren't faring well. Dara, who had initially seemed pleased at the dreadful sight below, now shook in Jessie's arms. Gina and Willa just clung to one another.

When Jessie finally heard voices, she jumped to her feet, leaving Dara on the ground with her arms wrapped around herself. *Those voices could be approaching hikers. What should I do?* Relief coursed through her body when she heard the agitated voice of her son.

"You should have called the police. The authorities need to step in. I told you, she's dead. Her face is underwater."

Ranger Jerome Goodroe said, "I'll be the one to make that determination. I can't call the police on your say-so alone. Besides, my boss told me to check it out first. We aren't even sure it *is* a person yet."

"Oh, yes we are! Do you think we're stupid?" Jessie was furious to hear that the ranger thought they were wasting his time.

"I told this youngster that I'll decide that," Goodroe said. "After all, how many of you have ever seen a dead body?"

"That's not the point. I know a dead body when I see one, and *that* certainly is one." Jessie pointed down to where the petite blonde woman was still stretched out. "And we can even tell you *who* it is, so you can't tell us it's some wild animal."

As the ranger looked down the hill, he realized they were correct. It was a person. "Oh? And just who is it?" he asked.

"Well, we don't know her name, but she's the one who had mice in her tent."

Ranger Goodroe didn't know whether to cheer or to cry to hear that it was the troublemaker. "Are you sure?" He moved forward. "You stay here while I look," he said as he began to descend the steep hill towards the stream.

"Do you think that's smart? Shouldn't you keep the crime scene intact?" Jessie asked.

"Crime scene? Who says it's a crime scene? Maybe she bent over to take a drink of water and fell in." Not to be deterred, he strode to water's edge. Perched on a large rock, he leaned over and pulled the woman's head up by her hair to see her face. He blanched before he let the head fall back into the stream and he pulled his cell phone from his pocket.

Jessie leaned forward and looked down to watch the young ranger. After he had what appeared to be a heated telephone discussion, Jessie saw him look around before he began to retreat inside his own soggy footsteps. From her vantage point, Jessie could see that the mossy ground was littered with small footprints around which blades of grass stuck up here and there.

She bet the ranger would be read the riot act. He should never have walked up to the body. Even Jessie knew this was a job for the Maine State Police. She'd read somewhere that they were always called in to take charge whenever someone died in a state park.

When the ranger looked up, Jessie and Jonathan were staring down at him. "You two stay where you are. We don't want any footprints messing up the area," he said.

Jessie couldn't believe what he was saying. *They* hadn't gone near the body. Only the park ranger had, which immediately put her on the alert. Had he already been here? Had he killed the woman earlier and was now attempting to cover his tracks? She could see from the look on her son's face that he was considering the same thing.

12

Rumor is a pipe
Blown by surmises, jealousies, conjectures.
        —Henry IV, Part 2, Induction, 15-16

It surprised Jessie how quickly the cavalry arrived in the form of the Millinocket police. "There's a body? Are you sure she isn't still alive?" The man in charge looked down the long incline towards the stream. When he looked back and noticed the five hikers, he glared at the ranger. "And what are *they* doing here? Are you giving a class in stupidity?"

"But, but..." The ranger didn't seem to know what to say.

"Sir," Jessie said, "we're the ones who found the body. And, yes, we are sure she's dead. She hasn't moved in over an hour. The whole set-up looked suspicious to us, which is why the ranger wanted us to stay put." She looked at the ranger with more sympathy than she felt the man deserved.

The officer in charge said, "Well, I'm going to have all of you escorted back to the campground. And don't leave the park," he said. Dismissing them, he turned back to the ranger. "You stay with us and tell us exactly how you determined that this is anything but an accident."

"Well, I went down and checked it out. She didn't have any bruises on her face, so..."

"You what? You touched the body? You traipsed all over the ground?" The man in charge yelled at the young ranger.

"But, sir, the manual says to not call the police until we know..."

"You know, young man, I don't give a flying leap what your manual says." And that was all Jessie heard as she and

38

Katahdin Drowning

Jonathan helped the younger women stand on wobbly feet, before they were ushered back to camp by a second policeman.

Katahdin Stream Campground was abuzz with rumors. Someone had died on the mountain. It could be foul play. It was a day hiker. No, it was someone from this very campground.

People were still speculating half an hour later, when Jessie, Jonathan, Dara, Gina, and Willa walked in accompanied by a uniformed officer. People rushed over to hear the news. "Stay away, everyone. These people are witnesses and no one is to talk to them." Turning to Jonathan as the group's assumed leader, he asked, "Where's your car? Maybe you should stay in it until my boss comes back down here. And I'll need your keys."

"We've been staying in camp, officer. Can't we wait at our campsite?" Jonathan asked.

"Well, why didn't you say so?"

"Maybe because you didn't ask," Jonathan said.

"Don't try to get funny with me, young man. Where's your car?"

Jonathan pointed. "That blue Chevy Blazer is mine, and the yellow Jeep beside it is my mother's. We all came here together."

"Give me your car keys, then." The officer held out his hand.

Jonathan and Jessie pulled their backpacks from their backs and unclipped key chains from each pack. Jessie took her car key from her keychain and handed it to the officer. Noting what his mother had done, Jonathan, too, handed over only the key to his vehicle.

With this simple act, Jessie turned her back on the law, rounded up the others, and ushered them back to their campsite. "We'll be over here when you want to ask us what we saw."

Jessie was relieved after her son had laid a fire and set a match to it, not because it was cold, but because everyone— including herself—was shivering. *We must still be in shock,* she decided.

They were all huddled around a blazing fire before Jonathan asked, "Is everyone okay?" They all simply nodded.

Jessie was surprised that none of them had been sick, but then again, no one looked the picture of health, either. She supposed they should try to eat something. Remembering the sandwiches Jonathan had made, she reached down to her son's discarded backpack and pulled out supper.

"Great idea, Mom, let's eat."

No one appeared especially thrilled with the idea, but once they had sandwiches in front of them, they all dug in. It seemed to be just the thing to keep them busy as the day stretched on. Jessie barely noticed as the shadows lengthened across the ground towards their site.

Once they had all finished eating in silence, Jessie, who began giving Dara furtive glances, suggested that the two of them go off alone together. Jonathan protested. "Mom, you can't leave the campground."

"Oh, we won't," Jessie said, "but Dara and I need a few quiet minutes together. You young people can entertain yourselves for a bit, can't you?"

When no one spoke, the two former college classmates strode towards a stand of trees. Had Jessie looked back she would have seen a worried expression on her son's face as he watched them go towards the edge of the campground's clearing.

13

Suspicion always haunts the guilty mind.
—Henry VI, Part 3, 5.6.11

Jessie needed a private place for her heart-to-heart with Dara. She looked around before she finally chose a shaded spot behind a stand of trees and motioned her college friend to sit.

"Jessie, is there something wrong?" Dara asked.

"You should be telling *me*," Jessie said before Dara could form an objection. "Dara, you knew this woman. Don't even try to deny it. This is just between the two of us, so spill it."

Dara's shoulders shook as she lowered her head. Because she didn't know what else to do, Jessie waited. After a short time, Dara looked up and smiled; she wiped the corners of her glistening eyes. "Yes," she said, "I knew her back home, but we weren't friends."

"She was from Augusta?" Jessie was surprised. She had assumed from the now dead woman's demeanor earlier in the day that she was from out of state. She supposed that wasn't a nice thought. She knew rude people resided everywhere.

No, not Augusta; my family moved there when I was still in high school. We're originally from Cornville. Bertha was from Cornville, too."

"Oh, I didn't realize that. The woman's name is Bertha?" Jessie tried to think back on all that had happened that day. Somehow that didn't sound like the name she'd heard.

"Yes, that's her name. She was two years ahead of me in

41

school. I didn't really know her, but small towns being what they are, we were all bussed to Skowhegan together. I knew who she was because she was mean to some of the others on the bus. Thankfully I was beneath her notice until I started high school. She almost immediately began to pick on me. She thought she was better than everyone. That was the problem."

"Problem? What problem?"

"Well, I was always quiet and shy. Then this one boy asked me out. He was in the same grade as Bertha and I now realize he was probably just looking for an easy mark. Bertha thought all the older boys should be drooling over her. She was beautiful and most of the guys ran after her all the time." Dara delivered her speech as though she had to get it out before she lost her nerve.

"Oh, Dara, what happened? Was she dating this guy?"

"No, but she didn't want him running around with a lowly freshman, either. I was her favorite target from that time on."

"Did you go out with the boy?"

"No, I never did. I might have been inexperienced, but I could tell that he wasn't really interested in me." Dara took a deep breath and exhaled. "Talking about it makes me feel better, but back then I didn't have anyone to talk to. Bertha was always harassing me. It was my rotten luck that her locker was near mine. Every chance she got, she would slam my fingers in my locker door."

"What did you do?"

"Nothing; I didn't dare to complain. Back then, Mom and Dad were going through a rough patch with my older brother. He'd just started college, and then he quit before he'd finished his first year. Added to that, Dad's job wasn't all that secure. But then a wonderful thing happened. A friend of his in Augusta called and offered him a fantastic job opportunity with the state. Dad's quite the math whiz and there was an opening in his friend's department. I jumped up and down with joy the day we packed up and moved to Augusta.

"I never saw her again, until this morning, that is. I heard rumors that she'd left home shortly after graduation, but I don't know if it's true." Dara wiped more tears from her eyes as she pleaded. "Please don't tell the police, Jessie. I don't see how they'll ever find out about me knowing her almost fifteen years ago."

"Of course I won't tell them. You have my word," Jessie promised.

14

Though it be honest, it is never good
To bring bad news.
— Antony and Cleopatra, 2.5.85-86

A short time later Jessie wandered back towards her campsite leaving Dara alone to think. Jessie sat and observed the police officer who'd brought them down from the falls. He must have his hands full trying to keep everyone apart, she thought, when she saw him throw his hands up in dismay. It must have seemed an impossible job when, as news traveled, people from other campgrounds leaked over into Katahdin Stream Campground. Jessie turned away from his woes when she heard a young man questioning other campers.

"Hey, do you know who died? I heard someone is dead," a young man asked one and then another person as he walked through the campground. "I can't find the lady I came up here with."

Jessie recognized the blonde, blue eyed man who had been with the angry woman earlier. "Who are you missing?" she asked, as she pretended that she didn't know who he had accompanied.

"Veronica Verne. She's the famous fitness expert from TV." He looked exasperated when Jessie gave him a blank look. "Oh, come on, the one with the mice in her lean-to. Don't tell me you didn't see her this morning. I saw you watching, like everyone else."

"But, oh," Jessie was momentarily speechless. That hadn't been the name Dara had given her. Then she realized that if the infamous Bertha *had* run away from home, she'd probably changed her name. "You mean that idiot who was afraid of a couple of tiny field mice? And you say she's famous? Never heard of her," Jessie said as she shrugged off the very idea that a fitness person would be of any interest to her.

"Oh really; you're trying to tell me that you've never heard of her? You must be kidding." The young cameraman shook his head. "Well, we got separated on the trail and now I can't find her. I wonder where she is. She's too mean to be dead, so she can't be the person whose death everyone is speculating about."

Jonathan soon came to the rescue. He had overheard the young man's call for help and retrieved the police officer. Jessie silently praised her son for having the foresight to palm this man off onto the police. Mother and son retreated to their campfire as the police took over.

The policeman walked Verne's cameraman across the footbridge, effectively separating most of the campers from them. The officer unintentionally escorted the young man towards Verne's former lean-to and sat him by the remains of a dead campfire.

"That guy over there told me he saw you with the victim earlier today. Just who are you?"

"V-victim? You mean she *is* the dead person everyone's talking about? Impossible; she's stronger than she looks," the cameraman said.

"And just who are you? And better yet, who is she?" The officer repeated his question.

"My-my name's Evan Kinderhook. I'm her cameraman. She's Veronica Verne."

"Veronica Verne? My wife watches her on the tube. Are you sure?"

"Of course, I'm sure. I was sent here to film her going up to the top of that mountain." He pointed up the trail and towards Baxter Peak.

"Well, that's not where she was found, mister."

"Well, she didn't want to continue past that big ledge. She made it up over it, but then she went white and turned around. She told me to go to the top and film everything. She insisted that we could piece her in later. She said she was going to come back here."

"Are you saying that's the last time you saw her?" the officer asked.

Kinderhook nodded. "Where'd you find her?"

"I'm the one asking the questions. If you came back down, how could you have missed her?"

"You mean you found her on the trail?" After thinking a few seconds, he said, "Well, as a matter of fact, I sat up there in the sun for quite a while before I came back down. It was so peaceful away from her that I fell asleep on the rocks. After I went back down the ledge, I sat in the woods for quite a while before I came back to the campground."

"Hey, you people, back away." The policeman had suddenly jumped to his feet when he noticed some of the campers creeping forward to listen. Because his boss needed to talk to this guy, he took Kinderhook by the arm and escorted him to the ranger station. From there he called the detective in charge and apprised him of his discovery. "Any one of these people could be a killer, sir. What do I do, sir?"

He was told to keep an eye on everyone, a job that became easier minutes later, when a state police cruiser and medical van pulled into the campground. One would have thought that, what with the speed limit being twenty miles per hour inside the park, that they couldn't make such a loud entrance. That wasn't the case as tires squealed and ripped into the dirt. Blue flashing lights announced the arrival of the Maine State Police from Bangor just as the sun was setting over the campground.

15

The sun brings to gild the western sky.
—The Two Gentlemen of Verona, 5.1.1

The Maine State Police Evidence Response Team had quickly vanished up the Hunt Trail, where they worked like a hive of busy bees, collecting evidence and photographing the scene. The sun had set before they had returned to the campground with what had once been Veronica Verne. As soon as her body was packed into the emergency vehicle, she would be making her final appearance at the Maine State Crime Laboratory in Augusta, where victims of suspicious deaths were autopsied.

The officer in charge from the Maine State Police went over to speak to the Millinocket detective. "I trust you and the rangers have made sure that no one has left the park."

"Yes, sir; we certainly have," Detective Walter Briscoe said. "We told the park director to close all the gates until you gave the go-ahead to begin letting people out. And, of course, no one was allowed in after we arrived, with the exception of your people."

"Good job, Briscoe." State Police Detective Hank Marley reached out and shook the man's hand. "It would be nice if we could have someone identify the body before it's transported. Was anyone here with her?"

"She had a cameraman. He's inside the ranger station. Too many nosy Parkers out here," he said by way of explanation. "Shall I bring him out?" Marley, who was keeping a close eye on watchers, only nodded.

Evan Kinderhook was escorted outside and shown the body. He almost collapsed before he said, "Yes, that's Veronica Verne."

The three men stood in silence as the body was loaded into the emergency vehicle. Once the vehicle had gone, Marley and Briscoe escorted the nervous young cameraman back into the rustic log cabin. When questioned, Kinderhook reluctantly admitted that there were a number of people back in Boston who disliked her. "But you can't think someone killed her. It was an accident, wasn't it? I mean, she wasn't the nicest person in the world, but she was okay."

"So where were you when your boss died?" Marley asked.

Kinderhook explained how they had started up Katahdin, but that Verne had suddenly changed her mind. "She told me to hike to the top and take pictures. I guess I was supposed to make it look like she was there with me."

"So you have pictures from the top," Marley said.

"Are you asking to see them? Why? It was an accident, right?" Kinderhook said.

"That's not what I asked," Marley said.

"Well, you see..." Kinderhook mopped his dampening brow. "Well, I dropped the camera between some rocks. It broke," he said.

"How convenient," Marley said. "Did anyone see you?"

"Yes, as a matter of fact, there was a man sitting on the rocks near where Ms. Verne turned back. You know, that man didn't go to the top, either. He followed her back down the trail. And I didn't see him earlier, not until he appeared on the rocks above us. I wondered where he came from. The trail isn't all that wide, so you get to see just about everyone along the way up. I didn't see him after that. He isn't in this camp, either; I'm sure of it."

"Well, you'd better give the ranger a description of the man. Maybe we can find him and save your bacon, just in case this turns out to be murder. Come with me." Marley took him by the arm. "The ranger will take down your name, address, and telephone number, before you go back to your campsite." Marley escorted an astonished Evan Kinderhook to an office at the back of the ranger station, where the park ranger sat compiling lists. Before he turned away from Kinderhook, Marley said, "Oh, and we will be confiscating your camera for now."

Kinderhook started to object, until he saw the determination in the detective's face. Dejected, the cameraman hung his head as he sat in a chair opposite the ranger and fumed on the loss of the station's video camera. He just hoped no one knew what a difficult time Veronica Verne had given him. *That was all he needed.*

16

The task he undertakes
Is numbering sands and drinking oceans dry.
— Richard II, 2.2.145-146

Marley and Briscoe stepped outside and looked around at all the visitors to the park. There were too many, Marley thought. They must do something, and soon.

"Until we hear back on the autopsy, we need to keep a tight ship. If Verne's death is ruled an accidental drowning, then we can let everyone go. But in the meantime, we need to proceed as though this is a murder." Marley shook his head in frustration. Because the state police were called in concerning park deaths, he knew just about how many people could be there right now. He also knew that anyone industrious enough could hike right out of the park without being seen.

As they walked towards his squad car, Marley said, "We have to get the names and addresses of everyone within the southern end of the park. I need all the help I can get. Can you stay on with me?"

Briscoe agreed. "Sure thing, sir, but I'm not sure how many officers my chief can send. How about using park employees? I've put young Goodroe to work, but maybe the park supervisor can find us more help."

"Good idea, Briscoe. Gatekeepers will be taking down contact information as people are allowed to leave the park. For now, we need to look over the check-in lists." Marley leaned against his car as he began to prioritize tasks. "I've been told that the rangers keep a close eye on the trailhead lists. I think we would be wise to look this one over before we proceed further."

Ranger Jerome Goodroe sat at his desk and looked over the names and addresses he had compiled on all the visitors to his campground. Sighing, he decided he had better turn copies of everything over to the man in charge. Just as he stepped onto his porch and shut the door on his formerly private haven, he heard the state police detective call for him: "Hey, you, over there; I need your help."

Goodroe dashed over to where police cars were blocking the tote road leading into the campground and beyond, but he wasn't about to complain. "What can I do for you?"

"We need to find out who registered to hike this trail, and then I want to talk to the people who found the body."

Goodroe handed over two lists: one of overnight campers staying at this campground and the other the trailhead list. "Here you are, sir. As you can see, I made copies of everything. The people who found the body are staying at lean-tos just across the stream, at numbers six, seven, and eight, to be exact."

"Good man." Marley turned to Briscoe. "Would you go over these lists and see if there's anyone who climbed today that isn't on the list of campers? We need to sort out the day hikers first, so let's start there."

Briscoe nodded as he took the sheets.

"I'll leave you to work on it while the ranger takes me over to see our witnesses. Lead on, young man."

Goodroe turned towards the bridge and escorted Marley across to the main part of the campground. In front of the closest lean-to, five people were huddled around a blazing fire drinking coffee. The young man stood to greet them. "Hello, sir. I take it you're looking for us. But before you grill us, would you care for some coffee?"

Coffee sounded tempting to Goodroe, but Marley dismissed him with the wave of a hand. Goodroe was more than happy to leave. He didn't want to hear these people tell the detective how he had messed up the crime scene.

17

The nature of bad news infects the teller.
—Antony and Cleopatra, 1.2.95

Marley took a seat on one of the stumps situated around the fire. "Yes," he said, "coffee—black, please—would be fine."

"Before you ask your questions, sir, I think we should introduce ourselves," one of the women said. "I'm Jessie Tyler and this is my son, Jonathan." She introduced the others before she said, "Now that you know who we are, I only drink coffee with people I know."

Because the detective approved of her direct approach, he complied. "My name is Detective Hank Marley, and thank you for the coffee." He took an appreciative sip. "Someone makes darn good coffee."

Jonathan smiled. "That would be me. My mother used to make great coffee, that is, before she started drinking instant."

Marley only shook his head and drained his cup. A second one had been poured before he proceeded to question the witnesses. "Which one of you found the body?"

"We all did," Jessie said. "We found her at three forty-five. We stayed up on the cliff overlooking the stream. None of us touched the body, or even went near it, for that matter."

Marley was surprised. He hadn't expected this woman to anticipate his questions. Before he could respond, she went on to say, "None of us had ever found a dead body until today." Jessie's voice took on an eager tone. "But I read mysteries, and we've been part of investigations before—back home on the coast—so we know how important timing is. That's why I looked at my watch."

Marley groaned inwardly. She reads mysteries *and* she's been part of investigations back home. He needed to put the brakes on this woman, and fast. "Whoa, we're the professionals here. I don't know how you people handle things *down on the coast,* but up here in northern Maine we don't welcome civilian help.

"I mean it, Mrs. Tyler. Let me be clear on this issue. You are not to stick your noses into state police business. We have plenty of professional help here." He hoped he had gotten his point across, but all five of them looked put out. "Now," he said as he brushed off any further attempts to discuss the issue, "were all of you together when you found the body?"

"Yes." Jonathan spoke before his mother could point out that she'd already told him that. "And we were together all day, right up until I ran back here for the ranger."

"How did you know the woman was dead?" the detective asked.

"Oh, come on, Mr. Marley." Jessie gave him an exasperated look. "That wasn't hard to figure out. She didn't move, her skin was blue, and her whole face was underwater."

"It's *Detective Marley,* and you could tell that from how far away?"

"We were close enough. We were looking right down at her body from above, so we had a good view," Willa said. "You'd better not try to blame one of us because we've been down that road before and Aunt Jessie, Jonathan, and my mom solved two murder cases all on their own back in Wyleyville." Willa's face glowed with pleasure.

"I told you not to go there. You are *not* getting involved in my case," Marley said as he rose and prepared to leave.

Jonathan stopped him with an unrelated question: "We planned to hike to Baxter Peak tomorrow. Is that still on?"

Katahdin Drowning

"We'll get back to you on that." Marley stalked off. He had too much to do, and he didn't have time to chat with these so-called amateur detectives.

No sooner had he walked away, than Jessie saw the dead woman's cameraman sitting near his lean-to. He appeared distraught, so Jessie motioned to Jonathan. After a quiet conversation, they crossed the bridge and approached the young man. "Hello, my name's Jonathan and this is my mother. You seem to be alone. How about joining us for dinner?" Jonathan offered.

"I'm not very good company right now, but thanks. Oh, forgive me; I'm Evan Kinderhook. I was sent here to film the *lady* for her television program."

"Hello, Evan. I don't mean to be pushy, but I bet you could use a good meal," Jonathan said. "My mother says it cures all ills."

"Well..."

"Oh, come on. You can cry on our shoulders, so to speak."

Kinderhook nodded and followed them to where a group of people with friendly faces sat around a campfire. After introductions had been made, he watched Jessie reheat the remainder of her homemade soup. Even though the others had dined on sandwiches, they all sat together and ate in companionable silence.

Jessie wanted to question Kinderhook, but she decided to wait. It would be rude unless he brought up the issue first, which he finally did: "I didn't like her, you know. I guess I'll be a suspect, once they know that."

"You mean they haven't questioned you yet?" Willa asked.

"Oh, they did talk to me, but they didn't ask me what I thought of her." Kinderhook shook his head in resignation. "I hated being sent up here with her. I'd been warned about her reputation, but I really had no choice. You know, she hit on me all the way up here on the plane from Boston. And she propositioned me again in the limo coming to the park."

"You rode here in a limo?" Dara's former foe certainly had come up in the world.

"Yes, Ms. Verne always insisted on the best." Kinderhook shook his head in disgust. "She got on her cell phone as soon as she saw these shelters, and she blasted her producer for not getting her a cabin." Kinderhook smirked with disgust. "I'm surprised she didn't try to take over the ranger's cabin."

Evan Kinderhook was still sitting with those who had befriended him when a limo pulled into the parking lot. The large white vehicle caught the attention of everyone as it sat with blazing lights illuminating the campground. This soon came to the attention of the police, as did the fact that the cameraman was sitting with the Wyleyville group.

"You!" Marley strode towards the Tyler campsite. "What do you people think you're doing? I told you to stay out of this investigation, and here you are cozying up to the victim's cameraman. I will not have you talking to him." Marley spun on Kinderhook and pointed towards the limo. "And what is that thing doing here? Do you think you're going to leave us? I know that's Ms. Verne's limo, so don't try to deny it." Marley grabbed Kinderhook by the arm and hauled him off towards the long white car before anyone could utter a word.

"Busted," was all Jessie could say as she watched their chance for information vanish into the night. "Where's your mother's murder board when we need it," Jessie said to Willa. Jessie sighed and tore a page from her spiral bound journal and began to write in defiance of police orders. *If that man thinks he's going to keep us out of the investigation, he is sadly mistaken.*

18

What a fearful night is this!
There's two or three of us have seen strange sights.
—Julius Caesar, 1.3.137-138

Detective Hank Marley strode over to the limo, where he spoke too softly for any of the campers to hear. After the driver shut off the engine and got out of the vehicle, the detective escorted him, along with Kinderhook, into the ranger cabin.

"Sit, both of you," Marley said. The men sat as Marley turned on the limo driver. "What are you doing here? I understood that you weren't due back here until tomorrow."

"Well, you understood wrong, mate. I was told to come here tonight and pick up this bloke and the famous lady." The driver's British accent was lost on the detective.

"That's not true," Kinderhook said. "We were staying here another night. Tomorrow afternoon we were supposed to return to the Bangor airport to go back to Boston."

"Not so, mate. You and that foxy lady are staying at a hotel tonight." The driver looked around. "Say, where is she? We need to get going. The room's waiting, with champagne and all the trimmings." The driver winked at Kinderhook. "Lucky bloke; I'll take your place if you want to stay here with these bumpkins."

Up until now, Marley had let the men talk uninterrupted. He'd discovered long ago that one learned more by letting people rant on. "So, you and Ms. Verne had a romantic evening planned back in Bangor. Interesting," he said.

"No, that was not the plan. I would never have agreed to such a thing," Kinderhook said.

"Well, I need a statement from you," Marley said to the driver. "Briscoe," he called over his shoulder. The Millinocket detective had taken over the ranger's office to make telephone calls. "Briscoe," he repeated. When the man appeared in the doorway, Marley said, "Get a statement from this man and send him on his way."

"Say, what's going on?" the limo driver asked.

"The lady is dead. She won't need your services tonight." The driver gasped in astonishment as Briscoe ushered him into the office. Marley turned back to Kinderhook.

Evan Kinderhook was under scrutiny for the second time in a matter of hours. He tried, unsuccessfully, to make the detective understand that he had no idea about Veronica Verne's plans. "I really don't know anything about what that driver said. I promise. I'd never do what he suggested. If we'd gone back to Bangor tonight, you can bet I would have found another hotel to stay in, very far from that piranha."

"Aha! So you admit she had her hooks into you."

"No, sir, but she was trying. She wasn't just after me, either. She tried to get her claws into any man walking. I know how to keep my distance."

Marley decided to let the issue drop for now. He knew where to find the boy, should more evidence crop up.

By this time, Detective Marley had made a wise decision. He would allow the Wyleyville contingent to hike the next day. *That will keep them out of my hair for at least one day,* he thought.

Ranger Goodroe was sent around to all the camps to give hikers the good news. He was also ordered to get an itinerary from each group. Meanwhile, Marley set up quarters in the ranger station. The park director had offered them a place to sleep nearby, but Marley intended to stay at the campground. Intuition told him that if this was murder—and he suspected it was—then the killer was nearby. He wasn't about to let any of the campers leave until he had questioned them all.

So he spent a busy evening talking to the day hikers. He let each of them leave once he had decided they weren't likely suspects. To be safe, however, he would send their names and addresses back to Bangor headquarters to have them checked out. If none of them were in the legal system or came up as having any connection to the victim, then he would take them off his list.

As he talked to those staying on, he soon discovered that no one had fond words to say about Veronica Verne. If this turned out to be murder, he would have his work cut out for him. In that case, he knew exactly what his next move would be.

19

Full many a glorious morning have I seen
Flatter the mountain tops with sovereign eye.
—Sonnet 33, 1-2

The new day began well before dawn for Jonathan as he brewed a pot of coffee and began cooking a hearty breakfast. He contemplated on how to get four tired women out of bed so early, but he needn't have worried. One whiff of his coffee and they were all up.

"I'll get up before the sun any day if I can have all this waiting for me," Dara said with appreciation.

"Dig in, Dara. You're going to need it." Jonathan spoke from experience when he advised them all to eat as much they could. "It won't pay to eat like birds today."

"Hey, I know you're talking about me. I can't help it if I don't eat much." Gina hadn't been fooled by Jonathan's blanket comment. "Yuck. I don't eat sausage," she said with a grimace on her face.

"Well, you'll need it this morning, all of it, so eat up. Right, Mom?"

"Sorry, Gina, I don't particularly like sausage, either, but it's just the ticket if you want to make it up this mountain. You need something that will stick to your ribs." She bit into her breakfast sandwich before she took her fair share of sausage and home fries. She washed it all down with coffee as she encouraged the others to eat.

Jonathan saw Willa oblige with no complaint, probably because she'd read up on hiking and knew he was right. Gina picked at her sausage until she was pressured into finishing every bite of her meal. Camp was soon disbanded as they all readied their packs. Each of them carried two bottles of water and clothing for warmth, just in case it turned cold.

Months ago, in preparation for this trip, Jessie had taken Dara, Gina, and Willa with her to shop at L.L. Bean for the store's warmest, yet thinnest waterproof pants and jackets to go over their hiking clothes. Jessie had even made sure they all had new hiking boots. Jonathan had firmly warned them to use the summer to break them in, but he suspected that Gina had not listened, as there was nary a scuff on her boots.

Jonathan had taken the lion's share of the load onto his back, including sandwiches for the peak. He'd also packed energy bars to be distributed, as needed, as well as extra water and packets of juice. The secret to making the hike a success was to keep everyone hydrated and give them just enough food to keep up their energy.

So off they went before the sun had shown its face. Jonathan had insisted they get an early start because they would not be hiking as fast as others. Overeager ones might not even make it to the top, but many would pass them along the way. The mountain might be a lonelier place today, however, what with all the activity going on in camp. He was sure some would stay behind just to keep up on the news, while others might have lost their taste for Katahdin after the dangers inherent to climbing were brought home to them.

But this hadn't stopped the Wyleyville hikers as they took the first leg of the trail they had traversed just yesterday. Jonathan led with a flashlight to illuminate the way through the woods. Even though he knew the path, he was glad there were white blazes on rocks and trees to keep hikers from straying off the path. It wasn't long before he heard the heavy breathing of struggling hikers. Jonathan slowed the pace slightly, but not enough to make it obvious that he was doing it for Gina and Dara. The two inexperienced hikers bravely said nothing as they struggled to keep up.

After the sun finally rose, they could see Katahdin

Stream as well as hear it. By the time the trail to The Owl split away from the Hunt Trail, they were near the bridge over the stream.

Despite small grumbles, the first mile was behind them as they approached the bridge. Once on the other side, Jonathan took pity on the women: "Time for a break, everyone." Jonathan felt they were making progress. He figured that Gina must be delighted for a chance to rest when he saw her sink to the ground without worrying about getting grass on her tan hiking shorts.

"Phew!" Dara was the first to speak. "How many more miles is it to the top?" As she sat, pulled off her ball cap, and wiped her damp forehead, she looked back in the direction of the falls.

Jonathan had carefully skirted past it today, for he was sure none of them wanted to revisit the scene of yesterday's death. He had an idea that was what Dara was thinking. In an attempt to comfort her, he said, "It's only a little over four more miles, Dara."

"But you made it past the worst part, at least to my way of thinking," Jessie said. "After we pass the tree line, there'll be more to see to take your mind off the hike. That is, of course, once we get around the ledge and over the bicycle bars."

"Bicycle bars?" Gina's voice held a trace of panic.

"Oh, for goodness sake, Gina, I loaned you my guidebook weeks ago. Didn't you read it?" Willa gave her older sister an exasperated look. "Aunt Jessie was being kind. It's really a cliff face we have to traverse even before the bicycle bars. That's the only part I'm concerned about."

"Don't worry, Willa," Jessie said with confidence, "Jonathan will help us. I couldn't get over it on my own the first time, either."

Jonathan laughed at the memory of his father pushing his mother from below and a stranger helping from above. "Yeah, Mom, you did it on your own after the first time, right?"

"Okay, so maybe I had to be helped the first two times. But I didn't need it the last time we came here."

Jonathan's body shook with mirth. "Mom, we took Abol the last time." The Abol Trail was shorter—and some say easier—because it is uphill all the way to the Tablelands. The drawback is that it's in the sun the whole way and involves climbing over smaller rocks that have a tendency to cause rock slides, should hikers be overeager.

"But we came *down* the Hunt Trail," Jessie said.

"Yeah, and getting down the cliff is much easier than pulling yourself hand over hand *up* the bars," Jonathan said. As they talked, other hikers continued to pass them. This would not be the last time faster hikers went by them, but Jonathan didn't care. He just wanted everyone to have a good time. "Don't worry, Gina. I'm sure someone will come along to help you women up the cliff face."

"Cliff face? What have you gotten us into? You're scaring me." Gina had apparently not been listening when Willa had mentioned the cliff face. Now she turned to her sister. "And, no, I didn't read your stupid book. I figured you read enough of it for both of us. You should have told me about cliffs and hand-over-hand climbing. *You* said it would be easy." Gina rarely argued with her sister, but this was too much. Willa *should* have told Gina about the dangers of the trail.

Before Willa could do more than shake her head, Jonathan came to her rescue. "Not fair, Gina. If Willa gave you the book to read, you can't blame her if you don't know what's coming." Jonathan felt bad about siding with Willa, but Gina just never listened. And the next phase of the trip definitely was the most dangerous part of the climb.

20

I must go and meet with danger there.
—Henry IV, Part 2, 2.3.48

All too soon they would be facing the aforementioned dangers. In the meantime, Willa was thrilled with her surroundings, especially when she discovered things she'd seen on Jessie's map of Katahdin. Cave Rock, a small slab of rock where one could escape from inclement weather, was one such example. It was all so exciting, she decided, as they walked past the cave.

Willa was energized. She was with Jessie and Jonathan on the trip of a lifetime. So okay, she admitted, it was mostly because of Jonathan, but that was her own deeply guarded secret. He loved Gina; she knew that. She would be content to cherish every moment and take tons of pictures for her scrapbook—including as many of Jonathan as possible.

Willa was fully enjoying herself as one spectacular view after another came into sight. And, of course, she loved hiking. She'd never had a chance to come to Baxter State Park until now. Before she knew it, they had emerged above the tree line. She thought about whether she could make it over the climbing bars on her own. She knew better when she saw the sheer rock wall on her left and the tops of trees to her right. She found herself pressing her back into the rock-face and wondered if those behind her were doing the same.

Willa watched in awe as Jonathan, who was in the lead, proudly walked right up to where the bars protruded from the rock wall above his head. Willa looked straight ahead as she tagged along at a slower pace. She hoped the others were following her lead and not looking down.

"Oh, my; there's no place to go." Willa heard Gina speak with a strangled gasp. Willa struggled with her nerves, which she guessed her older sister was also doing as treetops waved at them. They were standing on a ledge less than five feet wide before the sheer cutoff that separated the cliff from the forest below. The cliff face of about twelve feet in height was to their backs.

When Willa looked back and saw Gina waver, she threw her right arm across her sister's chest and looked for assistance from Dara. She, too, was pale as she stared at her surroundings. Catching Willa's look, however, Dara grabbed Willa's hand to pin Gina to the rock wall. "Open your eyes," Willa whispered into Gina's ear. "It doesn't help to close them. Dara and I will help you get over to Jonathan. Look straight ahead, and for heaven's sake, try to relax," Willa said, masking her own fear.

By now, both Jonathan in the lead and Jessie taking up the rear realized the risk they were facing. Before Jessie could react, however, Jonathan had it under control. He reached past Willa, who obliged by inching past him on the inside as she let go of Dara's hand. Jonathan gently grasped Gina's hand in his. "This is the worst of it, Gina. I promise. Even coming down, this will look like a piece of cake."

Another hiker, one who had passed them but a short time ago, looked down from above. As the hand-over-hand foot-wide horizontal bars loomed ahead for those below him, the man standing on the rocks above seemed to sense the potential danger. He reached down to help Willa. She wasn't too proud to accept the walking stick he stretched down towards her left hand. While she braced her feet on the rock wall, he pulled her upward. Because the cliff wall had a rough surface, Willa was able to use her feet for leverage.

One tug from the stranger and the six-foot tall Willa was able to reach the first bar—one that had seemed impossibly out of her grasp—with her right hand. Another tug propelled her upward and brought her within reach of the second bar. Willa let go of the walking stick and grabbed that bar. She was now able to bring herself up to within striking distance of the top of the cliff. When the man extended the stick once more, Willa grabbed the stick again in her left hand and was able to place her left foot onto the first bar. One more heave and Willa was on the top of the cliff.

"Thanks," she said to the handsome man who faced her. "I really appreciate it, but can you lend a hand with my sister and friends?"

"Not a problem," he said. "I brought my kid sister up here last year and she appreciated help from a kind stranger, too. But I suspect you didn't really need my help."

Willa wasn't sure about that as she lay on her stomach on the rocky surface to assist the stranger as he reached out to a shorter Gina. From below, Jonathan placed Gina's feet, one at a time, onto the rock face. Because Gina hadn't dared to look upward earlier, she hadn't seen the bars until they were almost level with her face. Gina reached up and grabbed first one bar, then another hand as they came into view. The stranger again used his walking stick. Willa hooked her hand into Gina's right elbow and she was dragged to the top. Once Gina was up there, she crab-walked away from the precipice and sat panting.

Since this worked so well, they followed the same plan with Dara. At the back of the pack, Jessie, too, agreed to have help. Jonathan joined them in short order. The women thanked the stranger as he tipped his ball cap and winked at Gina and Willa before he began scrambling like a mountain goat up large boulders and vanished from sight.

Willa sat to comfort Gina, who had found the experience nerve-wracking. Willa smiled towards Jonathan as he pulled water and energy bars from his backpack. "Wow, I needed that," Jonathan said. "See that up there?" He pointed up to a long line of boulders puncturing the horizon. They call that the Camel's Hump, but when I was a kid, my parents told me it was a dinosaur's back. Dad explained to me how these rock piles were left over from the last ice age."

Tension evaporated with Jonathan's story. "How old were you the first time you did this?" Willa asked. She was incredulous that a child could climb that last piece.

Jonathan broke out in a big smile: "Oh, I know what you're thinking. My dad hiked me up onto his shoulders and shoved me up the ridge while Mom reached down to us, just like that man did with you. Never be afraid to ask for help. And to answer your question, Willa, I was ten. I hear, though, that kids as young as six are allowed to climb, with their parents, of course."

As they stood to move forward, they considered themselves seasoned hikers. Jonathan had to remind them not to get too cocky and to watch out for where they placed their feet. One slip could pin a leg between large boulders and end their quest to reach the mountaintop. Added to that, the rocks were large enough for any one of them to lose sight of their party and wander off in the wrong direction. Willa remembered what she'd read in the guidebook: one must always look for white paint stripes marking the trail. It was easy to go the wrong way up here, so they all needed to stay close to one another.

This scenario put Willa in mind of another book Jessie had recommended. *Lost on a Mountain in Maine* was the true story of how young Donn Fendler had become separated from the rest of his hiking party. Of course, he had gone astray in the fog when he had tried to come *down* from the mountain alone, but even on this crisp, clear day these rocks could lead a single hiker astray.

21

Now I stand as one upon a rock.
—Titus Andronicus, 3.1.93

Less than a mile ahead they could see the Tableland, a flat plateau resembling the Arctic Tundra. But first they must traverse boulders during a steep climb. The view around them was a constant distraction, one that kept them from realizing the difficulty of the hike. It was a strenuous climb over and around the large boulders, but because it took intense concentration to not slip into crevices, Gina didn't realize that part of the journey was coming to an end until they were at The Gateway.

Gina listened in silence as Willa explained that The Gateway was what they called the last two large rocks through which they would be leaving the Camel's Hump. Willa explained that her guidebook called this part of the trail the Hunt Spur.

Gina leaned against one of the two granite stones and looked towards the flattest part of the trail yet. They had finally reached the Tableland, about a mile of flat land that would give Gina's sore calves a break. She was especially thrilled when Jonathan once more announced a rest break. She sat and thought about all that uphill climbing they'd done. It was over, she thought, just before she looked around and noted the fantastic views.

She was enthralled. "This is marvelous. I love it!" The vastness of the vistas astonished her. Now she knew it was all worth it as she stood in awe of it all.

Katahdin Drowning

"You just like the idea that there isn't much uphill left," Willa teased her sister, but Gina didn't mind.

"You got it." Gina revealed a genuine smile for the first time. "And I remember something about that travel book. There's a spring nearby named for a famous explorer."

They all looked towards Jessie, who explained that Thoreau Spring, which was about half a mile ahead, was named after Henry David Thoreau.

"But he was an author, too," Dara said as she enlightened the group. "He wrote *The Maine Woods* after he traveled all around the state." Looking at Jessie, she said, "Right?"

"Right; it was a fascinating book." Jessie pointed to Thoreau Spring in the distance. Jonathan rationed out packets of juice while they talked about Thoreau's adventures.

Listening to Jessie talk about Thoreau, Gina relaxed. She'd had mixed feelings about the whole trip. She'd been excited when plans had been made last spring, but that was because Jonathan had still looked upon her with adoring eyes. She supposed she was being selfish; after all, she had dated other men back at college. But he'd grown into such a handsome man and she had to admit that she really enjoyed having him adore her from afar. She had realized long ago, however, that he was too much like a brother. So why couldn't she just get on with her life and let him live his?

Revitalized, Gina walked across the flatlands as Jessie and Dara continued to discuss Thoreau's book. The spring was only a trickle as they passed it and began their last push for the summit. It was the easiest part of the hike, but by now they were less than a mile from the peak and everyone— including the more seasoned travelers—began to flag. They made a last push over the smaller rock climb to the top.

And it was all worth it, Gina decided, as they finally stood on top of the world. The sheer beauty of Baxter State Park stretching out below overwhelmed her.

22

I am a man.
More sinned against than sinning.
—King Lear, 3.2.59-60

Just as Jessie, Jonathan, Dara, Willa, and Gina were about to step atop Maine's largest mountain, a man back in Wyleyville was planning a covert mission. The timing was perfect. He knew that Jessie and Jonathan Tyler were away, so he could finally conduct a search of the workshop at Killdeer Farm. Ever since he'd helped look for an intruder back in July, Walker had wanted to return. He'd seen something for which he could find no rational explanation. An enlightened person would have said that he had seen a ghost. Well, he had seen something inexplicable—but he didn't believe in ghosts.

Wyleyville Police Officer Ebenezer Walker lived in a small apartment in a modern building on Cooper Street. He liked it that way. He wasn't into farming or old houses, which might explain why he didn't believe that apparitions existed. To him, ghosts were something that irrational people with too much imagination believed in. He might have roots going back generations in Wyleyville, but he was a modern thinker. He loved the beauty of the town and its environs, but in his personal life, everything must be new and shiny.

To that end, Walker had a sterile kitchen with a cook stove that had never been used and sink that had never seen dirty dishes. He ate all his meals out, most of them at the Maine Street Café. It wasn't because he couldn't cook; he just had no interest in it. His kitchen was bare, save for his radio controlled airplane kits. And why not, he would have insisted, if he'd ever had visitors who might ask him such a dumb question. The cafe had great food, so why should he mess up his spotless home with cooking. As a matter of fact, the food was so great that, Camilla, one of the waitresses, always teased him and asked, "How do you stay so darned thin?"

And he always responded in the same way: "I guess it's in my genes."

On this day, he made his plans as he ate a grilled cheese sandwich washed down with chocolate milk. Best to be bold, he decided. He'd learned that from his boss. So when Chief Michaelson had told him to cruise past Killdeer Farm to make sure everything was as it should be, Walker realized that Jessie Tyler and her friends were away on a crazy outing. He had been incredulous when the chief had explained their plans to climb Katahdin at Baxter State Park. They had gone out into the wilderness to scale a mountain, of all things.

Well, he guessed, it took all kinds. Besides, this would give him the chance he'd been waiting for. During his rounds he would go out to the Tyler place. Better yet, he could do it in the daylight, and should he be seen, he could say he was on the job. He couldn't get into trouble that way. After all, he was just following orders. And besides, he'd heard that the Lakewood clan had gone as well.

He was partially wrong there, but he wouldn't learn that until later. Cassie Lakewood, owner of the farm directly across from Killdeer Farm, didn't often leave home. She was a real homebody, and as an artist, she was able to work at home in her upstairs studio. She always used the excuse that she had farm animals to be tended. The truth was that she hated to leave home, so while Jessie was away, she watched over Killdeer Farm.

Walker didn't know this as he drove out of town and towards Killdeer Farm. Besides, he had another reason for going out there in the daylight, something he wouldn't admit to himself. If he was wrong about ghosts, he didn't want to meet one at night. As he turned his squad car into Merryfield Lane, he began to lose his nerve. After he pulled into the driveway of Killdeer Farm he didn't move for several minutes. He shook off a rising fear and kept reminding himself that he did *not* believe in ghosts.

And so he sat in his squad car working up the nerve to discover the secret of Killdeer Farm. When he finally got out, he walked around the house with trepidation. He knew the place was alarmed, but he was also under the false impression that the alarm system didn't extend into the outer building area. After all, he thought, most people in Wyleyville didn't even lock their doors. Jessie Tyler had only gotten her security system installed because her house had been broken into while she'd been working on a case that had been none of her business.

Eb Walker fumed over that one as he looked into ground level windows. He and his chief were supposed to solve the crimes in Wyleyville, not Mrs. Tyler and her band of friends. He had taken offense when Jessie Tyler and Cassie Lakewood—two middle aged women—had jumped in and caught the murderer last month.

After circling the workshop again and again, he checked all the doors. Locked. Then he saw something he could use to look into the second story. Jonathan had left a large extension ladder out back, under the storage area where the workshop didn't quite meet the ground. Walker hefted it with some trouble and fiddled with it for several minutes. He had no idea how to work these contraptions. The ladder suddenly began to extend, seemingly all on its own, and fell over backwards. He was almost trapped under it as it thumped to the ground with a mighty crash.

He cringed. He'd come scarcely inches from getting crushed. As he whistled at his close call and counted himself lucky, he noticed that the ladder had also just missed Jessie Tyler's vegetable garden. "Crikey, that's all I need. Why do people need to plant their own food? That's what restaurants are for," he muttered to himself as he put his hands on his hips to ponder his next move.

After much exertion, he lifted the ladder upright again and worked it up towards the upstairs window of the workshop. Much struggling and grunting ensued before the ladder was in place. He hated heights—something he didn't want his boss to ever find out—but he was on a mission. If he was to find out the secret of that supposed apparition in the upper regions of Jonathan Tyler's workshop, he must be bold. With shaking hands, he grabbed the sides of the ladder and on wobbly legs, propelled his feet onto the rungs, and slowly climbed. His face was just level with the window, when a voice almost dropped him to the ground.

"What do you think you're doing?"

23

Beauty too rich for use, for earth too dear!
—Romeo and Juliet, 1.5.47

"Wow!" This understatement came simultaneously from all three novices. Katahdin did that to people, Jessie thought, as she watched Dara, Gina, and Willa slowly turn full circle before each, in turn, settled on a favored scene. Dara honed in on the same thing that always awed Jessie: Chimney Pond. Gina looked far into the horizon towards Canada while Willa stared lovingly at Pamola Peak—or perhaps she was looking at the narrow path bridging the two peaks: Knife's Edge.

Before Jessie had a chance to discourage Willa about Knife's Edge, she saw Dara recoil in horror while peering straight down at Chimney Pond. Dara had been standing, transfixed for over a minute before Jessie had seen the fear materialize on her friend's face. "What's wrong?" Jessie linked an arm through Dara's as she followed her former college classmate's gaze. Deep blue water sparkled back at her.

"Oh it's, it's nothing." Dara gave an unconvincing response. Jessie let it go, but she was sure it had something to do with yesterday's shock. She knew that Dara wasn't ready to share her fears with the rest of their party. Jessie would just have to keep a close eye on her friend, she decided, as they stepped back from the edge. Chimney Pond—in Jessie's estimation—was the most beautiful pond in all of Maine. Nestled up against the back side of Katahdin, the pond was the focal point of the wooded campground below.

Katahdin Drowning

"Can we go over there?" Willa's words brought Jessie out of her trance. It nearly brought her to her knees when she saw Willa pointing towards Knife's Edge.

Jonathan laughed: "Not this time, Willa. Not with Mom along. Dad and I did it the last time we were here and Mom couldn't watch. I can't do that to her again."

Jessie wasted no time jumping into the fray: "Not a chance, Willa, and there's no next time, either." She recognized the look exchanged between the two adventurous souls. She and her friend Cassie had their work cut out for them. How would they ever manage to keep those two off Knife's Edge? She knew that countless others who had seen this stupendous bridge linking the two peaks had insisted on conquering it. They would not be denied. Well, she wouldn't—couldn't—think about that today. Luckily, thoughts were interrupted by a plea for food.

"You're the one who didn't think she could eat all her breakfast," Jonathan chided Gina.

"But that was hours ago," Gina said in what could only be called a whine. Jonathan laughed as he pulled out the sandwiches he'd made before the women had arisen that morning. He set out one for each of them and two for himself. Jessie was pleased to see Gina eat like a lumberjack.

The peanut butter and jelly sandwiches were truly delicious. Jessie pondered on how such simple fare always tasted perfect up here at the top of the world. She never tired of the view. All those mountaintops on the horizon were too beautiful to describe, she thought, as she finished eating. While sipping her water, she noticed that Gina had a puzzled expression on her face. "Gina, what are you thinking?"

"It's probably a dumb question, but why is there a mile-high sign stuck into that pile of rocks?"

Jonathan sighed and Jessie suppressed a smile when they heard Willa tease her sister for about the millionth time that day. "This peak isn't quite a mile high, dummy. Someone piled those rocks to make up the difference!" In truth, Baxter Peak rose 5,267 feet, the highest point in Maine.

"Hey, don't pick on her," Jessie said. "It makes for a great photo op for anyone brave enough to climb up here. We all need to have our pictures taken." Since everyone had finished eating, Jessie handed her digital camera to Jonathan. "Here, let's all have separate pictures and then maybe we can snag someone to take one of us together." A willing hiker who'd overheard the conversation agreed to snap off a couple of shots.

And all too soon it was time to leave. Jessie looked over to see how Dara was faring. She suspected that reality would soon come crashing down on her friend. Jessie knew Dara well enough that her friend was prone to internalizing her concerns, so she had reason to doubt Dara's earlier remark. "It's nothing," was anything but true. Granted, Dara was still a little shaky, but she seemed to be holding up as they made preparations to start back down the trail.

The trip down was always the hardest on the body because feet were sore and bodies tired. "We don't have much farther to go," said Jessie, who was in the lead for the first time. She, too, was anxious to get back to camp and rest.

"How much *farther?*" Dara suppressed a groan. She was ready to sit down and not move for the remainder of the day. Even their uncomfortable shelters were sounding more and more inviting.

"Well, maybe another mile," Jessie said as they all avoided the falls on their way to the bridge crossing Katahdin Stream. Jessie knew, however, that none of them would be passing up the chance to stop and soak their tired feet in the stream.

The resilience of the young had been tested even before the stream had come into view. Now thoughts of cool water on their feet overrode the memory of what they had found little more than twenty-four hours ago. All five sat on the riverbank and stripped off their boots and socks.

"Ahhhh!" Gina dragged out a sigh as she leaned over to cool her feet in Katahdin Stream. "This is much nicer than finding a dead body back at the falls. And I can tell all my friends back at school that I climbed Mount Katahdin!" Gina proudly beamed at the others as they, too, plunged their feet into the water.

"The book, Gina; I told you to read the book. If you had, you'd know better than to call it *Mount* Katahdin," Willa shook her head in disgust. "That translates into mountain greatest mountain."

"What are you talking about?" Gina asked.

Willa looked at the others and threw her arms up in disgust before she explained that the Indian word Katahdin meant greatest mountain. "So, if you had read the *book*, you would know that calling it Mount Katahdin is just plain repetitive."

"Well, no one told me that," Gina said.

Jonathan, who could tell that Gina was about to get into a snit, rescued her: "Willa, most people make that same mistake."

"But if she had..." Willa didn't bother to complete the sentence. She knew she was sunk. Whenever Jonathan stuck up for Gina, she might as well give up.

Jonathan smiled at Willa with sympathy. "I know you're right, Willa, but give your sister a break. We're all tired," he said as he laced up his hiking boots and stood.

Jessie was proud of her son for his sympathetic nature as he took Willa aside and gave her a brotherly hug. Jessie knew that Willa would always forgive him for siding with Gina. *And this whole trip has been so rewarding despite everything*, Jessie thought. She knew that it wouldn't be long, however, before they were back in camp and once again speculating about who killed Veronica Verne.

24

I can go no further, sir.
My old bones aches.
—The Tempest, 3.3.1-2

Camp never looked so good to the five tired hikers, even though their return was barely noticed, with one notable exception. Maine State Police Detective Hank Marley stood on the steps of the ranger station watching them as they stumbled towards their lean-tos. Jessie made note of his look of frustration. *He must not be able to pin the death on anyone,* she thought, which made her wonder if it meant that they were, indeed, dealing with murder.

Jonathan followed his mother's gaze. "Let them handle it, Mom. No one we know is in danger of losing their freedom this time. Let it rest."

Oh, little does he know, Jessie thought. If her feet hadn't hurt so much, she would have paid more attention to her surroundings, but most people who hiked more than ten miles—the last half downhill—were sore all over by this time. Downhill hiking was particularly hard on the knees, calves, and feet, and she was feeling every bit of it right now. But wait until tomorrow, Jessie admonished herself. If she thought this was bad...well, she wouldn't think about that right now.

Dara expelled a loud breath as she flopped onto the ground near the cold campfire. Even Willa, who was still riding on a high over the whole adventure, seemed glad for the chance to sit. "Wow! I can't say that enough times." She grinned from ear to ear. "That was the best thing I've ever

done. Thanks for inviting us, Aunt Jessie. You are awesome."
She turned to Jonathan and asked, "When can we come
back?"

Jessie cringed as everyone else laughed. Surely Jonathan
wouldn't bring Willa back here for that suicide walk. But
right now Dara's dilemma was of more concern to her as she
watched her son retrieve their cooler and a bag of supplies
from his truck. Before long he was making coffee and Jessie
began planning a light meal to cap off the day. She'd been so
busy with other issues that she didn't see two policemen
walk over to them.

"Welcome back." The state detective was accompanied by
the local police detective. "I have to admit that I thought that
you might sneak down one of the other trails to avoid me."

"And just why would we do that?" Jessie scowled at both
officers. "We have nothing to hide, and you're losing out on
an opportunity by keeping us out of the investigation."

Confusion was etched on Millinocket detective Briscoe's
face as Marley explained the situation to him. "These people
are what we call amateur detectives."

Before he could continue to put down her friends, Willa
spoke up. "Only Aunt Jessie and Jonathan are the detectives. We just helped compile data, right Gina?" Gina nodded.

"Well, it doesn't matter which of you are the amateurs
because none of you are going to interfere with *my* investigations. Is that clear?" Marley said.

"*Is* there a murder case here?" Jessie asked.

"Let's just say that none of you are going anywhere soon.
We need to do background checks on all of you to make sure
that none of you knew—or had reason to dislike—the victim,"
Marley said. As Marley shuffled his feet, he looked longingly
at the pot of delicious smelling coffee.

"Detectives," the park ranger yelled from across the
stream. Standing in the doorway of his increasingly smaller
ranger station, Jerome Goodroe was about to deliver bad

news to the strangers who had invaded his sanctuary. "I think you'll want to hear the latest."

"Goodroe, keep it to yourself until we get there." Marley admonished the ranger for speaking out of turn. *Amateurs!* They seemed to be everywhere. He silently cursed the loss of a decent cup of coffee as he turned and motioned the still silent Briscoe over the small bridge towards the ranger station.

They left a confused band of hikers in their wake. "What do you suppose that was all about?" Jessie asked. "I'm sure your coffee was beckoning Marley. We might have learned more if that ranger had just held off a bit longer. Maybe they've heard from Augusta."

"Augusta? Why Augusta?" Dara asked. "Isn't that state man from Bangor?"

"Well," Willa explained before any of the others could respond, "the state's medical examiner is in Augusta and he does autopsies whenever there are suspicious deaths. Right, Aunt Jessie?"

"Right you are, Willa," Jonathan jumped in while his mother just nodded. He'd seen the worry in his mother's eyes and wondered what was wrong. Before he had a chance to ask his mother what was bothering her, however, she'd grabbed Dara up for a short walk. *Hadn't they had enough exercise for one day?* Jonathan shook his head in puzzlement.

Jessie and Dara picked their way over to a short path near the edge of the campground. "Here, sit and let's talk," Jessie said after glimpsing around to make sure they were alone. Both women groaned as they carefully lowered themselves onto the ground. "Something scared you up on the mountain."

"Oh, Jessie, for a minute I thought I saw *her* floating in Chimney Pond." Dara wiped her damp brow and said,

Katahdin Drowning

"Maybe it's my guilty conscience for not admitting that I knew her." Dara peered around the trees and rocks before she whispered: "I've been wondering if I should tell the police about knowing Bertie."

"Bertie?" Jessie was confused. "Do you mean Bertha, aka Veronica?"

"Yes, you see, she always hated the name Bertha, so she made everyone call her Bertie. I guess she really went overboard if she changed her name to Veronica Verne." Dara shook her head, "Should I tell the police?"

"I don't know what to say, Dara. If it were me, I guess I'd keep it to myself. After all, if you haven't seen her in all these years, why would they consider you as a suspect? You can always say you didn't recognize her; that is, if they find out."

"I suppose you're right," Dara's thoughts were interrupted in the dim light as they heard a commotion back at camp. Startled, Dara jumped up and groaned. "Ouch, that hurt. We'd better get back and see what's going on. Maybe they found the killer." Dara was full of hope as the two friends linked arms and limped back into camp.

But it was not to be. The fuss was about a missing hiker. "I know she was right behind me," said a frantic young woman. "My mother's lost. Do something!"

"Look, before I go dashing off, I need more information. Calm down a minute." Ranger Goodroe was trying to get the young woman to sit and talk to him. "Let me see." He looked at the list of hikers he had just retrieved from the trailhead sign-in board. "Okay, I see that Marta and Melissa Walters have not checked in."

"I'm Melissa. Please find my mom!" The young woman was not faring well.

"I see. So Marta is your mother. How old is she? Does she have any medical problems?"

"What does *that* matter?"

"It's important because I need to know what to take with me. I also need to know where you hiked today." By now, most of the campground residents were huddling around, trying to hear about the lost woman. "Please stand back, folks. I have everything under control."

"She's healthy and she's forty-one. We went up the trail, but only as far as the bridge. We stopped to look down at the water for a while. I know she was right behind me when we got ready to come back down. But when I turned to find her, she was gone. Please, don't waste any more time. Go and get her."

"I wasn't wasting time. What you told me gives me an idea where to search. I bet she took the wrong turn where the two trails meet. I'll probably find her on the one leading to The Owl." The ranger looked around, as though hunting for someone to take care of the young lady while he went on his search.

Jessie stepped forward. "Come with us, Melissa. The ranger will find your mother." Jessie turned to the ranger as Dara escorted the young lady to their campsite. "Do you need any help? I'm sure my son would be willing to go with you, if that's allowed, of course." Jessie could see that the whole Veronica Verne business had taken its toll on the ranger. He seemed to be very tired and night was quickly approaching. He might make a mistake if he went into the woods alone.

"I am supposed to go alone, but..."

"Say no more," Jessie waved Jonathan over. He quickly agreed to help and the two went off together. After the ranger filled his backpack with first aid supplies and a flashlight, he and Jonathan vanished into the darkening woods.

25

What, all so soon asleep! I wish mine eyes
Would, with themselves, shut up my thoughts.
                                    —The Tempest, 2.1.191-192

Hours passed, or so it seemed to those left behind. Jessie regretted offering Jonathan up for a rescue mission. *What had she been thinking? She should have just let the park ranger do his job.* Well, there was nothing she could do about it now, she decided, as she attempted to keep herself busy preparing a light meal. Even though they invited the young Melissa to join them, the girl declined any food. While she sat by the fire, even Willa and Gina—who were close to Melissa's age—were unable to console her. It was a relief, therefore, when one of the officers took her off their hands and escorted her into the ranger station to sit in comfort while she awaited her mother's return.

After dinner, Willa and Gina went to bed early. Dara was in the lean-to she shared with Jessie, reading on the new Kindle she'd brought along. Jessie had been contemplating an e-book purchase for some time, but the librarian in her loved the touch of a real book in her hands.

Nothing to do about Jonathan now, she decided. She might as well keep busy. She groaned right down to the soles of her feet as she limped off to talk to some nearby campers. She soon found a couple sitting by a fire outside their tent. "Hello, my name's Jessie Tyler. I noticed that you came in about the same time as we did."

"I'm Tessa and this is my husband Roger. You hiked the big mountain today." Tessa rubbed her tired legs, which were extended towards the fire. "I'm afraid I'm not in good enough shape for that one. We've been doing the lesser trails around here. Roger is so patient with me. I told him to go for it, but he insisted on staying with me."

"Darling, I'd rather enjoy your company. The hiking trails around here are enough exercise for me." Roger waved for Jessie to sit. "Say, wasn't it you and your friends who found the body?"

"Yes, I confess." Jessie's eyes widened when she saw the collective look of horror in their eyes. "I mean, I confess that we found the body, not..."

Roger laughed. "I know what you meant." He leaned forward and lowered his voice. "We were up at the falls yesterday, too, only earlier. I'm sure glad we didn't know that lady, because the state policeman gave us a funny look when we told him we'd been there. I'm sure he's checking us out. Let him. The closest either of us ever got to her was when Tessa watched her TV show." Roger's voice lowered again, as though they were all in a conspiracy. "Not like that man in that tent over there." He pointed to the tent near the trailhead.

"Oh, Roger, you must have misunderstood him. And he didn't even call her by her name. He said something like Beeta."

"It was Bertha. And he was calling out to that TV lady, I know he was," Roger said.

Jessie stopped listening. Bertha? According to Dara, that was Veronica Verne's real name. Now what? How could she pass this information on to the police? "Sorry." She was brought back to reality when Tessa shook her arm.

Luckily Tessa had changed the subject. "I was asking about your son. Why did he go off into the woods with the park ranger?"

"Oh, you didn't hear? A hiker is lost."

"Oh, no, we were in the ranger's cabin being grilled by that policeman when a hysterical girl was brought in. I think she's still in there, but they ushered us out without saying why she was so upset," Tessa said.

"Well, that's the reason," Jessie said. "By the way, did you tell them what that other camper said to the victim?" She decided to let them spill the beans. That would keep Dara out of it.

"Well, no," Roger said. "Tessa was so positive that I was wrong."

"What are you doing, Mrs. Tyler? Didn't I tell you to stay out of our business?" Detective Marley sputtered. He had obviously overheard their conversation as he came up the path.

"But..."

"But nothing, Mrs. Tyler!" Marley knew all about her type: busybodies.

"But, she might be right," Tessa Rowley said. "I told my husband not to tell you because I didn't think he could be talking to *her*."

"Her, who?" Marley asked.

It was Roger Rowley's turn to speak. As he told the policeman what he had heard, Jessie melted into the background. All she needed was for Marley to give her more grief. He had his information, which is all Jessie cared about.

Back at the campfire, she sat and watched the glowing embers as the fire died away. She would get no sleep until Jonathan returned. She supposed she could hide in her lean-to, but she might as well let Marley give her a piece of his mind, if he was so inclined, which he did a short time later.

"I suppose you're proud of yourself, Mrs. Tyler, Well, don't get too cocky. I imagine that tidbit will prove to be nothing at all."

"But you're going to check it out, right?"

"Of course I will, but I want you to keep your nose out of my investigation."

"I'll try," Jessie said.

"You'll do more than try," he said as he stalked away from her and back towards the ranger station.

Dara crawled from their lean-to after the detective had left. "What was that all about?"

"Is that an extra blanket you have there?" Jessie asked. Dara draped one over Jessie's shoulders and wrapped herself in the second blanket. "Sit," Jessie said. "We need to talk." Jessie lowered her voice. "It seems that you aren't the only one who knew Bertha."

Dara frowned and looked around the dark camp. "What do you mean?"

After Jessie told her friend all about her interview with the tenters, Dara whistled. "Someone else from Bertha's past? I'm not sure that's good news for me. What if it's someone from our old high school? He might remember me."

26

All losses are restored, and sorrows end.

—Sonnet 30, 14

Barely two hours after the young men had taken off into the dusky woods, they returned with a sheepish Marta Walters. As the ranger had suspected, Walters had taken a wrong turn. When the daughter who'd been so difficult to handle learned of her mother's return, she came screaming from the ranger station.

"Mom! Are you okay?" Melissa raced forward and clutched her mother.

"Darling, stop," Marta cried out with delight. "I'm fine, but you're squeezing me too tightly. I'm just embarrassed about getting lost. I can't believe I went right when I should have gone left." Mother and daughter laughed and cried all at once. They thanked Ranger Goodroe profusely as he escorted them into the ranger station.

Jessie waited for the drama to end before she approached her son. "Well, that was quite spectacular. I guess you're a hero now."

"Nonsense, Mom. I just went along with Jerome. He was fantastic. I mean, I know it's his job, but Jerome was so confident. It was like another whole adventure for me, after we found the woman safe and sound. Jerome said it's all in a day's work. And he guessed right the first time. It turned out that Mrs. Walters *had* tried to get back to camp by taking The Owl trail."

"Well, I'm proud of you, son. You deserve a treat, how

about s'mores?"

Everyone perked up at that suggestion. Willa rummaged around in a spare backpack designated for non-perishables while Jonathan dashed over to his truck for sticks he had whittled for roasting marshmallows. Soon they were all joking over the last time each of them had enjoyed this delicacy. When Gina's marshmallow fell into the fire, Jonathan graciously pulled a golden one from his stick. He placed it on a piece of chocolate before he mashed both between two graham crackers and handed it to Gina. This process was repeated several times before Marta and Melissa crossed the bridge and approached Jonathan.

"I guess I was rude earlier. I'm sorry," Melissa said. "I want to thank you for helping find my mother." Melissa hugged her mother as they stood smiling at Jonathan.

"Won't you join us for s'mores?" Jessie asked.

Before her mother could decline the invitation, Melissa plunked herself down next to Jonathan by way of acceptance.

Marta smiled as she, too, pulled up a log and joined the fun. "This is delicious," she said as she tasted the s'mores, "but we just came over to thank you for rescuing me." Marta smiled at Jonathan before she turned to the others. "This young man was very helpful, you know. I got all turned around in the dark, but I didn't dare to leave the path. I was just sitting there, trying to decide which way to go because, by then, it was pitch dark. We didn't think to take a flashlight along; we were so sure we'd be back well before sunset. And then two heroes materialized out of the night. I was never so happy in my life."

"Hey, I was glad to help, but Ranger Goodroe is the one who knew what he was doing. I just tagged along."

"Oh, I'm sure it was more than that," said Melissa. Now that the scare was over, the girl's eyes sparkled with delight whenever she looked at Jonathan.

The party broke up after Gina and Willa lost all interest

in the party and went off to bed. Likewise, Melissa's mother retreated to her own site. Melissa chatted with Jonathan while Jessie and Dara retreated into their lean-to. Jessie's last thought before falling to sleep was, *Oh, dear, Jonathan has an admirer.*

27

Is it possible
That love should of a sudden take such hold?
—The Taming of the Shrew, 1.1.146-147

Every bone ached—or so it seemed—as Jessie gingerly rolled from her lean-to. She forgot her pain, however, when she saw Jonathan sitting around the campfire drinking coffee with Melissa. Jessie wondered if they had been sitting there all night. She shook her head to dispel the possibility. "Good morning, kids."

Melissa nodded vaguely in Jessie's direction, but she only had eyes for Jonathan. "You're so brave to have gone out into those scary woods to rescue my mother. I don't know what I would have done if you hadn't found her." The girl batted her eyelashes, but Jonathan didn't appear to notice. When he didn't respond, she expelled a huge sigh. "Well, I'd better go and see if my mother is up yet. Thank you for talking to me, Jonathan." Melissa gave him a coy smile before reluctantly walking away.

"No, Mom. We weren't up all night."

"I never said..."

"No, but I could tell, from the look you gave us, that you thought so. Melissa got up early and saw me from over at her site, and well, one thing led to another."

This exchange brought the rest of the party from their lean-tos. Once the others had poured and were enjoying their coffee, they chatted about last evening's excitement. As a result, only Jessie saw newcomers arrive when another state police vehicle pulled into the campground. Jessie groaned when she saw who emerged from the cruiser. "Jonathan," Jessie whispered. "Look."

"I see." Jonathan gaped at the newcomers. "This is *not* good."

"Tell me about it. I'd like to just crawl back into my lean-to and never come out again."

"You two look like you've seen a ghost." Dara teased her friend as she stood to pour another cup of coffee. The elegant aroma made her forget her painful muscles as she sipped and purred with pleasure.

"Quick, Dara. Sit over here," Jessie motioned for her friend to sit so as to block her from the two new state policemen striding towards the footbridge. "Maybe they won't see us."

"See us?" Jonathan laughed. "Mom, our names are on the park's checklist." Deciding to face the devil you know, he got up to intercept the two men before they could vanish into the ranger station. "Good morning, Detective Wilkins and Officer Milo." Jonathan produced an innocent smile. Before either could respond, Jonathan said, "So, it is murder."

Wilkins' eyes widened and his jaw dropped. "Do not tell me that you're here with your mother and her friend."

"Okay, I won't. Aunt Cassie didn't come with us, but aren't you lucky? Mom and I can help, just like old times."

"How often do I have to tell you people to keep your noses out of police business?" Detective Wilkins' fist crumpled over the coroner's report he'd been carrying. Before he could register his full displeasure, they were joined by Detective Marley.

Marley was surprised to have reinforcements already talking to one of his witnesses. "I see you've introduced yourself to one of the people who found the body, but first shouldn't we have a meeting about how to proceed?"

Jessie watched with amusement as her son was not to be denied a chance to shock the police. "Oh, we already know each another."

Over this revelation, Wilkins bellowed, "*You? You* found the body? Next you'll be telling me your mother was there, too."

"I guess you don't want to hear that," Jonathan said, "so I won't tell you, but she was."

Wilkins slapped his forehead and shook his head. After the officers introduced themselves to one another, he said, "Marley, I pity you. You have two of the worst pains in the..." Wilkins thought it wiser to say no more. "Let's go inside and talk. And, for heaven's sake, leave these civilians outside."

Before they had a chance to walk further than the porch, Jessie heard Jonathan drop the bombshell, "Then I guess you don't want to hear about the suspect my mother uncovered last night."

Nesowadnehunk Stream's Ledge Falls proved to be a great reprieve for the Wyleyville hikers. Since they were now allowed some freedom within Baxter State Park, they had followed up on their morning plans with a drive up the Tote Road to the falls. Jessie would rather have stuck around to see Detective Wilkins' reaction to her son's revelation, but the officers had retreated into Ranger Goodroe's cabin with little more than a backward glare.

The party had all piled into Jonathan's truck to make the seven mile side trip because none of them felt up to the walk. The slide—as many called Ledge Falls—was the perfect place to chill out. All of them took advantage of the cool water in which to swim and relax. Ledge Falls was fifty yards of huge flat rocks that water and time had smoothed out so that swimmers could start at one end of the sluice and just let the flowing water propel them down towards a pool that was deep enough in which to swim.

This outing was both relaxing and beneficial: every one of them was glad for a chance to cool down, loosen tired muscles, and let nature wash away two days' accumulation of trail dust.

"This is fantastic!" Dara grinned joyfully.

"I told you this would be great." This was always Jessie's favorite activity after a long hike. It certainly was the best way to relax after everything they'd been through. Jessie just hoped they would soon be allowed to go home. She wasn't confident, however, that this nightmare would be over any time soon because she feared that the police would learn of Dara's connection to the victim. If that should happen, she would just *have* to get involved.

28

For murder, though it have no tongue, will speak.
—Hamlet, 2.2.593

An ever-growing number of police officers sat staring at one another in silence after Wilkins officially reported that Veronica Verne's death was, indeed, murder. "Take a look at this." Wilkins handed the coroner's report to Marley. While he waited for the Bangor detective to read the coroner's results, Wilkins mentally ticked off the salient points.

Water in the victim's lungs proved that she did drown, but she'd had help. Bruising had been found on Verne's upper back in the shape of a footprint. The coroner theorized that the victim had been knocked down before she was drowned by having her head forced—and held—underwater until she had expired. This, along with the news that Jessie Tyler had found someone who knew the victim from years ago, had them all momentarily speechless.

"Okay," Detective Wilkins was the first to speak when he saw that Marley had finished reading the report. "Since we have a murder on our hands, I have a suggestion. This goes against everything I know about criminal investigations, but I think we need to reconsider the involvement of the Tyler clan."

After Wilkins had learned that his nemesis was here— and a key player as well—he'd decided something he never thought he would consider. Sometimes it was better to keep the enemy—or in this case, a rival for solving *his* murder— close by.

Katahdin Drowning

"You mean, you think one of them did it? But they were all together. If one did it, they *all* must be guilty. I suppose that's not totally impossible. I read an Agatha Christie novel once where all of the suspects were guilty," Officer Milo said.

"No, Milo." Wilkins gave his assistant a look of exasperation. "I'm talking about letting them in on the investigation."

"Wha-what? That's impossible! Civilians cannot take part in any of my cases." Marley sputtered his disapproval.

"Well, it just might cause you less headache. I don't say this lightly, you know." Wilkins went on to state his case before any objections could be formed. "I know, I know. When I found out that woman was here—of all places—I thought 'How can this be happening?' Here I am responding to a call for help in northern Maine, and one of the people who made my job difficult on more than one occasion is on the scene." To blank stares, Wilkins continued in a frustrated voice. "Look, I've had these people all over two of my cases, and you know what? They, not me, solved both of them. It was less than two months ago that I got egg on my face when I was carting the wrong man off to jail. I walked right past where Jessie Tyler and Cassandra Lakewood, that's Mrs. Tyler's friend, had tied up and were sitting on the real killer. Talk about embarrassing!"

Marley just shook his head. He wasn't convinced. "I don't think so, Wilkins. I know you have seniority over me, but I really don't want those people interfering."

"Then I suggest that you send them home. That's the only way you'll be able to keep them out of your hair." Since Wilkins was getting nowhere with this conversation, he changed the subject. "What about the man who knew the victim?"

"I talked to a Roger Rowley last evening. He's the man who overheard someone who supposedly recognized the victim. I haven't had time to pursue that angle yet, what with people butting into my investigations," Marley said. "It sounded like a dead-end to me. The man he mentioned didn't even call her Veronica Verne."

"I understand that things come up, but let's talk to this Rowley chap again and see if he sounds like he knows what he's talking about." Wilkins turned to his assistant. "Milo, fetch him for us, please."

After receiving directions, Milo took off with barely a nod. Wilkins smiled at his assistant's retreating figure. Wilkins had begun looking at his assistant in a new light ever since they had worked together in Wyleyville. The boy showed promise and he followed orders well.

Before Wilkins had time to further speculate on Milo's future, Roger Rowley had joined them. Rowley repeated what he'd heard the morning of Veronica Verne's death. "Yes, I *am* sure the man called her Bertha. He looked upset when she ignored him." After Rowley was excused, a short discussion ensued before the man in the last tent was summoned.

A nervous Barry Rockford was escorted into the borrowed cabin. "What do you want with me?" He fidgeted as he took the proffered hot seat. "I don't know anything about that dead person."

Wilkins sat back and let Marley run the show. He found that he frequently learned more by just listening.

"That's not what we hear. Someone heard you call her Bertha."

"Case of mistaken identity," said Rockford.

"Funny thing about that," Wilkins said. "You see, I have Ms. Verne's full case file right here." He slowly opened a manila file and flipped through the pages.

Rockford's face turned purple as he stammered. "But, but, that was a long time ago. I didn't know she'd be here, or I woulda stayed away. I never wanted to see that woman again. She was poison, pure poison, I tell you. I hadn't seen her in years!"

"Well, I guess it's a good thing Detective Wilkins looked into Ms. Verne's background before he arrived." Marley nodded his appreciation to Wilkins. "Just tell us how you knew her all those years ago."

"Back in school her name was Bertha Crumm, but she liked to be called Bertie. She always hated her name. I'm not surprised she changed it. I haven't seen her since we graduated from high school, really."

"So why haven't you been honest with us? You should have told us right away," Marley said.

"Well, I thought you'd blame me. Besides," he said as an afterthought, "I'm not the only person here who knew her. I saw someone else here from our high school, and it's someone who had good reason to hate her. Bertha was always nice to us boys, but she was just plain mean to the girls. She was a bully."

"A woman, you say? Who's that?"

"I don't remember her name. She was younger than us. It was something like Donna. I forget, but she's over there with those people that guy was talking to a little while ago." Rockford pointed at Detective Wilkins.

Just great! Wilkins thought as he looked over the list of names of people staying in the campground. There, he had it. Dara Kane was bunked down with Jessie Tyler.

In the meantime, Marley continued to quiz Rockford. "We need to know where you went on the day before yesterday. Give me a rundown of your day."

"I was with my family all day. We hiked together and never separated."

"Where did you hike?" Marley asked.

"We went up to Katahdin Stream Falls first, and then we went over towards The Owl. My daughter didn't want to do anything strenuous, so we came back to camp and wandered around close by. We were in camp most of the afternoon. Ask the ranger."

"We will. You and your daughter need to sign a statement. Was there anyone else with you?"

"Just my wife, Esther, but like I said, we stayed together all day."

"Good enough. I'll have someone take your statements. We'll begin with you." Marley looked around. "Darn, Detective Briscoe is at the main gate helping sign out people from other campgrounds."

Wilkins looked in Milo's direction. "Right, sir; I can do that," Milo said.

After Marley had set Milo up in the office with Rockford, he returned to have a chat with Detective Wilkins. "What do you think?" Before giving Wilkins a chance to respond, however, Marley pointed to the file. "It's a good thing you had that."

"Yes, it made a great prop."

"You mean that Veronica Verne's real name isn't in there?"

"Nope," Wilkins shook his head. "I was bluffing and it worked. But there's other good stuff in here."

29

He was my friend, faithful and just to me.
                              —Julius Caesar, 3.2.85

Marley smiled. He could learn from this man. Sometimes it paid to bluff, he decided as they scanned the file. "Say, Verne was married. I'm surprised, since she was so interested in nailing other men."

"That doesn't preclude fooling around. Besides, see right here," Wilkins pulled a page from the file, "she served divorce papers on her husband before she left Boston. Name's Richard Cameron; says here that he likes to be called Rocky." Alarm bells went off in his head. While Marley had interrogated the others, Wilkins had been reading all the check-in lists and he'd seen that name. Not Richard, but Rocky.

"I think I remember that name. Give me a minute." He reshuffled the sign-in sheets and began scanning. Nothing on any of the Katahdin Stream lists, but he found it on an Abol Campground list. Rocky Cameron of Boston, Massachusetts, had hiked Katahdin on the same day his wife had been killed.

Astonished with this new information, the officers wasted no time in tracking down the missing husband. The main gate reported that the man in question had left the park before the body had been discovered. He'd been a day visitor to Abol, one who had left without causing a stir. Marley suddenly remembered seeing a photo in the box of material they had collected from the Verne lean-to. The image was of a couple during happier days, but now it had pin pricks in it.

Veronica Verne must have been using it as a target for her wrath.

Marley had an idea. After rummaging around in an evidence box, he pulled out the photo, jumped up, and went outside, startling Wilkins with his abruptness. As Wilkins followed him onto the porch, he watched Marley stride over to a nearby lean-to and talk to the young man sitting there in gloomy silence. Marley crooked his finger at the man and the two soon returned to where Wilkins stood. "Detective Wilkins, this is Evan Kinderhook. He was Veronica Verne's cameraman." Marley held out the picture and waved it in front of Kinderhook's face. "Ever seen this man?" he asked.

"That's him! That's the man who saw me drop my camera. He was sitting on a rock above where we climbed the cliff face."

"Did Ms. Verne see him?"

"You know, I think she did."

Marley turned back to Wilkins. "Do you have any questions for this young man?"

"Not right now, but perhaps later."

As the relieved cameraman retreated back to the safety of his lean-to, the detectives began contemplating on which new suspect to question first. It wasn't a hard decision to make, since Rocky Cameron was no longer in the park. Wilkins informed Officer Milo to get on the horn to headquarters. "Find out where this Cameron guy is and have him returned here. I don't care if someone has to chase him all the way to Boston."

"On it, boss," Milo said before he retreated into the ranger station.

Meanwhile Marley and Wilkins turned their attention to someone they could lay their hands on. "This is not going to be pleasant, you know," Wilkins said. "That Tyler woman pulls out all the stops when it comes to protecting her friends."

"Well, that's just great." Marley groaned as they left the

porch to face the Tyler group. He loved police work most of the time, but not when he met up with people who tried to tell him how to do his job. This threatened to be one of those times as he and Wilkins strode over the small bridge and into the main part of the campground. Marley didn't waste any time. "Ms. Kane?"

Dara's face became etched with pain when she heard the detective single her out. "Yes? Did you want me for something?"

"You need to come back to the ranger station with us to answer a few questions."

"Hold it one minute, Detective Marley. She's going nowhere without me." Turning to Detective Wilkins, Jessie restated her case. "You know better than try to separate us, unless Dara wants to see you alone, of course, which I doubt very much." One look told Jessie she was right.

"I have nothing to hide, detectives, but I'd rather talk to you right here," Dara said.

"Well, I have no objections, but this is official, so I need someone to take notes." Wilkins looked back towards the ranger cabin and saw his assistant on the porch. He waved Milo forward and met the man halfway. After a brief discussion, the two men came forward and settled around the campfire.

"Milo, as some of you already know, works with me. He'll take notes and type up a statement for your signature." Wilkins turned to Jessie so there would be no misunderstanding. "This *is* official, so if you object to any of this, we can do this in a more formal setting."

Jessie and Dara exchanged looks before Dara said, "It's okay, but I don't know what I can tell you."

"Well, the first thing you can explain is why you didn't tell us that you knew Veronica Verne," Marley said. Taking a page from Wilkins' book, he bluffed. "And don't try to deny it, because we were told all about you."

"If you know all about me, then you know that I never

knew Veronica Verne. I knew Bertha Crumm. She always hated her name, so I'm not surprised she changed it."

Jonathan, Gina, and Willa gaped: *Dara knew the victim?*

"Are you saying that you didn't recognize her when you arrived at the campground?" Marley wasn't buying her story.

"Of course I recognized her, but it was only that first morning, when she made all the fuss about some tiny mice in her lean-to. That was the first time I'd seen her since I was in high school."

"And you had no reason to hate her?"

"I wouldn't say that I hated her. There was no love lost between us, but that was years ago. I'd forgotten all about her. I had no reason to want to revisit that relationship."

"Well, tell us all about that 'relationship,' as you call it."

And Dara did with complete honesty, which put her squarely on the growing list of suspects. Jessie silently groaned at her friend's candid disclosure.

30

For my part, if a lie may do thee grace,
I'll gild it with the happiest terms I have.
                    —Henry IV, Part 1, 5.4.157-158

Millinocket Detective Walter Briscoe had discovered something interesting while the others had been questioning Dara Kane. As he finished circulating the campground, he came upon Barbara Porter. Interviews had spiraled outward, using Veronica Verne's lean-to as the starting point.

Miss Porter had been adamant about what she'd seen. "I saw that ranger fellow ripping stuff from the outhouse near the dead woman's campsite, and then he threw everything into her lean-to. You should talk to him." She'd explained how she had been sitting near the stream, so she had overheard his tirade against the celebrity.

Briscoe approached the two state policemen. "Hey, detectives, I just learned something interesting." After these new revelations, a quick change in plans ensued. Park Ranger Jerome Goodroe came under suspicion.

"Why didn't you mention having a run-in with the victim?" Briscoe asked once they had Goodroe sitting in front of them. He thought it was too bad the boy had to be grilled in his own home, but they all had their jobs to do. "Before you deny anything," Briscoe didn't give the ranger a chance to speak, "let me tell you that we have a witness who said your face was red with anger as you yanked apart the blankets that the victim had draped in her outhouse."

"That's not true." The young man denied the allegations. "I mean, once I saw all the trouble she had gone to." Goodroe couldn't help but chuckle. "Sorry, but you should have seen the place. I mean, she had to have gone to a lot of trouble..."

"What do you mean by that?"

"Well, she had fancy pink curtains hung up on three walls. Talk about being prepared. The curtains were even held up by those spring-loaded rods." Goodroe paused. "Look, I never thought of it as being anything out of the usual. All in a day's work for me; people frequently complain about the lack of amenities. I can't let it bother me when they gripe about something. She was just one of those people who thought nothing was ever enough."

"Our witness said you acted as though it was more than the usual thing. She said that you told the victim she couldn't have her own outhouse, and then after she'd left, you went to the outhouse and threw her stuff into her lean-to," Detective Briscoe said.

"That's not exactly true," Goodroe said. "Yes, I removed the blankets, but I folded them neatly and placed them inside her lean-to. She also ordered me to clean her lean-to, but I do that only after someone has left their site for good. I didn't touch her place, beyond getting two tiny field mice out, but that was before she took off on her hike. I deal with much more serious complaints every day."

"Well, the witness didn't think it seemed like a normal encounter." The other detectives sat back and listened while Briscoe finished the interview. After all, he had been the one to discover the new information.

"Just who complained?" Goodroe asked.

"We can't tell you who said what, young man."

"Then how can I defend myself? Was it a camper who said all this? If so, how would she know what is normal for park employees to deal with on any given day?"

"How do you know it was a female witness?"

"You said 'she' when you told me what she said," Goodroe countered.

"Good point. He's right, Briscoe. But let's not get away

from the point. Are you saying that Veronica Verne's behavior was normal?" Marley asked.

"Oh, yes, you have no idea. We deal with unreasonable types every day, but this lady was just an annoyance."

"So you're saying that our witness was wrong about you removing the curtains?"

"No, your witness was only wrong about me being angry. If my face was red, it was from amusement when I saw what Ms. Verne had done to one of my outhouses." Goodroe grinned once more. "You see, some people just hate outhouses. I've seen all sorts of things tacked up to make the place more pleasing. But, gentlemen, I did not *rip* the curtains down or throw them. Like I already said, I neatly folded them and placed them nicely into one corner of the lean-to. And they should still be there. Go and check."

"We certainly will. Photographs were taken of the lean-to and all the items inside were cataloged. If we find that things aren't as you said, we *will* be talking again. I can't let you be involved in the investigation, at least not yet. Turn over all of the paperwork you've been working on to Officer Milo." Wilkins ended the conversation.

Ranger Goodroe suddenly felt deflated when he was told to get back to his everyday work in the campground. He was disappointed to be left out, and he certainly didn't like being added to the list of suspects.

31

The miserable have no other medicine
But only hope.
— Measure for Measure, 3.1.2-3

It wasn't long before the detectives received word that Richard Cameron had been found back at his office in Boston acting as though nothing had happened. The Boston police reported that he didn't flinch when told his wife was dead. He denied ever leaving town, but they soon dispelled that lie. With evidence faxed down to the Boston Police Department, they had convinced Cameron that it would be wise to return to Maine. After he had reluctantly agreed, a trooper was dispatched to accompany Cameron to the Maine State Police headquarters in Augusta for questioning.

Even though Goodroe was being kept out of the investigations, he heard things. He'd been in the office at the time, so he had overheard their discussion about the husband. Goodroe also knew that Wilkins had invited Marley down to Augusta on the following day to assist in interviewing the husband. Goodroe only hoped that they would all leave soon. For the time being, they continued to use his cabin as headquarters to conduct interviews and collect data.

Time seemed to stand still for everyone, especially for Goodroe, who was anxious to have his name cleared. He passed the time making the rounds of his campground. Since he had been told to stick close, he did the part of his job that he found most interesting: he visited the campers to find out if anyone needed anything. Of course, if he also found the woman who had told all those lies about him, he would be very happy, indeed.

He began his rounds—and the search for his persecutor—at the far end of the campground, where tenters were still in residence. The first tent was a larger one in which a family of three was making the best of things. Before he approached, he consulted his sheet. Barry, Esther, and Kim Rockford, he noted. "How are things going today?"

"Not good," a dark haired Esther said. "We'd like to go home now. My husband has to get back to his business, and my daughter's getting antsy. She has just so much music on her iPod." Mrs. Rockford looked lovingly over at her beautiful daughter. Kim stretched her dainty frame out on a blanket, her long blond hair covering most of her face, save the vivid blue eyes.

"Well, I certainly am sorry to hear that. If I get a chance, I'll ask the police when we can begin letting people leave. To be honest, though, I have little control over it."

"But Mom-m," the petulant Kim said, "I wanna go now!"

"We can't leave until we're told we can." Barry attempted to placate his daughter. Like his wife, he had brown hair and brown eyes, but unlike her plain-Jane appearance, he was very handsome. Goodroe decided that must be where the girl gets her looks.

Goodroe expressed his sympathy as he moved on. He wondered if it had been this Esther person who had lied about him. But there were more people he hadn't checked in with yet. Barbara Porter seemed to be pleasant enough as she flipped back her tent flap and came outside to greet him. She smiled winningly at the ranger. He wondered what it was about city women. Like Veronica Verne, this woman was blonde and beautiful, but since her hair was darker at the roots, he suspected it was dyed.

He moved on to campers in lean-tos. By the time he had reached the last group before crossing the stream, he was tired of all the complainers. He was ready for the friendly face that finally greeted him. "Hello, Jonathan." Goodroe shook the hand of the young man who'd helped him on his rescue mission. "How are you making out? I'm sorry you can't leave yet." He grinned with pleasure as Jonathan handed him a steaming cup of coffee. "Why, thank you. You're the first person to offer me anything more than trouble."

Jonathan laughed. "Sit and tell me everything you know."

Ranger Jerome Goodroe complied. He vented his frustration by talking about the trouble he was in. It wasn't long before he had an audience. Jessie and Dara joined them first, but Willa and Gina weren't far behind.

"You need our help," Jessie said. "You say that one of the women in camp told a lie about you?"

Goodroe found it a nice change to have a sympathetic audience. By the time he had returned to his porch, however, he had received bad news. Detective Marley had retrieved the evidence bags filled with Verne's personal belongings. The curtains had been slashed. The detectives were now theorizing on how Goodroe had taken his hunting knife to all the victim's personal items.

"But, I tell you, I didn't do it." Goodroe stared at the curtains inside the evidence bags. "Someone else did that." He turned on Marley, "You need to tell me who told those lies about me. She has to be the one who did it. It wasn't me. Please let me confront her."

Marley seemed loathe to comply, but Wilkins had no such compunctions. He would get to the bottom of this, one way or another. "Milo, go get that woman. What was her name?"

Since it was the Millinocket detective who had questioned Barbara Porter, he jumped up and offered to get her. He wasn't gone long before an ashen faced woman in her mid-thirties was ushered into the ranger station. "Here she is," Briscoe said. He motioned her to a seat across from Goodroe, who sat fuming in the woman's direction. So she was the one. He should have guessed, what with all that fake blonde hair.

"Now," Wilkins said, "We seem to have a discrepancy in statements, Ms. Porter. Are you sure about what you observed this ranger doing with those outhouse curtains?"

Porter sputtered before she came out with her story. "Oh, yes sir. I saw him tear those curtains down and drag them in the dirt before he dumped them into the nearest lean-to. He crawled inside and it looked like he was messing things up. When he came out and stalked away, I could tell he was angry."

Ranger Goodroe didn't know what to say; all he knew was that she was lying.

32

You told a lie, an odious, damnéd lie.

—Othello, 5.2.180

Jessie didn't waste time jumping into action. When she saw Briscoe escorting the blonde into the ranger station, she snuck over to the woman's tent and began rummaging around. It wasn't long before she'd found pinking sheers that had threads still stuck into them. Jessie thought they might be evidence, but she didn't stop there. She soon unearthed a picture of the woman as a brunette smiling at a man. What was more important was the second photo she discovered.

Searching the tent might not have been legal, but Jessie didn't care. She liked that young park ranger and this looked like a motive to her, so she decided to take both the sheers and the pictures over to the police.

She figured she would catch it from Wilkins, but she braved the storm and strode towards the ranger station. When Jessie entered, the policemen were sitting around in the living room facing Barbara Porter. "I said it and I stick to my statement." She was insistent before she looked up and blanched.

Jessie stood in the doorway with the pinking sheers in one hand and the pictures in the other. "Before you believe anything she says, perhaps you should look at these things."

"Have you been nosing around in our investigations, Mrs. Tyler?" Wilkins spoke sternly, but his lips curled in amusement. He shook his head, stood, and walked over to see what the amateur detective had brought them. His brows rose when he saw the picture of a brunette Barbara Porter and Veronica Verne framing an attractive man. "And just who is this man?" he asked.

Before she could respond, Jessie pulled the second photo from behind the first. It was a wedding shot of Barbara and the man. "Her husband," Jessie said. "So *who* had a grudge against Veronica Verne? She doesn't look pleased at all the attention her husband was giving Verne in that other shot."

"Oh, that was nothing." Barbara Porter tried to explain away the photo.

"Nothing?" Marley said. "You just got through telling us that you didn't know her. Explain that one."

"So what's the big deal? I didn't want you to know because I knew you'd think I had a motive. But that doesn't take away from what that ranger did," Porter said.

"Detectives, what color were the drapes?" Jessie changed the subject before they could let Porter get away with blaming poor Jerome Goodroe again. Then Jessie spied the drapes on the kitchen table just through the doorway into the kitchen. *Pink!* It was just as she thought.

"What does that matter? If Goodroe slashed the curtains with his hunting knife..."

Jessie jumped in before Marley could finish. "Well, that should be easy enough to settle. Were they slashed with a knife or cut with pinking sheers?"

Wilkins couldn't keep the widening grin off his face. Now Marley was getting a taste of what he'd put up with back in Wyleyville. And, unfortunately for Marley, Jessie Tyler had a point. It *would* be easy to tell them apart.

"What are you getting at, Mrs. Tyler? Are you saying that someone used scissors to cut the curtains? That still could be our ranger. I'm sure he has scissors somewhere in this place," Marley said.

"Why don't you try these first. There's a distinct difference between scissors and pinking sheers. I don't use them, but my grandmother did. Regular scissors don't cut the same way," Jessie said as she showed them the sheers she had found in the woman's tent. "And *these* have pink thread on them."

Wilkins took the sheers from Jessie, and compared the evidence with the sheers. "She's right. Those aren't knife slashes. So what do you have to say for yourself, Ms. Porter?"

While Barbara Porter fumed, Jessie glowed with pleasure. She was further thrilled to hear the woman finally tell the truth. "That woman stole my husband. She pretended to be my friend and then she took my man away from me. When I found out that she was coming here, I came to get even. And it would have worked out just fine if she hadn't been killed. I shredded her dumb curtains. So what!"

"Was that before or after you killed her?" Marley asked.

33

When I was at home, I was in a better place,
but travelers must be content.
　　　　　　　　　　—As You Like It, 2.4.17-18

It didn't take long for the police to decide that while Barbara Porter was a person of interest, they had witnesses who had seen her in camp for most of the day in question. It wouldn't have been easy, therefore, for her to slip away long enough to do the killing. They'd have to check into that one a bit closer.

Unfortunately, they had no solid suspect as yet, unless it was the man being escorted to Augusta. "I think we'll have to allow everyone here to leave as long as they keep us informed as to their whereabouts," Wilkins said, "unless you disagree, Marley."

"You're the senior officer, Detective Wilkins. I defer to you." Marley gave Wilkins a friendly smile. "Am I still on the case when we leave here?"

"Of course, but I don't think we'll be completely shutting down here. I want to keep someone on hand in case we need to come back. Officer Milo seems to be settling in well." Wilkins turned to his subordinate. "Milo, I want you to stay here in case there's anything we need to have looked into after Marley and I go down to Augusta."

Wilkins noted how Milo could barely suppress his enthusiasm. "Yes, sir!"

Wilkins had seen how relaxed Milo had been here. He wondered if it was the location, for Maine's northern woods held an irresistible appeal. Or perhaps it was Wilkins' own change in attitude. He had allowed Milo more responsibility ever since he'd learned that his assistant was studying for the detective's exam.

"You'll have to keep in touch with Detective Briscoe when he returns to Millinocket, and keep an eye on that ranger. I think he might know more than he's telling us. I don't want him in on anything confidential, but we'll let him think he's been cleared," Wilkins said.

"When are you leaving, sir?"

"Cameron should be in Augusta by mid-day tomorrow, so I think we'll leave first thing in the morning. How does that work for you, Marley?"

"Just fine; I'm looking forward to seeing how things work down in the capital. Perhaps someone can show me around your crime lab while I'm there?"

"Of course; I'll do it myself," Wilkins said. He was proud of the sophisticated lab they had at headquarters. It was one of the reasons he enjoyed being posted there. Of course, he also loved it for another reason: their troop was sent throughout the state to handle the most difficult cases. Even though from Augusta to the coast was his official beat, he sometimes got interesting assignments elsewhere—like now.

The time had finally come for him to do something he had been looking forward to. He would inform Jessie Tyler that her group could pack up and go home. "Marley, would you care to split up this list of campers? We can give them the good news."

Marley was up and ready when Wilkins nodded and handed him the list. "You take the top half and I'll handle the lower half."

"I see the Tyler group is on your list." Marley smiled. Wilkins knew that Marley wasn't pleased with how Jessie Tyler had ransacked Barbara Porter's tent. Wilkins, however, was glad the truth had been uncovered. Granted, the flap had apparently been open and Jessie had explained away her invasion of the tent by saying that she had seen the evidence clearly from outside. Not that Wilkins believed *that* for a minute, but he didn't let it bother him, as he made the Tyler campfire his first stop.

"Care to invite me to join you? I'd love a cup of that wonderful smelling coffee. I have good news."

"Already poured," Jonathan said by way of welcome as he lifted a steaming cup towards Wilkins and nodded for him to take a seat. "If you have good news for us, I'd better get the others out here."

Before Jonathan could call them, Jessie appeared from within her lean-to and said, "Only if the news is that we get to go home."

"It is," Wilkins said, "but I need one thing from each of you. I need addresses. I want to know where to find all of you, in case we have more questions."

Wilkins mentally checked off persons of interest while he listened to the excitement course through the group. Rocky Cameron topped his list, followed by Evan Kinderhook, Barbara Porter, Ranger Goodroe, and of course Dara Kane. Little did he know that Jessie Tyler would soon be compiling her own list, one that did not have her friend on it.

His thoughts were interrupted when Dara appeared at the campsite. "Did I hear that we can go home now?"

"Yes, Wilkins said, "but there are strings attached." His next words seemed to spoil the happy mood when he said, "You, Ms. Kane, need to remain available at all times."

34

Each hurries toward his home and sporting-place.
—Henry IV, Part 2, 4.2.105

Jessie was glad to be leaving the park. As soon as Detective Wilkins had walked away, she and her companions wasted no time packing up. They stowed their gear into their vehicles and made a hasty retreat. It wasn't long after they doused the campfire that Katahdin Stream Campground was in their rear-view mirrors.

Jessie and Dara rode in silence. This trip had not ended with the sense of elation Jessie usually felt after hiking. A cloud hung over them, sullying their memories. She only wished the killer had been found.

She barely noticed passing all the sights she normally enjoyed. The ride out the south gate and into Millinocket signaled the beginning of their trip home. Any other time, they would have taken the more rural and beautiful drive through the small towns they'd enjoyed on the way up, but today Jessie didn't have the heart for it. They went through Medway and were soon on Interstate 95. Jonathan must have been of like mind, Jessie noted, when his truck passed them; it wasn't long before it was out of sight.

Jessie wondered if there was any way for them to continue their search into Veronica Verne's death. This thought haunted her all the way to Wyleyville. The two friends eventually conversed about other topics, but they always came back to the murder.

Dara sighed with pleasure at first sight of Jessie's hometown. "Oh, Jessie, I'm always amazed at Wyleyville's beauty. It's such a quaint and lovely village. I envy you for living here, even though I love all Augusta has to offer."

Jessie had to agree as she detoured into town. She turned onto Maine Street and passed Preble Street, where the Wyleyville Public Library stood on a hill, proudly announcing the town's majesty of times gone by. Wyleyville, like most towns along Maine's coast, had been settled in the eighteenth century. The library itself had once been the home of a founding father. The town had purchased the beautiful building—topped by a mansard roof—in the early days of the twentieth century to house the library.

After Jessie and Dara passed the library, the Abnaki River loomed straight ahead, but Maine Street's business district came first, before the street gently sloped down towards the river. The historic flavor of downtown followed them on either side, with the town landing in the forefront. Jessie pulled up to the landing and sat watching the incoming tide. After a short stop, she turned and drove down River Street and looped back towards the other side of town.

"Thanks for that; I love it all," Dara said. Soon they were once more back on Maine Street and pointing away from town. It had cost Jessie to make that detour, for she would rather have dashed back to Killdeer Farm and, to her way of thinking, the most precious place on earth.

Jessie soon turned off Route 1 and onto Twin Pines Road, where a scattering of farmhouses and modern homes mixed into the wooded countryside. An old cemetery lurked on the left just before Jessie's Jeep rolled onto Merryfield Lane. And here was true country; farms from days of old inhabited this land. When Jessie pulled into her driveway, she noted Jonathan's truck sitting across the street at Cassie's farm.

Jessie retreated into the past as she sat with the motor running. This was *home*, home for the rest of her life—or so she hoped. Her eyes slid lovingly over the nineteenth century farmhouse she had visited as a child. It looked much the same, save a few improvements and a fresh paint job less than three years ago. Her two Jonathans had been responsible for the white clapboards that shone in the sunlight, Jessie mused, and for the roof that had been replaced shortly before her husband's death.

The two-story house had become hers—hers and her two Jonathans, she corrected herself—when her grandparents had still been living. After little Jonny had been born, Grandma and Grandpa had invited the young family to live with them at Killdeer Farm. They had all blissfully lived here until her grandparents had died, scarcely a year apart from one another. During the short years the family of five had been together, Jonathan had convinced Grandpa to let him build a porch off the kitchen. A new driveway off the kitchen was now where most people parked when visiting the farm.

Along the road side of the house were peony plants framed by burning bushes. Her grandmother had particularly loved pink and red plants, so by the time the peonies faded each summer, the burning bushes had begun to turn color. Fall must be on its way, Jessie realized, as she saw slight tinges of red on the leaves.

Jessie suddenly realized that she had been in her own world—for how long, she wondered. "I'm sorry, Dara." A silent Dara seemed to know what Jessie was thinking: this was her friend's home, her castle.

"Not a problem," Dara sighed. "It *is* lovely. All those plants: the bushes out front, the flowers rounding the corners of the house, an herb garden bordering the porch, and a vegetable garden down back frame Killdeer Farm perfectly. It's one of the most beautiful homes I've ever seen. If I weren't such a city girl..."

"I know you love your condo just as much as I love Killdeer Farm. I get it."

"Oh, I wouldn't say *just* as much, but it comes close." Dara was glad she would soon be home again, but she had promised to rest here one more night. Besides, it was too late in the day to pack her car and leave. She was just too tired. On that note, Jessie excused herself, for the first thing she must do was to greet Hamlet and give him a big hug. Her horse had galloped from a far pasture the minute he had heard the crunching of her vehicle on the gravel driveway. Dara sat in the Jeep and laughed. That horse sure had missed his master, she noted, as she saw Ham tip Jessie's ball cap onto the ground as he nuzzled her.

Jessie retrieved her cap and stuck it into her jeans pocket rather than cover her runaway auburn hair. She whispered in Ham's ear: "I'll be back later and spend some time with you, boy." Giving him a loving pat, she shooed Ham back to what he had been doing: grazing on green grass.

The next step was to unpack the Jeep. Jessie's cats were waiting for their share of attention. As she dragged her bags into the house, Mira and Juju came running. She recalled a cat her grandmother had had years ago: he had ignored everyone if he had been left alone long. He would always hide and no one would see him for hours, until hunger overtook pride. Jessie didn't have to worry about that with her two.

When Jessie saw Dara struggling with her luggage, she said, "Oh, do you need help with that?"

"I think you have your hands full." Dara grinned as she piled some of her gear in a corner of the dining room. Mira and Juju were yelling for attention and rubbing around Jessie's feet, threatening to topple her until she finally dropped her gear. Sitting on the floor, Jessie soon had two cats in her lap, both vying for attention.

Jessie could hear Dara's measured steps on the stairs, followed by her gentle tread as she entered the spare bedroom. Dara wouldn't unpack more than was in her overnight bag, Jessie knew. Dara was undoubtedly anxious to be returning to her own home and reconnecting with her own pet. She just hoped that Dara wasn't overly worried about still being a suspect. Jessie would just have to do something about that.

35

Such welcome and unwelcome things at once,
'Tis hard to reconcile.
                    —Macbeth, 4.3.138-139

Because Jessie and Dara had made that detour into
town, Jonathan had pulled his truck into the Lakewood
driveway some time ahead of his mother. The two girls
crawled out and limped towards home, but before they
reached the porch, Cassie was there with two dogs following
her. Castro, Cassie's elderly black lab, dashed forward and
began wiggling his enthusiasm to Willa and Gina. That was
nothing compared to the greeting Jonathan got, however.
Merlin, who had been visiting Castro while his master was
away, lunged himself straight into Jonathan.

Jonathan didn't have time to wonder what reception he
would get from his two cats back home as Merlin stretched
to full height with his front paws on Jonathan's shoulders
and washed his master's face. While they reconnected, he
heard Cassie ask her daughters to fill her in on all the fun
they'd had at Baxter State Park.

"Oh, it was fantastic!" Willa wasn't about to be stopped
by a few aching muscles. She was walking on air. Even a
death at the park hadn't stopped her from making future
plans. She *would* return, and soon. "Gina, care to go back
before school starts?"

As Jonathan continued to pat Merlin, he could see that
Gina thought her sister was nuts. Gina could barely walk.
She probably had blisters that would take weeks to heal.
Jonathan bet she hadn't taken their advice about breaking in

her new hiking boots.

Jonathan began to wonder if Cassie knew what had happened at the park when he heard her say, "I think you two have had enough excitement to last you a while, young ladies. I would rather you both get organized for school. After all, school starts next week."

"But, Mom, I am sure they'll have that murder business all straightened out soon," Willa said.

"What murder?" Cassie's voice cracked when she realized what Willa meant. "Don't tell me that death I heard about on the news happened near Baxter."

"Oh, not near, in!" Gina's voice held a trace of pleasure. Jonathan shook his head in amusement. He could tell she was getting a kick out of it.

"What do you mean by in?" Cassie asked.

"Not just in the park but in our campground, or near it," Willa said with pride. "And we found her."

"What? What? Surely you couldn't have been involved in something like that."

Jonathan had, until now, let the girls handle informing their mother of what had happened as they all entered the Lakewood farmhouse. He gave Merlin one more scratch behind the ears before he jumped into the conversation. "Aunt Cassie, we didn't have much say in the matter. We were out hiking, the five of us. We didn't run into a dead body on purpose."

"Dead body! I didn't send my girls away with you so you could find a dead body. I sent them off for a nice time in the woods." Cassie fairly collapsed into a kitchen chair at the thought.

"I guess you're right, but now that one's been dropped into our laps, why don't you go over to Mom's later and help her solve it," Jonathan said. "She'll be raring to go, especially since the police have no clue."

Jonathan left on that note because he had some fence mending to do at home with his cats, Arthur and Genevieve.

But before he returned to his own home, he had one last visit to make. He drove across the street, passed his mother's vehicle, and parked by the workshop/shed that was home to more than his carpentry business. With Merlin prancing around him, the two walked into the outer building attached to the kitchen side of his mother's farmhouse. There waiting for him was the ghostly figure of the man who had been his best friend since childhood.

36

We were the first and dearest of your friends.
—Henry IV, Part 1, 5.1.33

Ben Ames sat on his usual perch at the foot of the stairs and greeted the most important person in his life, so to speak. "My child, you have finally returned from the wilderness. I trust you found as much joy on your expedition as you did when you were a youngster."

Jonathan laughed when Merlin, too, greeted the ethereal figure of Ben. Merlin sniffed and attempted to set his chin onto Ben's leg. Ben, likewise, made a futile attempt at physical contact. Both ghost and dog sighed before Merlin settled down at Ben's feet. Jonathan had only recently come to realize that his dog was aware of Ben's presence. What a surprise that had been.

Ben had always been—to his mother's way of thinking—Jonathan's imaginary childhood friend. Only his father had taken on trust the stories that young Jonny had told him of his adventures with Ben in the upstairs storage area. Now that friendship had deepened into a lifelong commitment.

"Yes, we had a wonderful time, until we found the body."

"You found a body?" Ben shook his head with mirth. "You do love to tease me, Jonathan." When Jonathan didn't smile, Ben repeated: "Body?"

"I'm afraid so. Mom and I found a dead body at the falls."

"Where were the others who went with you?"

"Oh, sorry; Gina, Willa, and Dara found it, too."

"Tell me the whole tale, my lad. I cannot let you go off for a few days of enjoyment, but you *must* return home with a mystery. I am guessing that it is a mystery."

"Yes." And with that simple statement, Jonathan delved into his tale.

After Jonathan completed his visit with Ben, he departed for his own home. Merlin jumped around as the two walked towards his small log cabin behind Killdeer Farm. His father had helped him plan it, but had never seen it to completion. In the dark days after his father's death, Jonathan had built the place alone. It had been a healing experience and it had kept him from doing something stupid. Justice had finally been served earlier that summer, however, when another person had taken revenge on his father's killer.

Now he proudly stood, looking at his one-story log cabin with the porch running the length of the front. Merlin bounded onto the porch and anxiously waited for his master to open the door. The two entered as one, and received a greeting that Jonathan had not expected. His cats usually hid when Jonathan left them alone. Today was the exception.

Just as Jonathan bent over to set his backpack down, Genevieve wound herself around his legs. The greeting reminded him of how she had come to live with him. But Arthur, who had been a stray, had come first. Jonathan had scarcely gotten used to Arthur, when a second cat had shown up on his doorstep. He had chosen a male name for this one, too, until she had unexpectedly given birth. Lancelot had become Genevieve.

Genevieve had good maternal instincts, but when her time came, she had refused the box Jonathan had prepared for her. She'd repeatedly crawled under his bed and Jonathan had carefully extracted her over and over again. He was glad he'd taken a rare day off to watch over her. When all attempts at having her use the box had failed, Jonathan had sighed and placed towels on his bed.

Katahdin Drowning

Genevieve soon began alternately purring and breathing heavily. Apparently too tired to fight her master's wishes, she had stayed on his bed. Jonathan had read up on what to expect, so he had been ready. He'd sat at her side, patting her to keep her calm.

Genevieve's sides had begun to flutter up and down until a sac-covered kitten appeared. Genevieve had looked at it with curiosity until her instincts had taken over. She'd lapped away the sac and a wet kitten had emerged. It was mostly white, save a few gray splotches around its head and a gray corkscrew tail. After the kitten was clean, Genevieve spent more time washing herself than her new baby.

The kitten wiggled around and soon found her food supply. It ate merrily for what seemed to be hours. It was long enough that Jonathan decided there would be no more kittens. He'd wondered if his mother would adopt it. After all, he'd thought, it was only one tiny kitten and he already had two cats and a dog to care for.

But he'd soon realized that another kitten was on its way when Genevieve's sides began to heave again. A smaller black and white kitten wiggled towards one of her mother's teats just as the sun was setting. Well, he thought, maybe his mother would take them both. After all, he'd reasoned, one kitten would be lonely. He contemplated on how he would rook his mother into taking them.

It had been weeks before Jessie had agreed. In truth, it had only taken one visit to Jonathan's log cabin before she had become hooked. They were just too cute to pass up, Jonathan now realized, as his mother had kept him wondering for weeks, until she had chosen the perfect names: Juliet and Miranda.

Jonathan first cuddled Genevieve, and then Arthur, as both vied for his attention. It was great to be home, he sighed, but he had catching up to do. Because he owned his own carpentry business, he had to be careful how much time he spent away from the job. He had, however, promised weeks ago to take that mini-vacation to Baxter with his mother and friends.

Unlike his busy schedule, his mother still had several days off from her job as town librarian. He supposed that would give her plenty of time to delve into the murder. He wished he had time to look into the mystery as well. He knew that to be impossible as he picked up the blueprints he'd left on his kitchen table. This, he hoped, would keep his mind off what his mother was up to down at Killdeer Farm.

37

Make use of time, let not advantage slip.
                    —Venus and Adonis, 129

State headquarters was larger than Detective Marley had anticipated, and the lab tour had been fascinating. He was almost glad that Richard Cameron had been late because he'd had the opportunity to extend his visit. The detectives would later learn that Cameron had conned the trooper into making frequent stops along the way. The last break had been for lunch in South Portland.

Finally, Wilkins got the call that they had arrived. "Take him to interrogation room one. We'll be right there." Hanging up the telephone, he turned to Marley. "Well, it's time to get to work."

When the two detectives entered the dull gray room with a table and three chairs, the man seated across from them jumped up. The trooper standing behind him reached out to push him back into his chair, but Wilkins stopped him. "It's okay, trooper. You may go now." After the officer was gone, he said, "Sit, Mr. Cameron. We have questions for you."

Cameron bristled. "Am I under arrest? Why was I forced to come here? So I went camping. There's no crime in that."

"Then why did you deny it when the Boston policeman asked you about your trip to Maine?"

"I didn't think it was any of his business."

"Well, it was his business, just as it's ours. Tell us what you were doing at Baxter State Park. And don't try to tell me it's a coincidence that you hiked Katahdin on the same day as your wife. I don't believe in coincidences."

"Okay, so I wanted to talk to her." Cameron wiped his dampening brow. "No sooner had she left town than I got a letter from her lawyer. I had no idea she was filing for divorce. For goodness sakes, I thought we had a happy marriage."

"So you climbed Katahdin to confront her." Marley interjected himself into the questioning.

"No, yes, no..."

"Well, which is it?"

"Yes. I wanted to know what was going on. Wouldn't you? If you thought you had a happy marriage and you got a letter like that, wouldn't you go off the deep end? Since I'm the one who sent her up to the park to film her show, I knew where she'd gone, but I didn't want to confront her until I'd worked off some steam. I fumed all the way, and let me tell you, that was a long trip.

"I decided to park at Abol Campground because I didn't want to be in *her* campground. I'd read about the place so I knew that the two trails converge before the top of the mountain. I went up and waited. I even backtracked down the Hunt Trail, looking for the perfect spot to confront her. I stopped just above the cliff face because I thought she couldn't get past me without speaking."

"And what happened?"

"I was wrong. She turned around and went back down the way she'd come without saying a word. Oh, she saw me all right. Say, you should talk to her cameraman. He didn't like her leaving one bit. Just before she vanished down the cliff face, I heard her order him to keep going and film all the way to the top. I don't know what good that would have done the TV station, to have him film it without her in it."

"So did you follow her?"

"Of course not; her running away told me all I needed to know. She was through with me, and let me tell you, I didn't care by then. I got all dirty and sweaty just to see her, only to have her take off without an explanation. I decided to get the heck out of her life once and for all."

"That's not exactly what I heard." Wilkins shuffled papers in the file he'd brought with him. "We have a witness who says you followed her."

"Who? That little pipsqueak she was with? He was probably sleeping with her."

"Then you *did* follow her."

"So what; do you think that guy went to the top, either?" Cameron was getting flustered. "Say, just how did you know it was me? I've never even seen that cameraman before, so..."

"Well, it seems that your wife had a picture of you in her lean-to. Why would she carry it with her if she wanted a divorce?"

"How am I supposed to know what that woman would do? Women do the craziest things." Cameron changed tactics. "So it had to be that cameraman. He was in her lean-to, saw the picture, and now he's trying to blame me."

"As a matter of fact, the cameraman did recognize the picture, but we're the ones who found it in her lean-to. He told us he saw someone on the rocks, someone who seemed to frighten his boss, so we showed him your picture," Wilkins said. "He identified you. And, yes to your earlier statement, he did say that he went to the top of the mountain to take pictures."

"With what? He threw the movie camera into a crevice. I saw him do it, so don't tell me he has footage of himself hiking up to the summit, either." Cameron shook his head. "Look, I only followed her a little ways. When I lost sight of her, I just went back through her campground and over to Abol, where I'd left my car.

"You should ask the cameraman what *he* did the rest of the day. I saw him just sitting on the rocks with his broken camera. I tell you, he broke it so he could turn around and follow my wife back down the mountain."

After that, Cameron had no more to say and demanded

to call his lawyer. Since they didn't have enough evidence to arrest him—at least not yet—they told him to keep in touch and sent him on his way.

Wilkins watched their only viable suspect walk down the hallway and into the outside world before he took Marley to his office. At his messy desk, Wilkins began compiling lists. He wrote as he recalled the mental list he had formulated earlier. The short list of potential killers was still topped by Richard Cameron, followed by Evan Kinderhook. He also speculated on Dara Kane. Was it ever too long ago for someone to carry a grudge? Kane remained on their list because Wilkins had learned from experience that hatred knew no boundaries.

"Barbara Porter is still a possibility. Her marriage was destroyed. We should also talk again to some of the witnesses who seemed to be watching the comings and goings of everyone in the campground."

Marley agreed, but still wondered about the park ranger. "You know, I like that Goodroe kid. I know he's the least likely of them all, but in my experience, someone like that sometimes turns out to be the killer."

Wilkins nodded in agreement. "Now, as for witnesses, I know we need to show pictures of all the suspects to everyone who stayed at the campground. I want to show them Cameron's picture right away, before he has a chance to hightail it too far. Care to go with me?"

"Who do you have in mind?"

"Well, that Barry Rockford lives in a small town called Cornville. That isn't too far off 95 going north. I'd also like to see if the wife or child saw anything. And that Rowley guy who heard Rockford speak to the victim seemed observant. Tessa and Roger Rowley live in Dexter, which isn't far out of the way, either." Wilkins looked once more at the list in his file. "Say, I need to interview that woman who got lost. Marta Walters and her daughter, Melissa, it says here, seemed so shook up that we let them leave without asking them about the victim. They live up your way, too. Care to join me?"

"I'll say. When do we leave?" Marley was anxious to get back to his office, but this was a heaven-sent opportunity to tag along.

"Actually, I was thinking about waiting until morning. There's plenty to do here in the meantime, if you'd care to help me. And I have an extra room at my place, if you'd be willing to stay down here overnight."

"I'm sure that'll be fine, as long as I can check in with my office. Do you have a phone I can use?" Marley asked.

"You can use Milo's space. His desk is just outside my office." Wilkins led Marley to a large area with several desks. "Here," he pointed to a desk that was neat and orderly. When he sensed Marley's surprise, Wilkins said, "Yes, Milo is a neat-freak, unlike me."

Marley laughed. "Actually, your office is more like my workspace. Say, I'm famished. I need to find somewhere to eat soon, but I don't want to disrupt your day."

"Now that you mention it, I'm pretty hungry, too. If your stomach will hold off for a few more minutes, we can go out together. I have a phone call to make," Detective Wilkins said.

"Fine with me," Marley said.

"Great." Wilkins returned to his office and left Marley to make his call from Milo's desk. He didn't want to admit to Marley that he was curious about what Jessie Tyler and her son were up to down in Wyleyville. It was time to call on Wyleyville's chief of police for a favor.

When Jeb Michaelson answered on the first ring, he was surprised to hear the voice of a man who only called when there was trouble brewing. "Detective Wilkins, what can I do for you on this fine day?"

"I thought we were on a first name basis, Jeb. It's Charlie, remember?"

"Of course, Charlie, but you never call."

Wilkins laughed, which was something Jeb had never

heard him do before. He wondered what this meant. It wasn't long before he found out. Charlie told Jeb all about the murder at Baxter State Park and Jessie Tyler's involvement. Michaelson pitied Wilkins, for he knew from experience that keeping Tyler and company out of a murder investigation was nearly impossible.

"So you want me to keep an eye on her and make sure she doesn't mess up your case," Jeb Michaelson said.

"Not quite, Jeb. I want you to keep an eye on her to make sure no one tries to kill her this time. I'm tired of being late to the party. I've decided to let her in so that perhaps she'll keep *me* informed in my own case."

Jeb couldn't help but snort at that one: the state police being led around by Jessie Tyler. He almost, in the process, missed Charlie's closing comment.

"...and I'll be down there in a couple of days to have a talk with her and the others in her party. They were good witnesses and so far most of them haven't been implicated in the death. But you and I both know one cannot eliminate the person or persons who find the body."

38

At your return visit to our house;
let our old acquaintance be renewed.
                    —Henry IV, Part 2, 3.2.293-294

Jessie arose earlier than usual to visit Ben. She hadn't taken that opportunity the evening before because she didn't want to have to explain her ghostly friend to Dara. She carefully crawled out of bed and—for a change—left her cats still sleeping. After throwing on old clothes so as to later clean Ham's stall, she crept past the guest room and slipped downstairs without waking her friend. Dara must be very tired, Jessie thought, as she bypassed her usual coffee and went straight to her destination.

"Ben?" Jessie called out as she descended the short staircase bridging the gap between her home of the living and the land of the dead.

"Jessie, I am delighted to see you." Ben materialized near the bottom of the stairs leading to his permanent home. "I was surprised that you did not come out to see me last evening; that is, until Jonathan explained that you have a visitor. He told me about the body you found and the involvement of your friend. I understand that she is still your house guest."

"Yes, Dara's still here. I really wanted to visit you earlier, but I doubt that Dara is up to meeting you."

Ben laughed. "You are a caution, my dear," he said before turning serious. "But not everyone feels that way. I had a guest while you and Jonathan were away, one who seemed determined to meet me."

133

Janet Morgan

Before Ben could continue, Jessie asked, "Cassie? Did Cassie come in here?"

"No, young lady, it was not your friend Cassandra. The closest your friend ever came to me was to check the workshop doors every day. Of course she entered your house a number of times each day to feed your cats and I observed her caring for Hamlet." Ben pointed to a window that looked out towards the barn. He was grateful for it because it also gave him the opportunity to watch over Jessie whenever she was outside with her horse.

"Then what are you talking about, or should I say who?" Jessie wondered if the twins had been poking around.

But then Ben said the totally unexpected: "It was that young police officer who assisted Jonathan after your house was broken into last month. You know the person to whom I refer. He is the youngster who is a relative of mine, after a fashion."

Several weeks ago, Jessie had discovered an interesting fact about Officer Ebenezer Walker. Over coffee at the Maine Street Café, he had admitted to being related, through marriage, to the brothers who had built Killdeer Farm. It had come as quite a shock to Ben that his brother's wife still had relatives in town.

"Young Ebenezer looked through all the downstairs windows on the first floor of this building," Ben said. "After he finished spying around, he vanished out back. I could hear him thrashing out there, before I witnessed something that fairly scared the wits out of me. I spotted a face looking into my upstairs window. My guess is that the officer found one of Jonathan's ladders to achieve that feat."

Jessie didn't think much of a local policeman skulking around her home while she was away, but it wasn't as though Jonathan hadn't warned her about Officer Walker's interest after he had seen Ben. "I know you can make yourself invisible whenever you want to, but did he see you this time?"

Katahdin Drowning

"I do not know if he saw me or not, but I certainly did use all my powers to make myself invisible until he went away. I did not have to remain invisible for long, however, because I heard your friend Cassandra berating him. She did this as young Ebenezer stood with his beady eyes looking into my room from just above the bottom of the window frame. He must have gone back down the ladder with some speed, for his eyes vanished very soon after your friend spoke. I could hear him fumbling around on the ladder." Ben laughed. "What with all the noise he made getting down the ladder, I would not have been surprised had he tipped the thing over. I heard your friend giving him quite the talking to. She made him put the ladder back before she sent him away, with his tail between his legs, no doubt."

Jessie laughed. She was relieved that Eb Walker had been unsuccessful, but it concerned her that he had come out here at all. "Did anyone else see him?"

"Oh, my, no; that was not the case. Your friend Cassandra was quite enough. And that boy did not like it one iota having a woman give him a dressing down. I heard him tell her that he was here on official business. From the pitch in his voice, I am sure he was all puffed up with self-impor-tance. I heard him tell her he was going to produce his badge. She said he was an idiot and that she already knew he was a police officer." Ben shook his head, "Jessie, you never told me that young man was a fool. I thought that any relative of mine would have more sense."

"I'm sorry, Ben, but you're right about Eb. He's a nice person, if a bit inept, but I heard the chief say once that he hopes the boy will season well."

"I certainly desire that result, myself. After all, it would appear that he is my only living relative." Ben gave Jessie an enquiring look. "Or do you know of any others?" He appeared hopeful.

"I have no idea, Ben. Perhaps sometime soon I can ask around—after we're done with this mess up north."

Ben nodded. "That certainly takes precedence right now. You must clear the name of your friend first. And when you have that deed done—for I know that with your abilities, it will happen—then it would make me happy if you could determine if I have any other living relatives. If not, I certainly hope that your police chief has extremely *high* hopes for young Ebenezer improving with age."

39

I have of late—but wherefore
I know not—lost all my mirth,
forgone all custom of exercise.
                    —Hamlet, 2.2.295-297

After their discussion had wound down, Jessie said good-bye to Ben and went outside to do her barn chores. She groomed Hamlet with special care before taking him out to one of the pastures that still had plenty of green grass. She had several pastures that were large enough for him to run around in and get plenty of exercise.

The original barn had blown down during a particularly strong hurricane when Jessie had still been a child, but she remembered that barn well. She, Cassie, and Cassie's numerous siblings had spent many a day playing in the second story hay mound and swinging on ropes onto the dirt floor below. That had been back in more innocent times that Jessie missed.

Once they had moved to Killdeer Farm, Jonathan had built a smaller barn in anticipation of one occupant: a horse for Jessie. Hamlet had fit the bill. Fencing for him had come next. Ham was rotated between pastures so that there was fresh grass for him all summer. Neighbor Mark Merryfield always hayed both her extra fields and Cassie's, thus providing enough hay for Ham and Cassie's creatures to live the life of luxury throughout the winter.

While Jessie reflected on the past, she cleaned Ham's stall and straightened up inside the barn. She had enough space for another occupant, but right now Ham was all she had time to tend. Cassie had cows, chickens, pigs, and two horses, which worked well for her because she didn't have to leave home to work.

By the time Jessie returned to the house, the day had heated up. She had one thing left to do, however, before she showered. After filling several quart canning jars with dried spearmint leaves from her herb garden, she added water and set the jars on the doorstep to catch the sun's rays. The resulting sun tea was always a delicious concoction that would make the perfect refreshment for later. She showered, even though she had already bathed the night before. A few days in the wilderness made her appreciate the amenities. By the time she had dressed in fresh jeans and a t-shirt, Dara, too, had risen and taken her turn in the shower for the second time in less than twenty-four hours.

"What would you like for breakfast?" Jessie asked as Dara appeared in the kitchen. Dara smelled the brewing coffee and pointed.

"Cereal will be fine, once I've had coffee. I've eaten altogether too much during the last few days." Dara cringed as she carefully sat down on a padded kitchen seat. Unlike the handmade nineteenth century maple dining set in Jessie's dining room, her kitchen set was of art deco design: chrome legs and frame with a white Formica tabletop and kitchen chairs with padded, red plastic cushions. Straight out of the nineteen fifties, the set was a Christmas gift Jessie's grandfather had purchased for her grandmother before Jessie had been born.

"Me, too," Jessie said. "And yes, it will get better. Some say the first day after a long hike is the worst, but to me the next ones are the most painful."

"It was those stairs. Last night going up was bad enough, but coming down this morning..."

"Oh, Dara, the first time I hiked Katahdin, you should have seen me after we got home. I was so tired that after getting Jonny ready for bed, I crashed. The next morning I had to sit and lower myself down the stairs one at a time." To

Dara's laugh, Jessie shook her head in amusement. "That's not the worst of it, though. I heard laughing and looked up to see my Jonathan standing at the top of the stairs. I wanted to sock him, until he, too, had trouble getting downstairs. I guess that gave me the last laugh."

"So what did you do?"

"We took a walk around the neighborhood after breakfast. Mind you, we wouldn't have won any races."

"Does it help?" Dara's greatest desire was to crawl back into bed and rest her aching bones.

"Actually, it does. Care to try it after breakfast?"

Dara was saved from replying when they heard the porch door slam and Cassie Lakewood walked through the connecting door and into the kitchen. "Hi, guys. Made any plans yet?" she asked.

"Plans? Whatever do you mean?" Jessie knew full well what Cassie was talking about, but she pretended not to. "Oh, yes, we do. If Dara isn't too tired, we're taking a hike this morning."

"Hike? I meant detect, you fool." Cassie looked hopeful.

Jessie was just thinking that at least she doesn't have her murder board with her, when Cassie said, "I brought my easel and drawing pad. They're just outside the door. Shall I get them?"

To the look of confusion on Dara's face, Jessie explained how twice before they had used Cassie's art supplies to set up Jessie's dining room as murder central. "We got right into it," she said before she turned back to Cassie. "You might as well bring them in, but we're hiking first. Care to join us?"

"Sure. You can catch me up on the case while we walk," Cassie said. "I didn't come over last evening as Jonathan suggested. I figured you two needed to rest before we dug into the new case."

Jessie could only laugh while they enjoyed coffee. Dara tried to linger over breakfast, but Cassie would have none of it. "Hurry up. The sooner we hike the sooner we detect."

"Let's go up back," Jessie said. Once breakfast was over, they each took one of Dara's arms and pulled her up and outside. "Cassie and I frequently ride on the trail behind Jonathan's house." Jessie led the way across a narrow wooden bridge over the stream between Killdeer Farm and Jonathan's house. Because Jessie saw Dara limping, she kept the pace slow.

Dara wasn't sure she was up for much of a walk, but as it turned out, they did more talking than hiking. Despite Dara's pain, Jessie could tell she enjoyed the scenery that was new to Dara, who had never been on the trail behind Jonathan's house before. In the past whenever Dara had visited, Jessie had either taken her around Merryfield Lane, or they had walked the paths behind Cassie's place. Here at Killdeer Farm, the trees had been allowed to touch the sky, but the ground around them was kept relatively clear of underbrush. As a result, they frequently saw small creatures darting across the ground and up into nearby trees.

"Oh, what's that?" Dara took a step towards a porcupine.

Jessie pulled her back. "Dara, you are *such* a city girl." She laughed as she told Dara how dangerous it could be to approach some creatures. "But unlike what some say, a porcupine cannot throw its quills at you. You have to get close enough to touch him before you're in trouble."

Dara visibly cringed. "No, thank you, and does that apply to skunks as well?"

"Skunks don't have quills," Cassie teased. When Jessie saw Dara wrinkle her nose, she laughed as Cassie explained: "No, it doesn't apply to skunks. I don't know how close you need to get to be sprayed, but that's something I do not want to discover." Cassie turned to Jessie. "Remember when Castro came home after tangling with a skunk?"

"How could I forget; Castro is Cassie's dog," Jessie said to Dara. "You'll be happy to hear that we've reached the end of the trail. But be careful. That cliff is steep." Jessie gently pulled Dara back. "Not too close, but look down. That's the

Abnaki River. If it weren't for that bend in the river," she said as she pointed east, "you could see into town."

"It's beautiful." Dara stared into the depths of the blue-green river. She stood entranced until Jessie said it was time to turn back. Jessie loved the view from where the back part of her land faced the Abnaki River, but today she was distracted.

Cassie knew the whole story by the time they had turned around. Dara had even told Cassie about her past history with the murder victim.

"Wow! We need to solve this one before that mean Detective Wilkins comes down on Dara," Cassie said.

"I don't think Wilkins is such a bad guy after all," Jessie said. "He was actually nice to us. I think he gave us up as a lost cause. I guess he decided that he couldn't keep us out of his investigation."

"Well, that's a new one. He was mad as all get-out at us less than two months ago."

"Things change, I guess, but you're right about one thing. We do need to make sure Dara doesn't hit the top of their murder board. We need to check into who had the best motive. I heard that the real reason we got to leave the park is that they found out that Veronica Verne's husband was there on the day she was murdered."

"How did you find that out?" Dara was amazed. *How did Jessie do it?*

"Oh, while you took a walk with the girls yesterday, that nice ranger came over and chatted with us." Jessie went on for Cassie's benefit: "He's a suspect, too, because the victim was mean to him. The police seem to think that's enough of a motive."

"So, he goes on the list?' Cassie asked.

"Well, at least the police list. Dara, too," Jessie gave Dara a sad look. "Sorry, but we won't put you on ours."

Jessie could tell that Dara was happy to hear that as they once more entered the house. Jessie poured sun tea as they chatted before entering murder central.

Cassie's easel and drawing pad once more sat at one end of Jessie's dining room table. "I wish we could convince the police that Dara is *not* a viable suspect," Jessie said. "Then there's the park ranger. Jerome Goodroe could be the killer, but I'm not convinced. I like him, but he still goes on the bottom of our list."

"Then just who are good suspects?" Cassie asked. If they kept this up, they wouldn't have anyone left. Cassie had been doodling while she waited to fill the paper with names.

"Hold on, Cassie. We have a few. First, we have the husband, for obvious reasons. Second, the cameraman, from what I heard, had a motive. His name is Evan Kinderhook. This Verne woman was giving him a really hard time. Then there's Barbara Porter, who lied about the park ranger being angry over the outhouse deal. She admitted that she tried to set him up when they began to close in on her. She and her husband became friends with Verne, and the next thing you know, her husband wanted a divorce so he could be with the fitness star."

"She fits the bill for me." Cassie looked over at Dara, who had a funny look on her face. "What do you think, Dara? Is something bothering you?"

"Well, I'm not sure about motive. To be honest, when I saw Bertie lording it over everyone, I wanted to swat her myself. Drowning was too good for her." The vehemence in Dara's voice startled Cassie, but not Jessie. She had known Dara long enough to realize that even the most placid of people can have a passionate side.

"Oh, Dara, don't worry. We'll find the killer. And you had four witnesses who can vouch for you, so I doubt that the police are interested in you." Jessie turned back at the list Cassie was slowly compiling. "Personally, my money's on Veronica Verne's husband. I heard that young cameraman telling someone that he was there, on the mountain when he and Verne began the final ascent."

"That's it?" Cassie seemed disappointed that the list wasn't longer. "There must be more people we could add."

"Well," Jessie said, "of course, there were others in the park, but we don't know enough about them yet. There's the mother who got lost, for instance, and her daughter. Then there's the man who knew Verne years ago. I wonder if there was anyone else we could check into."

"I think we have enough for now," Dara said. "After all, it's likely that the husband did it. Why else would he be there with no one knowing, including *her?*"

"*Her* being Veronica Verne, I take it. What did you say her real name was?" Cassie asked.

"Bertha Crumm," Dara said. She smiled at Cassie's grimace. "I know; no wonder she decided to change it. Even her nickname, Bertie, wasn't particularly elegant." Dara sighed. "I wish I could stay longer, but I have to go home and begin preparation for my classes."

"Please stay for lunch," Jessie said. "I have a great veggie meal planned for the three of us, but first we need to visit the garden to select our lunch. We'll also get some things for you to take home." Jessie led her two friends into the kitchen where they were each given a basket. "Let's go."

They spent a fun-filled half-hour rummaging through Jessie's garden, collecting tomatoes, green peppers, radishes, cucumbers, summer squash, carrots, and the last planting of lettuce. Then more goodies were collected for Dara to take home when Jessie dug up some new potatoes and onions. On the way back inside, she snipped some herbs and dropped them atop Dara's basket.

Once back in the kitchen, they made huge salads and poured more sun tea. They enjoyed a leisurely lunch before Dara reluctantly decided it was time to leave.

"Not yet." Jessie pulled out some garlic she had retrieved from one of her storage bins inside the shed. "These are for you, too." Jessie plopped them atop the other things Dara was to take home with her. Dara made a nominal protest.

She loved garden fresh food, so she didn't complain.

"Thank you, Jessie. I owe you lunch the next time you're in Augusta." Dara made a snap decision. "Why don't you both come up to my place as soon as this crime is solved. I just wish there was some way I could help out, too."

"We'll think of something," Cassie said. "And, yes, I'd love to come up to your place. I've never seen it. Jessie says you have a lovely condo."

As they walked outside carrying Dara's basket and bags, they promised to keep in touch. Dara just hoped that Jessie was right to so easily eliminate her as a suspect. She only wished that the police felt the same way.

40

What says she, fair one?
That the tongues of men are full of deceits?
> —Henry V, 5.2.117-118

While Dara worried about being a suspect, the two Maine State Police detectives drove north on Interstate 95 towards Newport. Their first stop was to see Barry Rockford. Since Rockford worked at home, Wilkins hoped to see the whole family. And he lucked out. As they drove into the driveway of a rustic farmhouse, an old station wagon pulled up beside them. Wilkins looked across and saw a sulky blonde girl sporting earplugs slumped in the passenger seat. Beyond her, the girl's mother glared at them from between lank strings of dark hair as she slid from the driver's seat.

"This doesn't look like it's going to be a friendly visit," Wilkins said as they climbed from his cruiser.

"Mrs. Rockford, we need to talk to all of you again. May we come inside?" Wilkins walked towards the front door, but paused for the ladies.

"I suppose so, but my husband's a very busy man. He runs his own business and he already lost work after you made us stay in the park two extra nights." It would seem that Esther Rockford didn't care for this intrusion into her privacy. "He's a stonemason, you know. He builds stone walls that are a work of art. He's the best in the county—heck, in the whole state," Esther proudly stated with vehemence. "Come along, Kim." She ushered her daughter towards the house. "I'm sure these men don't need to talk to you."

"Mom-m," Kim stretched out the single word. "It's not..."
Her mother cut her off. She pushed her daughter forward
and into the house with a wave of the hand. "Come in, if you
must," she grudgingly said, "but you'll have to settle for talking to me."

"I'm afraid that won't do. We need to talk to each one of
you, and in private." When Wilkins sensed an objection forming, he said, "Unless you want me to have you all escorted to
headquarters in Augusta."

That shut Kim's mother up. She slammed the door. "Go
in there." she pointed towards a large room straight ahead.
"Sit in the living room while I go and see if Barry is free to
talk to you."

"Why don't we begin with you, Mrs. Rockford?" Wilkins
signaled for her to sit as well.

"I have nothing to say. I didn't see anything. I don't know
anything about that woman's death. So what could I tell
you?"

"Well, for one thing, in looking into Bertha Crumm's history, we discovered that she graduated from the same high
school as your husband." Wilkins stopped to let her mull
that one over.

"Okay, so Barry knew her slightly. It's a small town.
Everyone knows everyone here; that doesn't mean anything."

"But you failed to mention that you, too, graduated with
Crumm. Are you saying that you didn't recognize her at the
campground?" Wilkins asked. "Think a moment before you
answer me. You aren't denying that your maiden name was
Carson, are you?"

"No. But so what? I told you Barry only knew her slightly. The same goes with me."

"And, so when you two married right out of high school,
Bertha didn't come to your wedding?" Wilkins asked.

"She left town right after graduation was over. She didn't
even wait a minute. She was gone the next day. I don't know
why this is important. We were together all day, my family

and me."

And so the conversation went. Barry was no more inform-
ative than his wife. He, too, insisted that the family were
joined at the hip all day. Neither of them recognized
Cameron's picture.

As for Kim, she just sat listening to her iPod until Marley
had made her remove her earplugs. "I never saw that person
before," she said. After repeating what both her parents had
told them about hiking together all day—and after also denying all knowledge of Veronica Verne's husband, she said,
"And I don't care what happened to her." With that, she
jumped up, grabbed up her iPod, and dashed up the creaky
stairs.

"Well, that was productive," Marley said as the two men
headed north once more, this time towards Dexter, which
was the gateway to Moosehead Lake. "Was it my imagination,
or did their stories sound just a little too rehearsed?"

"It did sound at though they thought they needed alibis."
Wilkins nodded in agreement. "That family bears further
investigation. Everyone in camp vouched for them being
together that day, so I don't know what they can be hiding. I
could swear they know something, but people frequently
hold back vital information because they don't want to get
involved." Wilkins began considering the possibility that one
or more of them had seen someone or something they didn't
want to talk about. By this time they had arrived at their next
destination, so Wilkins was saved further speculation.

41

An honest tale speeds best being plainly told.
　　　　　　　　　　　—Richard III, 4.4.358

The Dexter interview elicited no more information than they had received earlier. Neither Tessa nor Roger Rowley recognized Richard Cameron's picture. They also collectively said that they had never met the Verne woman before. Tessa confessed to sometimes watching Verne's show, but that was it. "Unless you count me not liking her superior attitude on the tube as a motive," she said. "If so, maybe you should haul me off in chains. And I wasn't overly impressed with the way she treated everyone in the campground."

"Which people did she treat badly?" Marley took the lead.

"Well, that young cameraman had a hard time of it. I could tell that she was sending him strong, sexual vibes. Had she lived, he would have been lucky to make it back home without her having her way with him," Tessa said.

"So he didn't reciprocate?" Marley asked.

"I'd say not." Husband and wife both chimed at once. They looked at one another and laughed. "You see," Roger said, "He seems like a nice young man. He tried to please her by being her gopher, but I don't think he was interested in her. After all, he's younger than her." Roger stopped them with a raised hand, "I know, sometimes younger men do have affairs with older women, but in this case, he didn't seem interested."

"But you said everyone. Was there anyone else she wasn't nice to?" Marley asked.

"It wasn't so much that she was rude to others; it's more that she ignored everyone as being beneath her notice. It looked to me as though no one particularly liked her." This was Tessa's final statement.

"So that's it?" Marley noted their comments on the pad of paper that he had been using since their interview had begun.

"The ranger," Roger said as an afterthought, "but you know about him. She was just plain mean to him, unlike that Kinderhook kid, who she was seriously trying to seduce. She treated the ranger like a slave. You know, she expected him to clean her place out while she was hiking." He grinned at the memory of the mice. "And that incident with the poor field mice was rather funny. Everyone in camp laughed. That sure made her mad."

"Oh? Who saw what happened?"

"Well, us and the cameraman. I think that mother and daughter next to us were up and cooking breakfast by then. And, of course, those nice people in the lean-tos down below us, they saw it all. You know, Jessie Tyler and the others. I know her name because she's the one we told about that man who called the Verne woman by a strange name I now forget. It began with B," Roger said.

"Did he look angry with her?" Marley asked.

"No, not at all; actually, he seemed pleased to see her. I didn't see the wife, but the daughter didn't seem too pleased with her father calling out to the luscious blonde."

"Well, well," Wilkins said as they walked down the steps of the lovely cottage belonging to the Rowleys. "Perhaps there could be something funny going on in the Rockford family after all."

Marley contemplated Wilkins' remark about the Rockford family as the cruiser headed towards Bangor. *Perhaps that family could stand another looking into,* he thought.

Just south of Bangor, they checked in with the last witnesses of the day. Marta Walters, who they found at work in a local florist shop, was willing to answer their questions. "I want to say right away that the young ranger is not capable of murder. He went out into the night and saved my life."

"We aren't out to arrest an innocent person, but rescuing you is part of his job." Marley changed the subject. "We're just checking back with everyone to see if they remember anything new. You know, people sometimes forget things."

"I cannot say that I saw anything, but I thought those nice women with that Jonathan boy seemed a little tense. Melissa went over to thank the boy the next day and she thought they seemed distracted." Marta scratched her nose as she worked on making a floral arrangement. "I hope you don't mind if I work while we talk. We have a large wedding later today, and I have all these orders to fill." She pointed to a stack of paper receipts.

"Not at all," Wilkins waved off the suggestion that they take a seat. "But I would like to talk to your daughter again. She might remember something that you didn't notice."

"Oh, Melissa is out shopping with friends, but I'm sure she was too upset to notice anything, what with me being lost and all. She wouldn't have seen a thing," Marta Walters said. "School starts soon, so she needed to pick up a few last minute items."

"One last question: have you ever seen this man?" Wilkins asked as he held up the photo of Cameron.

"No," Mrs. Walters said as she scarcely gave the picture a glimpse.

Wilkins shrugged and decided to let it drop for now. Since he was dropping Marley at his station in Bangor, Wilkins would have him stop back on another day to talk to the daughter.

42

One feast, one house, one mutual happiness.
—The Two Gentlemen of Verona, 5.4.173

Reesie meowed her greeting when Dara picked her up at her neighbor Betty's condo. Dara and Betty usually helped one another by watching their respective felines during one or the other's absence. Jockeying mail and cat, Dara opened her front door. Once inside, the first thing she wanted to do was to spend time with her condo mate. The gray and white tabby was the love of her life.

Dara had adopted Reesie a little over two years ago. She had originally gone to the shelter to find a dog for protection. Living on her own for the first time, Dara thought it would be wise to have something that barked when someone knocked on her door.

Dara preferred Dachshunds, but there were none to be adopted. She had returned home disappointed. She was still in the process of deciding if she wanted to replace the cat she had lost a year earlier, when Jessie had called. She knew someone in Augusta who had a four-month-old kitten she couldn't keep. The woman had just married, only to discover that her new husband was allergic to cats. She hadn't wanted to take Clarice to a shelter, so she'd put out a call to friends.

When Dara had gone to see Clarice, it had been love at first sight. So her guard dog had become a cat with a pink, jeweled collar. The collar was Reesie's first Christmas gift. Reesie interrupted this reverie with a yelp. *Boy, Reesie really*

151

missed me, Dara noted as she turned her attention back to her loving cat. It was fate that the name morphed into Reesie. Somehow, Clarice hadn't really fit this lively cat's personality because Dara thought of Clarice as too calm a name for Reesie, who demanded attention in a loud—and what some could call an obnoxious—voice.

Dara thought about this as she unpacked and began doing laundry. After the first load was thrown into the dryer—and after Reesie had been carefully extracted from it—Dara and Reesie played. When Reesie finally tired of chasing Dara around the condo, she crashed on the couch. Dara took the break from entertaining her cat and cleaned. She always kept her place as neat as a pin, but she felt there was always room for improvement.

Next, she retired to her home office and set to work on her course files. She had two classes to teach this week and she needed to put the finishing touches on them. Her first class was European literature. Partway through Dara's work, Reesie awoke and took up her usual perch on the shelf above Dara's desk. Her raccoon-striped tail dangling down towards the desktop, Reesie purred with contentment. Still less than three years old, Reesie never tired of playing. Today she reached down and batted Dara's pencil, frequently interrupting her master as Dara scratched out notes before transferring them to her laptop.

With her classes ready to go, Dara decided it was time to give Reesie a good brushing. Dara sat on the floor and called her cat over. Reesie sat patiently while her back was brushed, before she flipped over to have her sides, and last her tummy, groomed. Dara didn't get much hair off Reesie, but she knew how much her cat loved the ritual.

Afterwards, Dara stayed on the floor with her legs outstretched as she pressed the remote to turn on the news before dinner. Reesie walked the length of Dara's legs and curled up in Dara's lap. They stayed there for some time before both were hungry enough to eat. "Time for dinner,"

Katahdin Drowning

Dara said as Reesie stretched and jumped from her master's lap. Dara groaned as she rolled over and rose to her feet.

After a big salad for Dara and a can of tuna for Reesie were consumed, Dara sat down to her computer and looked up things for her Edith Wharton class. She needed to see what was happening at The Mount, Wharton's one-time home in the Berkshires. Dara visited the western Massachusetts community of Lenox at least every other year. It was an excuse to brush up on new info about the author, but in reality, she loved Lenox. She frequently went online to check out The Mount even when she taught no Wharton classes.

As an afterthought, she searched online to see if anything had been posted concerning the death of Veronica Verne. Perhaps the police had released more than they had shared back at the park. She saw that there was little to be learned, so she almost turned off her computer. Then she had another thought. She went onto Facebook and looked around. Sure enough, Verne had a page.

Dara began to feel sick to her stomach at all the hate mail. She never liked the woman, but this was too much. She persisted in reading everything only because she thought that she might find something useful.

Several people did not like her show because Verne was so condescending. But that was only the beginning. A number of people said that she must have slept her way to the top and that she would be punished by God someday. Another said that she only got the job because her husband helped her get it.

Someone named Michael said that she was a terrible lover, and he was not the only one to post this view. Several men talked about her in the same manner.

Women talked about her stealing their men. "You will get yours some day, and I hope it's soon," Cassidy said.

Another angry woman wrote, "You stole my husband and I'll get even. He loved me until you showed up and spoiled

153

our perfect life." Well, lady, your marriage couldn't have been *that* perfect! Dara was glad at times like these that she was self-sufficient. Or maybe it was because she'd never met the perfect man.

Another diatribe ended in a vitriolic spewing of hatred with, "I hate you. You ruined my life and I'll never forgive you. You are such a b..." Well, Dara got the point. The person was among quite a number of people who had nothing good to say about Veronica Verne.

Dara noted that some comments were posted on the day before Veronica Verne's death. Surely the woman had not read them, since that was the same day they had first seen her in the park.

Dara emailed Jessie the link to Verne's Facebook page. Not that Jessie would necessarily see it. She was still on vacation and rarely checked her messages from home. After sending the information she had discovered, Dara called Killdeer Farm. "Hey, my muscles are beginning to loosen up. I can walk without being in so much pain now."

"Glad to hear it. Are you ready for another hike?" Jessie teased.

"Very funny, but that's not why I called. I found some stuff on Facebook that you need to look at. I sent you a message about it, but I know how you are about using your computer at home."

"I know. I usually have my face in a book when I'm not outside, so I'm glad you called to let me know. I'll check my messages in a little while."

"So what did you do today?" Dara asked. Jessie was such an outdoors person, that Dara never knew what she was up to.

"Oh, I worked in the garden for a while. It's almost harvest time, but for now I collected some fresh stuff for my larder and some to share with the neighbors."

"And does that include the handsome Henry Evans?" Dara asked.

"Well, Jonathan took him some stuff, but he has a small garden of his own. Most of it went to the Merryfields. They're so generous with their meat birds, so I try to help them out. And I gave everyone some of my garlic, too."

Well done. Dara noted how smoothly her friend had glossed over the 'handsome' neighbor remark.

"Speaking of that, thank you again for the things you sent home with me. I hope you don't mind, but I gave some to Betty. She was so nice to watch Reesie for me, and you sent too much for just me to eat." Dara sat patting Reesie while she talked.

"You don't have to keep thanking me. I always seem to grow too much, and I certainly don't mind sharing," Jessie said. "It's only the apples that I save for Ham. He loves them, so I keep a barrel full in the barn. Speaking of him, he was feisty on our ride this afternoon. The twins and Cassie took him out while we were gone, but he seems to save his wild side for when I'm on him."

"One of those tiny little girls rides him?" Dara was surprised. Hamlet was such a large horse.

Jessie snorted. "Ham loves the girls. He'd never act up for them. Animals are smart. They know when to be bad. He saves it all for me, but all in fun. We had a great time."

Dara closed the call on this note. She loved small creatures and had no room in her life for farm animals. She thought once more about what she had discovered on Facebook. Did it really amount to anything?

43

Peace to this meeting, wherefore we are met.
                    —Henry V, 5.2.1

Jessie was still thinking over what Dara had told her when she heard a knock on her porch door. There stood Police Chief Jeb Michaelson. Jessie inwardly groaned, but she put on a happy face as she strode forward and invited him inside her home.

"Hello, Chief. Long time no see." She motioned him through the porch and into the kitchen. "My son tells me you like iced tea." To his simple nod, she said, "Well, this is your lucky day. I made sun tea for my friends, and there's still some left. Have a seat," Jessie said.

"This tea is marvelous." Michaelson said after taking a sip. What a welcome respite. He'd had a busy day and this had been his first chance to check in on the Tyler family.

"I know you sometimes stop by my son's place for pleasure, but my guess is that this is Baxter State Park business."

"I'm afraid so, but I hope you won't consider it an intrusion. Charlie just wanted me to ask you and your son if you've remembered anything new."

"Charlie? Who is Charlie?"

"Oops, sorry, I've recently found myself on a first name basis with Detective Wilkins. I forgot myself for a moment."

Jessie beamed with pleasure. "So his name is Charlie. You know, he was actually pleasant to us this time. To be honest, I think he's given up trying to keep us out of things."

"You are one smart woman. That's it, exactly. He told me

156

that he didn't want to be left in the shade while you scoop up all the accolades."

Jessie laughed out loud. "I'm glad to hear that he's finally come to his senses. I bet you had something to do with that." She gave the chief a mischievous grin. "Oh, don't deny it. You've been good to Jonathan and me ever since you stopped trying to arrest us for murder."

"Admit it, young lady. You had a motive where Alfonse Sweetzer was concerned."

Jessie couldn't disagree with him, since Sweetzer had been the one who had run down her husband two years earlier. "Maybe so, but murder? I might have thought of it, but I'd never do such a thing, and neither would Jonathan."

"I know that now, but what about your friend Dara?"

"Not a chance. She's less the violent type than me." Jessie eyed the chief for a minute. "Say, did Charlie—as you call him—send you here to find out about Dara?"

"Actually, he didn't. I got the impression that she wasn't one of his top suspects. He wants me to keep in touch with you to make sure you don't go running off on your own to find the killer. He would prefer that if you have to be involved, you tell us of your suspicions. And before you object, think about two things: he wants you safe and he knows that he can't keep you out of things, so it looks like he's stopped trying." Michaelson smiled winningly and asked, "So, who do you suspect?"

44

I have unclasped
To thee the book even of my secret soul.
                    —Twelfth Night, 1.4.13-14

Ben was waiting for Jessie when she entered his domain for the second time that day; she'd promised to come out and update him if she learned more about the murder.

"I observed that you had the pleasure of a visit from the chief of police. I hope that he has not decided to involve you again."

"That depends on what you call involve." Jessie went on to tell Ben not only about the visit, but also about the data that Dara had emailed her.

"What is Facebook?" Ben asked. "I recall what you told me about computers, even though it still confuses me. Is Facebook another type of strange machinery?"

"No," Jessie said with a laugh. "I'm sorry; I shouldn't make fun of you. It's so good of you to be curious about new technology. Remember what I told you about the internet?" To Ben's serious nod, Jessie went on. "Facebook is a social network. It began as a way for college students to get to know one another. You can profile yourself to meet new people online and then they can correspond with you."

Ben nodded even though Jessie was sure he had no idea what she had just said. She didn't blame him, since he was born in the first half of the nineteenth century.

"I do not know what to say about this situation. Please explain about the comments of those people and we will leave it at that."

"Yes, that's best. You see, it looks as though Barbara Porter has more animosity towards the murder victim than she admitted. I'm wondering if Dara should tell the police about it. The other people who said mean things about Veronica Verne might be possibilities, too."

"I agree with you. Your friend Dara *should* talk to the officers of the law. Am I to assume that you will not stay out of this case?"

"Oh, Ben, we have a vested interest as long as Dara is a suspect. So I guess I *will* be involved." When she sensed an objection forming, she said, "I can't leave a friend to be hung out for the wolves to tear apart."

At this, Ben grinned. His pale skin shone brighter and his body almost held form for a second. "I did not think that I would be able to stop you, young lady, but you must keep me apprised of what you are doing. Will you please promise to do that for me?"

Jessie had a question for Ben, so she made a compromise. "If you tell me something personal, I'll agree to keep you in the loop."

"Jessie, my dear, the things you say always amaze me." Ben raised a pale arm up to his face and pushed back what had once been a lock of dark hair. "I think that I understand why you use that word 'loop' but that only comes from so many years of listening to your son." Jonathan had been a companion to Ben ever since the boy had been five. Young Jonny had always recognized Ben and they had become life-long companions. Jessie only wished that she had been open-minded enough to be part of the experience years ago. She had only opened up to Ben's existence since her husband's death.

But she must not think about that now, for she wanted to plant flowers on Ben's grave. She knew that he had been buried beneath an apple tree, but that was many years ago. The tree was undoubtedly gone now. Could his grave be near the two apple trees that her grandfather had planted? Just

where were Ben's bones? All she knew was that his brother
had secretly buried him on the farm.

Ben had followed his heart south during the American
Civil War and had paid for his mistake. He had joined the
confederate army to please his true love, only to have her jilt
him. He had fought for the wrong side and ended up killing
a friend on the battlefield just before he, himself, had been
wounded. After he'd made a torturous trek back north, Ben
had died in the attic above Jonathan's workshop. Ben's
brother Ebenezer had not known what to do. He had wanted
to sneak Ben's body down to the cemetery on Twin Pines
Road, before he had learned that the bodies of many soldiers
had never been returned home. That was when Ebenezer had
decided to keep Ben's body close to him. *Could his unmarked
grave be near the pond Jessie now called Ames Pond?*

After much teasing, Ben had once admitted that his only
grave marker had been an apple tree planted atop his bones.
Jessie had been denied a chance to place a stone on his
grave. Ben had insisted on this many times, which was why
he had not told her where his bones were buried.

"What would you care to ask me, Jessie my dear? I will
do what I can to comply as long as you keep me in the loop,
as you call it."

"Oh, Ben, please tell me where you're buried so I can at
least plant some flowers. If you prefer, no one needs to know
what they're for, except Jonathan and me."

Ben sighed. He had slowly unveiled information about his
past, so perhaps it was time to tell Jessie about the journey
of his bones. Why not this small thing?

"Jessie, I might never have known exactly where my
bones reside today had I not met a man named Fernald
Colby." Seeing the look in Jessie's eyes, he said, "Yes, that is
your great-grandfather."

"You knew my great-grandfather?" Jessie was astounded
until she thought it over. After all, Ben had died in the 1860s
and, therefore, must have seen a number of people over the

years.

"Ah, I see. You never considered how many people I might have met since my demise. I did not have the heart to stay hidden forever. Or are you surprised because you did not know about your great-grandparents?"

"Oh, I knew that Grandpa's parents were Fernald and Jessie Colby. I'm named after her, as you probably know. You never cease to surprise me. Are you telling me that you knew him?"

Ben nodded to both. "Yes, and I also knew that your parents decided to name you after your mother's grandmother. Your mother was very close to her grandmother, but perhaps you did not know that."

Jessie had not known. "Will you tell me about my great-grandparents and what that has to do with your bones?"

"I shall do that, but you must let me tell it in my own way. It is a long story. You see, I watched Fernald Colby from the time he bought this place. It came about after Ebenezer had passed on. When my brother died, his spirit visited me once and only once. He said good-bye to me and I am certain that he went straight to heaven. His widow, Florence, only lived here for a few more years. By this time, my parents were also gone.

"This place came to your family in 1895. Back in my day, a few miles was a long distance to travel for social reasons alone. This is the reason why Florence elected to move into town. Her sister had recently been widowed as well and they decided to share her place.

"Fernald told me all this later, when he revealed some of his childhood memories. He had always been a town boy, one who always felt out of place there. He loved to plant things in the small back yard behind their home."

When Ben saw Jessie open her mouth to speak, he said, "Patience, my dear, and I will tell you the complete tale. There will be time for questions when I am done." Jessie nodded a silent agreement as Ben continued: "You see, Fernald and I had many long conversations over the years and he told me of his aspirations. Farming had been the one dream that he finally had a chance to pursue when Florence sold the house to him. At first I was sorry to see the place leave my family, but I soon learned that I had inherited another, more precious gift than I could ever conceive: friendship.

"Fernald had saved money all his life for just such a chance. He finished his education at age eighteen and began working full-time. He was twenty-three before he was able to cash in on that dream. When Fernald insisted on purchasing this farm, his father had tried to talk him out of it." Ben smiled at the memory. "He told me that once he had looked the place over, reality had set in. He had wondered at his ability to make a go of it. After all, he had only raised vegetables in a small plot of land thus far.

"But this house, the barn, and over one hundred acres of land were just what he wanted. My sister-in-law had even thrown in her team of horses and the farm wagon to sweeten the deal. That did it for your great-grandfather. He would own it; even his father had failed to dissuade him.

"Fernald plunked down his money and all too soon Florence moved out with her bedroom furnishings and the living room furniture. Fernald later told me that since she would have limited space at her sister's place, Florence had left most of the furniture in his care. He told me how he had felt bad when he saw her rub her hands lovingly across the maple dining room table. 'My husband made this set with his own hands,' Florence had told him. Your great-grandfather, being a kind man, had promised to take good care of everything she had left behind and should she ever want any of it back, he would turn it over to her." Ben's face held a sad air as he paused for a moment. "You see, Jessie, I watched my brother build that furniture. That is why I was pleased that she never took it away, even if I was never able to see it again. Somehow, it does not matter, for it is still in this house."

"Oh, Ben, I wish you could come inside and see it." Jessie

was sad for Ben.

"Never mind about that now, Jessie; I know it is there and that is enough for me. In the intervening years, Fernald and I talked about my brother's extraordinary abilities as he, too, learned the art of furniture making." Ben smiled. "I guess it runs in the family. Jonathan comes by it naturally." Jessie swelled with pride, but said nothing.

"But before she left the farm, I had listened to Florence talk to Fernald. For the first time I realized how lonely she had been, even before the death of my brother. Poor Florence had been all alone in the house while Eb was out here with me, but she had never complained. She told your great-grandfather how a change had come over Ebenezer after I had died. Of course, he had told everyone that I had died down south, but all Florence had known was that my brother grieved at the loss and had locked himself away out here." Ben's sad countenance held a trace of regret. "You see, he had been with me all that time, and Florence never knew it. I regret all those years that Florence might have shared with us, but at the time I figured Eb was the only person with the ability to see or hear me.

"I began to think that perhaps I had been wrong on the occasion when I first saw your great-grandfather. I wondered if he was sensing my presence when I saw a convulsive shiver wrack his body when he stood in this building for the first time. Florence, bless her, kindly led him back into the house. I never saw Florence again.

"And then one day I literally ran into Fernald and I discovered that others *could* see me. Ever since my brother's death, those people have all been members of the Colby family. But I get ahead of myself. I watched Fernald from a distance before we ever met.

"I could feel the pride Fernald Colby had for this place, so while I resented the farm that Ebenezer and I built going outside the family, I finally accepted it. I saw Fernald work every day as he planted new gardens.

"I watched as he slowly made the farm look as it had before Ebenezer had passed on. Fernald would frequently sit by the nicely flowing stream that ran across the land scarcely a dozen yards to the rear of this building. I could tell that he was planning something. He had such a look of determination on his face; I feared that it involved my tree. Fernald would walk around it and stare at it. It had never given up apples even before Ebenezer died, but my brother had refused to cut it down.

"Florence had shown no interest in the tree and it had slowly died from neglect. So why did I care? I cared because it was my final resting place. I watched from my upstairs window with rising horror as I guessed what your relative was planning.

"And I was correct. Because Fernald needed digging tools, he entered the shed for the first time since Florence had gone away. I saw him grab a sharp saw, a shovel, and a pickaxe. I wanted to stop him, so I reached out and attempted to touch his shoulder. He shook with fear and dashed out the door. The implements jostled in his shaky hands as he ran away before I could make myself seen."

"Did he destroy the tree?" Jessie asked.

"Yes, Jessie, he did, but it took him quite a long time. As I watched, the tree seemed to be fighting him. It was quite small; its branches hung over to touch the ground like an old man with arthritis. I could see him become chilled and sweaty with exertion all at the same time. The tree seemed to defy his attempts to cut into it, but that young man did not give up. He sawed on the trunk until he discovered that the tree was hollow. That was when it fell to the ground.

"But that was not the end of Fernald's labors. He began digging away at the bit of trunk that was left. All the time he attacked the roots I tried to stop him. Oh, I could not go outside and push him away from my tree, but in my mind, I fought him. I have to admit now that I felt sorry for him. Just as he finally began making headway, a hole formed and began filling with water. It turned the soil into a heavy, mucky mix of clay and rocks. It was as though Ebenezer were up here, too, helping me put up obstacles. I should have known better, but I wanted my tree back in one piece.

"I almost missed what happened next. The mud seized him as though it were pulling him into its depths. He could not get loose. As I watched, I felt as if he were being sucked into the very bowels of the earth. His high leather boots were rapidly being covered with heavy, oozing mud. He struggled, but it was not working. He needed help. He yelled, but no one came to his rescue."

45

What have you done, my lord, with the dead body?
—Hamlet, 4.2.5

Jessie gasped. "Ben, what happened next? I know he did-
n't die, or I wouldn't be here."

"You are correct, Jessie. He did get loose, but he fought
like the devil for quite a time before he got out of that mess.
By this time I realized that I had been selfish. So what if he
found my bones and threw them out. I did not want this
young man to die. I prayed that he would not succumb and,
after a time, I saw his left foot released from the muck, leaving the boot behind.

"His right foot was still stuck into the thick mud, but he
pulled and pulled until it—boot and all—was released. He lay
on the ground and grabbed at his left boot. I heard a great
sucking sound emitted from the hole as the boot was set free.
He looked into the hole left by that boot and instinct told me
what he saw.

"He stretched out over the hole as it slowly began to fill
with muddy water and grabbed out one of my bones. I
watched as he cleaned the mud off before he took it away. It
was some time before I found out that he had taken it into
the house and set it on the mantle piece.

"The next day he crossed the stream, took up a shovel,
and began digging quite a distance away from my old apple
tree. He dug all day. I still did not understand why he was
making a new hole. The tree was gone, but he did not go near
the ground holding the remainder of my bones.

166

Katahdin Drowning

"You know, Jessie, I learned much later that Fernald had feared that my brother had killed someone and had buried the body out there. That was why he stayed away from the spot where my bones were buried—that and fear that the land would swallow him up."

"He thought your brother had killed someone? If so, why didn't he call the police?" Jessie asked.

"Your great-grandfather was a kind man. He did not want to see a scandal raised. After all, what good would it have done? He was afraid that Florence would be hurt by even the possibility of her husband having killed someone."

"Then why was he digging that other hole?" Jessie began to understand what Fernald Colby had been doing. "Was he digging a pond?"

"Yes, the pond was your great-grandfather's creation. He wanted a pond to water the livestock he planned to purchase in the spring, but we are getting ahead of ourselves."

"Oh, I'm sorry, Ben. Please continue."

"That is fine, Jessie. You are a smart girl." Ben was as proud of Jessie and her family as though they were his own. And in a way, they were. "As the season progressed, Fernald stored the farm implements in the barn. He did what you call 'busy work' until the time came when he decided to get to the bottom of his fears. He had figured out that someone was watching him and he was determined to find that person.

"And so he tricked me. One day while he was working on his pond, he must have seen movement from upstairs, because I saw him suddenly throw down his shovel and dash for the shed. I knew that he was sensitive to my presence as he ran through the nearest door and dashed for the staircase. He took the stairs two at a time, but I had vanished before he reached the top.

"After several more failed attempts, he tricked me good and proper. One day he ambled towards the rear of the shed with great nonchalance. I watched him fidget with the shovel's handle. I did not know it then, but he was pretending to fix the handle as he slowly moved close to the shed wall where I could not see him. I did not know, therefore, that he had crept to the far side door. Once at that door, he dashed through it and raced up the stairs. Unfortunately for him, he had forgotten to fix a loose handrail. It gave way under his left hand just as his right foot touched the top step."

Jessie's eyes widened in horror, but she said nothing. Ben smiled with reassurance and finished his story. "I might not have wanted this man to learn of my existence, but I could not let him be injured. As he fell backwards with a piece of broken rail coming away in his hand, I grabbed him by his shirt collar." Ben chuckled for the first time since he had begun his story. "With his flight suddenly halted, the man was shocked to discover his feet dangling in midair. I guess I held his shirt collar a bit too tightly, for he passed out.

"I placed him on the floor and waited. When he finally awoke, he must have received the biggest scare of his life. He told me later that he saw beams of sunlight pierce my body and my smoky eyes glowed. I apologized for frightening him.

"You know, your ancestor was brighter than I would have anticipated. He asked me if I was Ebenezer. I could not help but be cheered by that comment. He knew right away that I was a ghost and he accepted it.

"I told him, that no, I was not Ebenezer, for sadly, he was gone forever. I was not sure what to say next, but I decided that it was best to tell the truth 'I, sir, am Ben Ames, and what have you been doing out back?'

"At first he did not seem to believe me. He had heard how I had died at the Battle of Fredericksburg back during the American Civil War, so he did not see how my ghost could be in Wyleyville, Maine, even in death. 'Ben Ames died down south and his body was never recovered from the battlefield. Everyone in town says so,' he proclaimed.

"I told him what I thought about that. I said something to the effect of, 'Well, young man, everyone in town does not know what they are talking about. I did return to Maine, but I was gravely ill and I died right here.' I pointed towards my cot with its blanket neatly tucked into its mattress. The physical presence of my cot seemed to be enough. He just nodded in acceptance.

"That was when I told him my story. I explained that I am destined to stay locked away in this building forever. He empathized with me. I explained how I had come here to die and that my brother had found me. He was shocked when I told him how Ebenezer had buried me near the stream and planted an apple tree over my grave as a memorial.

"'Th-those are your bones out there?' he stuttered. I told him that yes, they are mine and that is why I had been watching him from my window. I also told him that I had been spying on him from the very beginning. Fernald told me that he had felt something cold every time he had entered the shed and workshop. He shook his head with resignation. He said that he had known all along that something was off about this place.

"It was then that I asked him what he was planning to do with my leg bone. He seemed perplexed, so I asked him if he would please put it back with the rest of my body."

Ben smiled up at Jessie as the story closed: "He promised to do that for me, but he asked if he could plant two new trees beside my final resting place. He also told me that he was digging a pond, which I had already guessed. 'I would like to call it Ames Pond, after you and your brother, if you do not mind,' he said to me. I was touched, just as when you mentioned giving the pond the same name."

"Oh, Ben, you never told me that the pond already had a name." Jessie's eyes twinkled with suppressed tears.

"I would say that over the years the name had become lost, but now it has been found again." Ben's grin fairly split his face. "Fernald Colby became my lifelong friend from that day forward. We talked almost every day, until he passed away."

"Why didn't he introduce you to my grandfather? Why did Grandpa have to find out about you on his own?" Jessie asked.

"Well, dear, I never push myself onto people and most of them do not think that anyone else believes in ghosts. Almost everyone—save young Jonathan—has kept me their secret."

Of course Jessie knew all about that: a five-year-old Jonathan had told his disbelieving mother about his invisible friend. She lived to regret her close-minded nature, but after her husband's death she'd found out her son had been telling nothing but the truth. When Jonny had told his father, Jonathan had also developed a friendship with Ben. Father and son had kept Ben to themselves after Jessie had fluffed off the relationship with such platitudes as, "That's nice, Jonny, but you should spend time with real people, with children your own age."

Now Jessie blushed at the memory. Ben, who noticed and correctly guessed what she was thinking, did not further embarrass her, but changed the subject. "Jessie, the truth of the matter is that those trees are not the ones that Fernald planted. They, too, died. Your grandfather planted those trees to replace the ones that his father cherished for many a year. They, like these trees, did bear fruit. Fernald planted them on either side of my grave and Jackson did the same."

"So your grave is situated right between the two trees that are out there now?" Jessie finally had her answer. She could do something special for Ben to see from his upstairs home. She would plant flowers and surprise him very soon.

46

Whither I go, thither shall you go too.
　　　　　　　　　—Henry IV, Part 1, 2.3.115

The workday was far from over for Detective Charles Wilkins when he turned his police cruiser towards Baxter State Park to retrieve Officer Milo. During his solitary trip into the park, Wilkins mulled over what he had learned. He was beginning to have second thoughts about Goodroe. Everyone he had talked to had good things to say about him, besides which the only evidence against him had turned out to be bogus.

Wilkins drove with great care during his approach into the park. Vehicles frequently had to share the road with wildlife, and Wilkins didn't want to hit a moose, or anything else, for that matter. As the park gate loomed up, Wilkins slowed to show his identification before he was waved through.

Detective Marley had been a good sort to work with, but Wilkins didn't know him well yet. Since talking to Jeb Michaelson, Wilkins was a bit sorry that it wasn't the Wyleyville police chief who had accompanied him. He sure missed the chief's keen wit and his willingness to do whatever Wilkins suggested. He thought that it was too bad this murder hadn't taken place in Wyleyville.

Earlier, when Wilkins had dropped Maine State Police Detective Hank Marley off at his Bangor office, Marley had promised to go back to see the teenaged Melissa Walters. He would show her the photo of Cameron, as well as conduct a follow-up on her statement.

Today, Wilkins and Milo would be returning to Augusta. Wilkins parked his car in the campground parking lot and sat observing Park Ranger Jerome Goodroe as the youngster assisted a couple in putting their tent up.

Goodroe excused himself and trotted over to the detective when the tent erection was under control. When Goodroe learned that he had been downgraded to a person of interest, Wilkins could see the relief in his eyes. "Well, that's something. Is there anything I can do here to help you? Assisting visitors to the park is my number one priority, but if you need anything, please let me know."

"I'm taking Milo with me, so you're back in charge here at your campground, at least for now. If I need anything, I'll call you. I would appreciate it if you would keep your eyes and ears open. Call me if you learn anything new, but do not try to investigate this case without our help. It's far too dangerous."

"Yes, sir, I can do that," Goodroe said with renewed enthusiasm. "It'll be nice to get back to concentrating on the job I was hired to do."

Wilkins smiled appreciatively before he went off to round up his assistant. As they drove away from Katahdin Stream Campground, Wilkins hoped this would be his last trip into the park, but he very much doubted it.

On the way back to Augusta, Detective Wilkins and Officer Milo had made a side trip to Skowhegan, where Verne had attended high school. An hour later, Milo whistled as they walked down the school steps. "Well, the things you learn about small town life. I'm glad I went to a large school, where everyone didn't know one another."

"Yes, small towns can be a hotbed for gossip." Wilkins was thinking about what the high school guidance councilor had told them. Secrets …

"Oh, by the way, when we get back to headquarters, how about checking on that movie camera. Even if it is broken, there must be a hard drive we can look at to confirm Kinderhook's story."

"Sure thing; I'll get right on it," Milo said as he pulled the cruiser into the parking lot. As it turned out, he had to wait on that job, for their arrival coincided with a visit from one of the suspects. Dara Kane looked up from a bench in the hallway and smiled as they approached. "Do you have time to talk to me for one minute?"

"Only one minute?" Wilkins kidded her. "Actually, I would like to talk with you. Please come in." Wilkins escorted Dara down a long hallway and into a large room with several work stations. He walked past them all, and into his office. Milo retrieved a notebook from his desk and followed. As Milo seated himself inconspicuously to one side, Dara told them all she knew about Veronica Verne, aka Bertha Crumm. Wilkins was glad Dara was forthcoming with them. Perhaps she'd had time to realize that the woman's death could have its roots in Bertha's past.

"Why did you want to know about her boyfriends?" Dara asked.

Wilkins decided to tell her what they had learned when they had visited her old high school in the hopes of shocking her into disclosing something new. "Bertha seems to have been pregnant during the summer before her last year of high school. She was away until October that year, before she came back with a baby."

Dara produced a look of astonishment. "But Bertie didn't seem the type to allow herself to get caught like that. I don't know what to say." She looked from one man to the other. "Yes, she dated, but she was never with one boy for long. She preferred sports heroes. If they weren't on the football varsity squad, they were beneath her notice."

"Surely you know more than that," Detective Wilkins said.

"Oh, but perhaps you don't understand. My family moved away before then." Dara mulled over her last year there. "You know, that man at the park might have dated her. He was one of those sports jocks. That's all I can tell you, but I did discover something else that might interest you." Dara pulled several sheets of paper from her bag and handed them to Wilkins. "I found this online. You might want to go onto Ms. Verne's Facebook page and check it out. I bet I only touched the surface of how people felt about her."

47

In companions
That do converse and waste the time together.
—The Merchant of Venice, 3.4.11-12

Jonathan had spent a long day catching up on several small jobs before he stopped home to check in on his cats. He and Merlin, who had kept him company at work, next hiked a back trail to visit his new friend.

After Henry Evans had moved to the old Dexter Farm, Jonathan had wasted no time getting acquainted. A couple months ago, Henry had sold his New York business and moved to the farm he had inherited. He lived off-the-grid, a lifestyle that fascinated Jonathan, more so because Henry was repairing a Jacobs wind charger to augment the photovoltaic panels he had installed to generate electricity.

Jonathan knew that Henry spent most evenings in his barn tinkering with the wind charger. Jonathan, therefore, came over to watch Henry whenever time permitted.

"Hello, Henry. How goes it?"

"Well, long time no see, stranger. I thought you'd be busy catching up on business after returning from your trip."

"Oh, I am busy, but I have to take some time out to relax, too. Not that the trip is really behind us." Jonathan watched Henry fiddle with parts while he told Henry about finding the body and how his mother had been disappointed that they hadn't solved the murder before they had left Baxter State Park.

Henry shook his head in amazement. "You people always seem to become embroiled in murder."

Jonathan knew Henry had a point, but he hoped that distance would keep his mother from trying to discover the murderer this time. *Fat chance of that*, he thought, *as long as her friend was a suspect*.

Henry had a quizzical stare on his face when he looked up from his work. "Are you thinking that your mother will try to get involved, even from back here?"

"How'd you guess? Oh, I'd better tell you everything."

After Jonathan had told him all the details, Henry asked, "Her friend, this Dara Kane, knew the victim?" Jonathan simply nodded. Henry shook his head and set his screwdriver down before wiping his hands. "This calls for a break. Let's have a beer."

"Sure thing," Jonathan said and followed Henry into the house. Once they were sitting at Henry's table sipping what Jonathan called near-beer, Jonathan finished the tale.

"Are you telling me that this friend of Jessie's is really a viable suspect?"

"So it seems," Jonathan said. "Dara was told to stay available for further questioning. Before the police talked to her, she'd only told *Mom* about her involvement with the victim. Dara seemed ashamed when she finally told the rest of us why she disliked the Verne woman. They'd been in school together and the woman had bullied her. I guess she felt better after Willa, Gina, and I told her we'd been bullied, too. Mom was just shocked. She had no idea. Of course, none of us told our parents, but I'm glad she knows now because it put Dara at ease. I think it made her feel closer to us."

"Bullying isn't as rare as most people think. I know it happens more today—or maybe more kids are speaking out—but it's nothing new."

Jonathan agreed before he changed to a lighter topic. "You should have seen my mother's face when Willa said she wanted to walk across Knife's Edge!"

"I've heard of that place. Isn't it dangerous?"

"Not too much. You do have to be careful, but it makes

176

climbing Katahdin the ultimate experience. Dad took me over it once." Jonathan grinned. "Mom hated it. She wouldn't go across and she refused to watch until Dad asked her to take pictures."

"That must have pleased your mother no end."

"True, but she survived it that time. I'm not so sure about the next one. Willa has her heart set on it, though. She's nothing, if not determined. At first, she was all set to go right back to the park, until I told her I couldn't get away again this fall. So now she's planning a spring climb."

"Do you think Cassie will let her go?" Henry asked.

"Willa is too determined. She'll be eighteen soon, so she figures no one can stop her. She has it all planned out. She hopes to convince her father to take her and there's nothing Joe Royce won't do for his daughter. She wants me to go, too, probably because she saw the gleam in my eyes when I recalled my last trek over the Edge." Jonathan thought he saw a longing on Henry's face. Perhaps—when the time came—he would invite Henry, too.

After they had depleted that conversation, Jonathan looked around. "You're next on my work list, that is, if you still want me to help you around here."

"Of course I do. I need a new roof on both the house and barn and then I need to scrape and paint both buildings. I'd also like to hire you this winter; this kitchen sure needs sprucing up." Henry looked around at the dismal kitchen. He needed new cabinets. He hoped Jonathan would design them; he'd heard the boy was a fine finish carpenter.

"Say, why don't you drop by my shop tomorrow? I'll be working there first thing in the morning," Jonathan said. "I'm working on some cabinets I need to install in a kitchen I've been renovating. That way, you can see if I'm suited to the project you have in mind."

"I'd love to do that. What time shall I come over?"

"I start work at seven, so anytime after that. And since my mother will probably be home—she's still on vacation—I bet we can get a cup of coffee out of her."

Henry promised to be there bright and early as Jonathan said good-bye and left for home.

On the way back, Jonathan thought about his plans for that night. He had met a new girl in town. Well, she wasn't exactly new because she'd lived in Wyleyville as a child, but her family had only recently moved back. He didn't know why he was keeping their dates a secret. Perhaps it was because he couldn't see a future in their relationship. And perhaps that was why he hadn't introduced her to his mother.

48

Finish, good lady, the bright day is done,
And we are for the dark.
—Antony and Cleopatra, 5.2.193-194

During Jonathan's visit to the Dexter Farm, Jessie continued her talk with Ben. Besides learning more about Ben's past, Jessie had been given a glimpse into her own family history. It was exciting to learn more about her great-grandfather, but she wondered something else. "Say, did you ever meet Jessie Colby?"

"No, Jessie, your great-grandmother frequently came out to watch her husband in his workshop, but whenever I was present, she seemed oblivious to my presence. I guess she did not have the gift to open her mind to otherworldly possibilities."

Jessie was disappointed. Perhaps she was more like the other Jessie than she realized—or used to be. Still, she had hoped to learn more about her namesake. Maybe Ben knew more than he realized, but there was always time to quiz him about her at a later date. Right now, something else had Jessie curious. One part of his story had confused her. How had he lifted her great-grandfather up by his shirt collar?

"Ben, don't get me wrong. I'm not saying that I don't believe your story, but you can't pick people up. Every time you try to touch someone, your hand goes right through them. How did you do it?"

Ben was silent for a moment. "This is something that has had me puzzled for over one hundred years. I have never had the ability to repeat that feat. I have thought this over for

179

many years. I have tried many a time to replicate it, but I have always failed." Ben gave Jessie a sad smile. "I would love nothing more than to place my hand in yours or put my arms around you when you need my support, and that saddens me. I wish it were not so. I have developed a theory, however, one which might answer your question. Perhaps, in moments of extreme distress, my body takes on more substance. I know this is not much of an answer, but that is the only solution I have ever been able to envision."

Later Jessie sat in bed thinking about what Ben had told her. She contemplated whether his ability to physically help someone would return if a drastic event should occur. She wondered what it would take, but the thought of extreme danger to a loved one was just too scary to consider.

So she turned to more pleasant matters. She was looking forward to the dinner party Cassie's sister, Mary, was having the next evening. Jessie was thrilled that it was Mary and not Cassie who was giving it, for Mary and her husband Bart were wonderful cooks. They owned the Great Taco Bazaar, Wyleyville's only Mexican restaurant, and it wasn't surprising that the two knew their business.

Mary had extended her invitation to most of the neighborhood, so their small ranch house would be full of people. Because Jessie had offered to bring pies, she would be busy tomorrow morning. That should keep her out of trouble for one day, and perhaps distract her from thinking about the murder.

She sighed as she picked up and began rereading *Othello*. While it had once been one of her least favorite Shakespeare plays, she had changed her mind when she had seen it performed. Shenandoah Shakespeare Express had visited Maine a number of years ago when she was still a student at the University of Maine at Augusta. They did *Othello* on stage in a two hour rendition they were so famous for. 'We do it with the lights on' was their battle cry, which meant that house lights were on during the whole performance in an attempt to replicate the original play. In Shakespeare's day, the stage was open to the daylight sky.

Their back-to-basics performance with minimal props and plain black outfits talked to Jessie. She had loved it and so had begun her love for Shakespeare. Back at school, the professor had also shown them a black and white movie starring Orson Welles. That, too, had thrilled Jessie. Its stark imagery was more realistic than most color movies. Black and white had been just right for *Othello*, Jessie thought, as she fell asleep before finishing the first act. The book fell from her hands and onto the floor just after Iago began plotting Othello's downfall.

49

A dream itself is but a shadow.

—Hamlet, 2.2.260

Jessie awoke with a sense of elation. She'd done it. She'd seen Alfonse Sweetzer's car careen over a cliff, leaving the helmeted motorcyclist intact. Then reality set in: her husband Jonathan was still dead! Oh, why did life have to be so difficult? Jessie shook her head. It was still dark outside but she knew she'd get no more rest as she crawled from her warm bed, plucked *Othello* from where it had fallen on the floor, and moved to a nearby chair.

Juju changed her master's dark mood when she left her bedtime pillow on Jonathan's side of the bed—for Jessie would always call it that. Juju, who had taken over Jonathan's pillow, now drifted over to the chair and curled up in Jessie's lap. "Oh, you're such a sweetheart." Jessie scratched her gray and white cat. Not to be outdone, Mira rose from the foot of the bed and stretched before joining her sister on one chair arm to get her share of attention.

Mira and Juju always seemed to know when she needed a little extra TLC. Jessie chatted with them as they nuzzled her before both cats decided it was time for breakfast. With collective "Meows," they were off and running. They were barely out of the room and into the hallway before their small feet could be heard pattering down the stairs.

Jessie laughed. She'd get no reading done this morning, she decided, as she set the book aside. She dressed quickly and followed them downstairs to feed them before delving into the day's project.

She'd already planned to get up early to make the pies she'd promised for Mary's dinner party, so she decided to get started. By the time she made her appearance to visit Ben, Jessie had rolled out dough for four pies and the two apple pies were in the oven baking. She would put together the two blueberry pies after she talked to Ben.

And that was where she was sitting, quietly chatting with Ben, when she heard voices coming from outside. "It would appear that your son has company." Ben stood. "I will be seeing you again very soon, I trust." He winked out as he silently retreated upstairs. He had vanished just before Jonathan opened the outer door leading into his workshop beneath Ben's permanent home.

"This is where I create." Jessie could hear pride in Jonathan's voice as he spoke to an as-yet-unknown person. Before Jessie had a chance to withdraw, her son appeared in the shed through the interior door. A friend followed closely behind.

"Did I hear you talking to someone?" Henry Evans said to Jessie by way of greeting.

"Oh, I'm just talking to myself," Jessie denied his claim. "I'm planning my day over coffee. I've been waiting for Jonathan."

"Yes, Mom always has coffee brewing when she knows I'll be around." Jonathan looked at his mother with concern before he sniffed the air. "Oh, I can tell what you've been up to." Jonathan knew full well that his mother had been visiting with Ben, which is why he had announced his presence in a louder-than-usual voice.

"You can smell the coffee?" Jessie teased.

"Now that you mention it, yes, but you know that's not what I meant."

"Good morning, Henry," Jessie said. "Do you drink coffee?"

"Yes, as a matter of fact, I do."

Jessie waved her now empty coffee cup towards the kitchen as she motioned both men inside. She wondered if she'd just been tricked into showing her new neighbor around Killdeer Farm.

"I should have called you, Mom," Jonathan said. "When I was visiting Henry last night, I invited him over to my workshop this morning. He needs to see what kind of work I do, in case he wants me to renovate his kitchen."

After they stepped into Jessie's kitchen, she said, "Well, my kitchen is old-fashioned, but it fits my place. I thought of having new cabinets in here, but I decided to keep it the way my grandparents had it."

"Yes, it does fit. I wouldn't change a thing," Henry said as he looked around at the older cabinets. Jessie wondered what he was thinking. She sighed as they sat down and had coffee together before showing him the rest of the house.

50

It never yet did hurt
To lay down likelihoods and forms of hope.
—Henry IV, Part 2, 1.3.34-35

Henry Evans had been dying to see Killdeer Farm ever
since he'd met Jessie Tyler. When Jonathan greeted him outside his shop with: "Welcome to Tyler and Son," however, the
full realization of Jonathan's loss hit Henry. The boy had
planned to spend the rest of his life working with his father.
Granted, Jonathan gave the appearance of a well-adjusted
young man, but this shop must be a constant reminder of
what might have been.

Henry silently drank in his surroundings, nodding his
approval as he said, "This is a very nice workshop—and
neat." His own shop was anything but. He was essentially an
orderly man, but he had yet to straighten up the mess his
uncle had left behind. He couldn't blame Uncle Walt—after
all, he'd been feeling poorly for quite some time before he'd
taken the fall that had landed him in a nursing home. It had
been one short step to his death after he'd been separated
from his beloved home. Henry shook off regret at not being
able to shut down his New York business sooner to move his
uncle back home. When Henry had inherited the farm, he'd
felt even worse, but now he worked hard to make it a thing
Uncle Walt would be proud of.

"Oops, sorry; wool gathering," Henry sighed. "Your place
reminds me of what I want my place to look like some day. I
only wish Uncle Walt could be there to share it with me."

"Oh, I know the feeling," Jonathan said.

Of course he did. Henry could have kicked himself for the stupid remark. "I say..."

"Don't. I know what you meant. I guess we both have regrets." Jonathan seemed anything but chipper for a second, before he gave a wide smile of contentment.

And then Henry suddenly felt a tremor go through his body; it was as though something not quite human had walked into the room. Jonathan seemed to sense the difference in Henry, or so Henry guessed.

Before he had a chance to question the feeling, they moved past Jonathan's neat and orderly workshop filled with his handsome cabinetry and into the shed. There Henry saw Jessie sitting alone on a short set of stairs. He had been so embroiled in his thoughts, he almost missed something: he'd heard Jessie talking. Someone else had been in the shed, he just knew it. He wondered if she'd been talking to her dead husband, but he let it pass. After all, these two had suffered a great loss. Henry was perceptive enough to understand that they were still grieving.

Before he had a chance to contemplate further, Jessie invited him into the house. He knew she had been acting stand-offish about having him see her home, and he fully understood her hesitation. They shared something. He wanted to get to know her better, but he wasn't sure how she felt about that. Well, he would take it slowly and see what came of it, he thought, as Jessie conducted a tour of her home.

It was a great house. No wonder she was so proud of it. He became momentarily distracted by an item sitting on the dining room table. It was an easel with names written on the attached tablet. Above the names was one word: Suspects. So Jessie was embroiled in the murder up north. The image followed him throughout the house. Killdeer Farm *was* Jessie Tyler. As the tour ended, Henry was all the more determined to get to know her better.

Even if Jonathan had not been such a good carpenter, Henry would have hired the boy to work on his house for a very selfish reason: Henry wanted to see Jessie again, but he respected her privacy and he was a patient man. For now, he would take friendship, if that was all he could get.

51

Thus men may grow wiser every day.
　　　　　　　—As You Like It, 1.2.137

Gran moved as one with a purpose when she toddled into Jessie's house. She had heard all about her granddaughter's adventure in northern Maine and she was furious. "How dare you take your murder out of town so I couldn't be in on the action?" Jessie's paternal grandmother glared at her.

"I did not!" Jessie sputtered with surprise. She usually heard Gran arrive with a bang. The eighty-eight-year-old woman was spry for her age, despite two problems: she was hard of hearing and her driving abilities were practically non-existent. It was rare for Gran to show up at Killdeer Farm without hitting a tree or anything else that got in her way. Since Jessie had been standing in the dining room looking over the murder board and could easily see out a window towards what had once been the front yard, she had seen her grandmother's accident-free entry into her old driveway.

Gran always parked there, something Jessie had long since given up trying to stop her from doing. It turned out to be the safest place for her grandmother's dented red Volkswagen bug to park anyway, because no one else was likely to have their car there for her to hit.

"Did, too! It's all over town. You found a body up north," Gran said in an accusatory tone.

"Oh, Gran," Jessie laughed as she took Gran's arm and crossed into the kitchen. "And how was I supposed to let you share on that? Did you want to climb a mountain with us?"

Katahdin Drowning

"Of course not, but you should have called me the minute you got home. Those old folks at the home know more than I do about your adventures. Now is that fair?" Gran stuck out her lower lip in protest. "It's just not right!"

"Of course it isn't. I'm sorry, Gran. You're right. I *should* have called. Come, sit down and I'll tell you everything. You can go back to your senior housing complex," Jessie corrected Gran, "and fill them in on stuff that no one else in town knows yet." And so Jessie did as they sat in the kitchen that, by now, smelled of blueberry pie. The two discussed the murder; they sipped tea as Gran collected inside information to rub into the faces of her neighbors.

Jessie had already told Ben most of the details about their trip and the murder, but she could tell that he wanted more. After Gran had left, she had plenty of time to visit with him again, before she went over to Mary's place.

While the last pies were cooling, Jessie decided it was now or never. Between Henry's visit—and then Gran's—they hadn't had another chance to chat. "Ben," Jessie called out as she strode into the shed, "are you here?"

Ben's chuckle came from deep within his throat. "You are a constant source of humor, my dear. You know I am *always* here."

Jessie had expected such a response. She hadn't been thinking when she'd made the remark and Ben had called her to task on it. "I know, but what should I have said?"

Ben only shook his head and changed the subject. "Did I hear your grandmother leaving?" To Jessie's nod, Ben said, "You know that woman is not safe. She has no business driving one of those newfangled contraptions. Even in my day, she would have been a danger to others, should she have been allowed a horse and buggy. But it is the other visitor I want to discuss with you, the one Jonathan brought in this morning. If I recall correctly, that gentleman is Jonathan's

189

friend from a nearby farm."

"Yes, that was Henry Evans, Walt Dexter's nephew. You must have heard Jonathan talking about him." Jessie knew she had failed to keep a neutral face.

And now Ben knew he was correct. *Those two have an interest in one another, but neither one of them will admit it.* Letting Jessie off the hook with pretended nonchalance, he began asking questions about the murder.

After Jessie had spoken and Ben had quizzed her over some of the details, he shocked her with a proclamation: "You should go back to that park and finish this business. I only know what you told me, but I have an idea who the murderer might be."

And he told her. Jessie was surprised with what he suggested. He had pushed aside several possible suspects and had honed in on two people. "Of course, I think that my first choice is the killer, but do not discount the second person."

They talked for quite some time about why Ben had picked those particular people and when they were done, Jessie said nothing. She just didn't see it, but Ben was a wise man and he was rarely wrong.

Jessie needed a respite from all that baking—and a chance to be alone, so she tacked up her black and white paint and donned her hard hat before escorting Ham outside the barn. Ham's hooves clacked on Jonathan's wooden bridge as Jessie rode up towards the woods behind her son's house. Once in the same woods that she and her friends had hiked just a couple of days ago, Jessie slowed Ham to a walk in order to think over what Ben had told her.

A kaleidoscope of ideas ran through her head as she contemplated the murder of Veronica Verne. No, she just didn't see what Ben had suggested. Surely, Ben's theory had to be wrong. Even as she wondered how she could get all the witnesses and suspects back together, the plan was already

Katahdin Drowning

being set in motion from Augusta.

52

Society, saith the text, is the happiness of life.
— Love's Labor's Lost, 4.2.161

Meanwhile, Mary's kitchen was a virtual hive of activity as she and Bart were in the throes of preparing a meal. They had never invited so many neighbors over to dinner before; it was an oversight they were rectifying tonight. Mary had pulled out her mother's recipe for lasagna with four cheeses and sweet sausage. They would be filling three pans, two with the complete recipe. Cassie's twins were leaning towards vegetarianism, so the third pan would have no meat.

Dinner guests would include Julia and Mark Merryfield; Jessie and Jonathan; Cassie and her four girls; and their new neighbor, Henry Evans. They would be seating twelve in their small home with a large kitchen.

The meal had initially been planned as one for Jessie, Jonathan, and her oldest sister's family, but it had soon evolved into a block party. Cassie had started it all by hinting that Henry should be invited. *Are Cassie and Henry at the start of something?* Mary wondered as she worked. Once the lasagna was ready to be baked, Bart slid the pans into their industrial sized stove. They had purchased the large stove in order to do some of their restaurant cooking from home, but it came to good use today.

They had purchased a building downtown and had opened the restaurant soon after their marriage. Bart, a graduate of chef school, had subsequently taught his wife much of what he knew. They were having the time of their lives owning their own place.

Their second love was gardening. This had the added bonus of providing much of the produce they needed for the restaurant. They had grown enough tomatoes, peppers, onions, and herbs to make a marvelous salsa.

Great Taco Bazaar thrived as the recipient of most of their homemade concoctions. Jessie and Cassie, who always canned their own tomatoes together each fall, always gave Mary and Bart their extras for the restaurant. Harvested herbs from the small herb garden outside Mary's kitchen window were added to the tomatoes as a source for making her own spaghetti sauce. Bart's garlic put the finishing touch on this and other recipes.

Bart had created his first garlic bed three years ago. When Jessie, too, had shown an interest, he had helped her plan her first garlic bed. Bart had harvested his just a couple of weeks ago; he was proud of the plump bulbs sitting on the kitchen counter. He and Jessie both shared garlic with all the neighbors. It would soon be time to plant another crop, as garlic stays in the ground all winter and into the summer. Jessie stuck to one-year bulbs, but Bart experimented with a mix of two-year garlic grown from seeds and one-year garlic bulbs from individual cloves.

Mary knew that Cassie wasn't the greatest cook in the world, but she could trust her older sister to bring a salad filled with ingredients from her own garden. With Jessie bringing the pies, and Julia Merryfield offering up her homemade bread, the meal was complete.

Mary had taken off work in preparation for this feast and Bart had come home early to help her put the final touches on everything. He was now able to even take an occasional day off because they'd recently hired a new fill-in cook.

The twenty-nine-year old Mary was especially excited today. She and Bart had a secret. Tonight they were planning to share it.

Cassie was the first to arrive with twins Kailey and Kelly. They came on foot with each girl balancing an oversized bowl in outstretched, skinny arms. "I know," Cassie said when she saw the look of panic on Mary's face. "They insisted, but they promised to be careful and not drop them." Cassie lunged forward and grabbed Kelly's bowl just before the twelve-year-old tipped it onto the doorstep.

Mary laughed as she rushed over to assist Kailey. "Thank you, girls," she said as they all entered the focal point of the house: Mary's kitchen. This surprised no one who knew Mary and Bart. Glistening steel appliances stood out, offsetting the oak cabinets and a huge oak table at the far side of the room.

Before they had a chance to settle in, Gina breezed through the doorway with other guests behind her. "See who I found walking down the street."

Mark and Julia Merryfield were followed by their closest neighbor, Henry. After Mark had handed over several loaves of bread, Henry passed two bottles of wine to Bart and gave Mary a large jar of honey. He had a box filled with additional jars, one for each household in the dinner party. Mary was still cooing over the bread, wine, and honey, when Jessie and Jonathan arrived empty-handed. The twins groaned. Their faces became crestfallen, until Jonathan laughed and explained that he'd already delivered the much-cherished pies. Once they knew that the most important part of the meal was here, they skipped off into the living room.

Surprise erupted on Mary's face when she noticed the looks exchanged between Jessie and Henry—or quick avoidance on Jessie's part. Mary looked around, but saw that her big sister was the only other one who noticed. Mary wondered if she had been wrong. Something is going on with those two, meaning Jessie and Henry, and here she'd been thinking that her big sister had set designs on their new neighbor.

Cassie interrupted Mary's thoughts. "Willa should be here soon, but she said not to wait. She went to an end-of-summer celebration at the newspaper office. You see, some of the staff members are high school students," Cassie said as she helped load the table with food.

Willa arrived before food was served and—to her delight —was seated next to Jonathan. Gina leaned forward from the other side of Jonathan to ask Willa about the party at the *Wyleyville Express*. While the two girls talked, Bart asked Henry to help him pass out drinks. Gina, who had just turned twenty-one, gratefully accepted a glass of red wine from Henry before he moved on to the next guests.

"Care for a glass?" Henry offered a glass of wine to Jessie.

"Oh, that looks good." Jessie stretched out a hand before she said, "No, I'd better stick to water."

"Even one..." Henry started to ask.

"Even!" Jessie said with such ferocity that Henry looked at her with strange speculation. Bart handed out the water while Henry proceeded down the line. The two men sat when everyone had liquid refreshments. Everyone dug in. One thing Mary learned from the meal was that Kelly and Kailey weren't the only ones who liked her vegetarian lasagna. She was fortunate that the twins ate like birds, for in no time at all, the vegetarian pan was empty.

And then the dessert was served. After the twins snagged pieces of both apple and blueberry pie, everyone sipped hot drinks and ate. Not a scrap of pie was left when Cassie turned talk to the murder in Baxter State Park.

"We haven't worked on our murder board," Cassie said. "The case will be solved without us if we don't get on with it."

Mary teased Cassie and Jessie about their murder board. She let them talk on about the case until Jessie said, "Cassie, we do need to talk about the case, but not now. How about nine o'clock tomorrow?" To Cassie's nod of approval, Jessie turned to Mary. "I believe you got us all here for another reason, besides feeding us all this wonderful food." When Mary blushed, Jessie said, "Come on. I know you've been dying to tell us something all evening."

Mary grinned so hugely that Willa gasped with pleasure. She threw back her chair and bounced over to Mary and hugged her. Willa had been the only person she had told about her secret wish.

"Mary is pregnant," Bart said with a beam of pleasure. Everyone gave a round of applause. All the women hugged first Mary and then Bart. The men shook Bart's hand before they, too, hugged Mary. This announcement erased the very thought of murder from their minds as another round of wine was poured. As before — had anyone noticed — it was only Jessie and Mary who stuck to toasting the blessed event with water.

53

Our hands are full of business, let's away.
—Henry IV, Part 1, 3.2.179

Bright and early the next morning Detective Wilkins decided it was time to visit Wyleyville. Yesterday, Wilkins and Milo had spent a busy day at their desks, rechecking facts. Wilkins had perused witness statements and talked to the coroner once again.

Milo had been given the job of doing online searching. Dara Kane's printouts had led them to more in-depth information, which Milo printed for his boss.

Today, Wilkins sent his valued assistant back to the victim's alma mater to check out the rumors about Crumm's pregnancy. Wilkins went to see a friend.

Police Chief Jeb Michaelson was pleased to see him. Jeb never thought the day would come when the two wouldn't be at loggerheads about which one got credit for solving a case, but that day had finally arrived.

"Well, Charlie, it's nice to see you when we're not both trying to solve the same murder."

"Yes, that's true. But I'm here, in part, to see if you can give me any insight into my case. I also want to talk to you about your local contingent. I really believe that Jonathan Tyler and his mother could be an asset to this case."

"Well, well. I thought I'd never hear the day." Jeb shook his head with pleasure. "Would you care to tell me more?"

So Charlie told Jeb the whole story. Because Michaelson was also in law enforcement, Charlie left nothing out. Jeb knew when to keep his mouth shut; he just listened. When Charlie was done, Jeb said, "So you assume that the only reason Jessie got involved in your case is because her friend Dara Kane is a suspect?"

"Something tells me that you disagree."

"Well," Jeb considered, "Jessie seems to be getting right into this sort of thing. I would bet that if Dara had not been there, Jessie would have taken up the cause of another suspect, say, for instance, that park ranger."

"I see you have gotten to know Jessie Tyler well," Charlie Wilkins said. He had been thinking the same thing. Once a person gets a taste for detection, investigating crimes seems to overtake common sense. "So, how about coming with me to her place? I'd like to know if she's been nosing into our business."

"When there's a way..." Jeb left the statement unfinished as they left his office.

"Walker," Michaelson said in an attempt to catch his patrolman's attention. "Walker!" This time he raised his voice. "Are you listening?"

Officer Ebenezer Walker just grunted and nodded his head.

"We're headed for Killdeer Farm. You're in charge."

Walker only gave his boss a startled stare as Chief Michaelson and Detective Wilkins headed out the door. "I don't know what's gotten into that boy lately. My secretary's on vacation, so he's the only other person on duty today. If I'd said 'You're in charge' any other time, he'd have been fairly dancing with joy." Michaelson shrugged. "I guess I'd better get to the bottom of that situation, and soon."

54

Today will I set forth, tomorrow you.
—Henry IV, Part 1, 2.3.116

Cassie sat in Jessie's dining room looking over the murder board. She seemed distracted, or perhaps, Jessie wondered, she had an idea about the killing. Before Jessie could ask, however, Cassie said, "Did you know you had an unexpected visitor while you were away? You might have told me that you had the police watching your place."

Jessie sputtered over the dregs of her coffee. "What?" She knew perfectly well what this meant, but the timing surprised her. She'd expected Cassie to mention it sooner. She'd wanted to ask about the incident, but how could she before Cassie brought it up? She wasn't supposed to know anything about it.

Cassie just laughed as she set her own cup of coffee down. "So you didn't know! I thought not. Now I'm sorry I didn't say anything sooner. But it was so strange that I had to think it over a bit."

"What happened?" Jessie wanted to hear the story from her friend's perspective.

"Well, I spied Officer Walker skulking around Killdeer Farm. I did wonder about you having the place checked out. After all, you'd just had that security system installed after the July break-in. Walker looked so normal, walking around your property, but when he went out back and didn't reappear from behind the house, I went looking for him."

"What was he doing?"

"He was on a ladder, peeking into one of the upstairs windows of Jonathan's workshop. Now let me tell you, I gave him a piece of my mind. If the chief *had* sent him out here, he surely wouldn't have told that pipsqueak to look into your upstairs windows."

"And he gave no explanation?" *Darn,* Jessie thought. Now she'd have to follow up on the situation with Eb. She had been wondering how long it would take Cassie to tell her about Walker's visit.

Cassie soon tired of the subject and turned to the murder board. "Tell me about these people," she said as she sipped coffee and silently mouthed off the names:

Suspects
The husband
Barbara Porter
Evan Kinderhook
Park Ranger Jerome Goodroe

One by one, they revisited why each was on the list. "I wish we knew the husband's name," Jessie said. "He *must* be the primary suspect. From what I understand, he was in the park and even saw her on the mountain."

"It's too bad that we can't question him and the others. Even those witnesses you have listed here might have valuable information." Below the suspect names were three families listed as witnesses: Rowley, Rockford, and Walters. "What can you tell me about them?"

A long discussion got them nowhere, so Jessie decided she'd run Ben's idea past Cassie—as her own—of course. But first, she returned to the kitchen to make another pot of coffee. While she stood, pouring water into the coffeemaker, and still contemplating what Ben had told her the day before, she saw something that surprised the heck out of her. A Maine State Police cruiser had just stopped in her driveway.

"We have company." Jessie called into the dining room as

she walked out to her screened-in porch to greet Detective Wilkins and Chief Michaelson.

"Welcome to my home, Detective Wilkins. The chief has had the pleasure a few times in the past, so he knows that he is always welcome."

Wilkins was perplexed for a moment, but he shouldn't have been. He always used to think that local policemen got too familiar with the public. He now realized the benefit of it. With no further ado, Jessie had seated them on the sunny porch and was offering them liquid refreshments. "The chief is partial to iced tea, but I just made a fresh pot of coffee. Which would you prefer?"

Both men opted for iced tea; Jessie poured two tall glasses of tea and two cups of coffee. Wilkins was still contemplating the two cups of coffee when he heard Michaelson say, "Jessie, I thought we weren't standing on ceremony these days. You may call me Jeb in front of Detective Wilkins."

"Since we're being informal, you may call me Charlie," Wilkins shocked Jessie. Before she could think of a response, he finished with, "but only when we're alone."

Jessie surprised him with, "It's a deal, Charlie, but we aren't alone." The sight of Cassie strolling onto the porch surprised Wilkins. Jessie laughed at his expression. "You didn't think Cassie was staying out of this, did you?"

"May I call you Charlie, too?" Cassie asked.

Charlie Wilkins doubled up with laughter. He should have known that Cassandra Lakewood would be here.

"I've been caught. Charlie it is, Cassie. Now, before you hit me with complaints, Jessie, I promise that I'm not planning to arrest your friend Dara. She has increasingly become less viable in that respect, but I suspect that she told you about her online searches." To Jessie's nod of approval, he asked, "And what about you? What have you two been doing?"

Jessie was reluctant to tell him, but when he saw Jeb's grin of approval, she said, "Not much. We created a murder board, but we're too far away from the suspects to test it out. And I just came up with an idea, one I haven't had a chance to share with even Cassie." Jessie felt funny about taking credit for Ben's ideas, but the alternative was not an option.

"Well, let me see that murder board, as you call it," Charlie said.

She went inside, but before she returned with it, she quickly jotted a new name at the top of the column of suspects, along with upgrading another person. Charlie Wilkins was shocked to see the top two names. "I have to say, this time you are wrong. One of them isn't even a suspect, but a witness."

Jessie just shrugged, but her new friend Charlie wasn't letting her off that easily. He probed until she said, "Well, then, who do you suspect?"

"I cannot tell you that now, but I will give you a name you have missing. You can change 'the husband' to Richard Cameron. And he *is* a suspect."

"Tell us more about him, if you will," Cassie said.

Wilkins shook his head, "I think I'll leave that for later. I've decided to recreate the scene, or at least as close to it as possible. Are you free to return to the park tomorrow?"

Jessie didn't even have to think it over. Labor Day weekend was fast approaching and after that she would be back to work and on a five day schedule every other week. Since the weekend was not for a few more days, however, she agreed. Wilkins told her that he would like as many of her party as possible to return with her.

When the men were gone, Jessie looked to Cassie. "Care to go, too?"

"You know me and unplanned travel. I better stay home with the twins and livestock, but I'll help you round up the group."

"I hope we won't need to stay long. I want this done and over with so we can get back to our regular lives," Jessie said. While Cassie waited, Jessie called Dara. She was available and excited to be included in what she hoped was the conclusion of the case. "Let's see if your girls can go," Jessie said. She picked up a paperback and slid it into the back pocket of her jeans before they stepped outside and crossed Merryfield Lane.

"Sorry, Jessie," Cassie said, "but Gina's decided to head back to school tomorrow. She and Willa are in town. Gina's saying good-bye to a couple of friends and Willa is at the newspaper office. Willa told me that she's trying to get them to let her write about her visit to the park. I bet if you guys do go back, she'll be bugging them to let her do a story on the outcome of the murder." Cassie led the way into her house as the conversation continued.

"The *Express* should let her," Jessie said. "I remember when Willa brought that article about Ruffy Island over for me to see. She was so proud to get published. She did a fantastic job with how she presented the plight of native Mainers. I still remember her explanation of how some out-of-staters have been buying up our land." Jessie thought back on their last case. The murder victim in Wyleyville just over six weeks ago had been a person who was trying to cheaply purchase all the prime waterfront property in the area and on nearby Ruffy Island. The islanders had almost become the victims of Reginald Trilby's venture.

Cassie beamed. "I'm so proud of my daughter. You know, Willa's still carrying that article around in her pocket."

"I'm sure there will be many more articles," Jessie said as they went upstairs to await Willa's return. Meanwhile, Jessie would take a look at Cassie's newest painting, but before Jessie could coo over the seascape on the easel, Cassie interrupted her thoughts.

"Oops, I was in such a hurry to get to your place this morning, I left my brushes in to soak. As Cassie cleaned her brushes, she asked her friend if she had begun the book she recommended.

"You know me and books, Cassie. I started it yesterday

and finished it this morning." Jessie pulled the paperback from her back pocket.

"Oh, I wasn't sure you'd read it. I thought you didn't care for science fiction." Science fiction was Cassie's favorite genre. She'd been surprised that Jessie had agreed to read *Invasion of the Body Snatchers*.

"Of course I read it. Thanks for suggesting it. I'd never read it, but I have read Jack Finney before. You should read *Time and Again* sometime."

Cassie started to ask Jessie about *Time and Again*, but she heard the kitchen door slam from below. "Oops, the girls are back. I'm done here, so let's go and check in with them."

Downstairs Gina was bummed to hear that she'd be missing out on a return to the park. Not that she wanted to hike again, but she sure would like to be there when they arrested the killer. Willa, on the other hand, was ecstatic. She couldn't wait to get on the phone and talk to her editor. If she were to be there when they slapped the cuffs on the murderer, she would have the story of the century. "When do we go?"

As the afternoon dragged on, Jessie decided to go into town. She had two missions, the first being to visit the new bookstore. She wanted to pick up a book to read during an upcoming visit to her parent's camp. Leslie Wheeler's *Murder at Spouter's Point* was just the thing to take with her.

When the object of her second mission walked through the door of the bookstore, Jessie turned her back, pretending to look at a shelf of local titles. She listened to Eb Walker talk to the girl behind the counter. "Hi, I'm in charge today. If you see anything suspicious, let me know," he said without his usual enthusiasm. When the girl didn't respond, the patrolman left without making further conversation.

Jessie quickly paid for her book and left to follow Walker on his rounds. The young man looked miserable, so Jessie decided to be nice to him. "Hi, Eb," she said when she caught up to him. When he stumbled, Jessie took him by the arm and escorted him to a bench. "Say, are you okay?"

"Why shouldn't I be?"

"I just wanted to thank you for watching my place while I was gone. I know the chief didn't ask you, but it certainly was nice of you to take the initiative."

"I, I just..."

"Oh, I bet you wanted to see if there was anything strange going on at the farm." Jessie laughed. "People find old buildings to be scary. I know Jonathan said his workshop had you spooked, but it really is okay," She attempted to reassure the young man. "Your boss doesn't have to know."

Officer Ebenezer Walker just stared before he tipped his cap and went on his way, this time with a jaunty gait in his step. Had she read his mind, she would have realized that she had not fooled the young man one bit. Killdeer Farm hadn't seen the last of Officer Walker.

55

O, I have passed a miserable night,
So full of fearful dreams, of ugly sights.
                              —Richard III, 1.4.2-3

Morning couldn't come soon enough for Jessie. The dream she so hated had reappeared with a vengeance. She had awoken at midnight with a scream on her lips. She would have raided the liquor cabinet two years ago, but that had been emptied long ago. She did something more productive instead: she visited Ben.

"Did you ever try that idea young Jonathan suggested to you?" Ben attempted to reassure her.

Jessie didn't know why she was surprised that Ben would know about Jonathan's solution to her nightmare problem. "Ben, I did, and it worked, for a while."

"I would suggest that you try it again, for I understand that you have a busy day ahead of you tomorrow. You undoubtedly need your rest." Ben would have given her a pat of reassurance, but since he couldn't, he just encouraged her to go back to bed.

She eventually returned to bed, where she tried to redirect her dreams into something innocuous. Sleep had failed her until she finally drifted off shortly before dawn. She was tired in the morning, but all too soon it was time to leave. Fortunately, Jonathan had offered to drive. They would only be a party of four this time and they wouldn't be dragging all their camping gear to Baxter, so everyone would fit in his extended cab pick-up. With Willa ensconced in the front seat beside Jonathan, Jessie stretched out and slept.

Katahdin Drowning

Less than an hour later, when they picked up Dara in Augusta, Jessie was surprisingly refreshed. "Hello, Dara," Jessie said after her friend had tossed an overnight pack into the back of Jonathan's truck.

"This should be fun." Dara's enthusiasm almost matched Willa's. Jessie and Jonathan just looked at one another and groaned. *Those two!*

Willa and Dara chatted non-stop all the way to the park while Jessie and Jonathan just listened. Jessie decided that Dara was light of heart because she felt she was in the clear. Willa and Dara—who had never been in on the conclusion of a case before—were so excited that they were still high on adrenaline when the south gate of Baxter State Park loomed ahead. At this point Jessie wouldn't have been surprised to see them actually fly from the truck and into the air. Instead they bounced out and danced across the grass as soon as Jonathan had parked at Katahdin Stream Campground.

Most of the faces were familiar to Jessie, but there were a couple of strangers present. Jessie was sure that one was the husband. The other was in the uniform of a park ranger. As Detective Wilkins promised, the campground had been cleared of hikers. She did not know it, but their time here was limited. People not involved in the case had been escorted to other campgrounds until later in the day. Those hiking up Baxter Peak via the Hunt Trail had all left and weren't expected back for several hours. Since they—not this crew—would be allowed back to Katahdin Stream Campground by evening, everyone involved in the case—should they be detained overnight—would be spending the night in town.

"Hello, Mrs. Tyler." Wilkins greeted her before the others in her group. "Ms. Kane, it's nice of you to return. I see one from your group is missing."

"Yes," Jonathan said. "This is Willa Royce, but her older sister had to return to college. Is that a problem?"

"Not really. I don't recall that she had noticed anything that the rest of you hadn't seen. I'm glad, however, that four

207

of you could join us. As I told your mother, Jonathan, we've decided that we can use your insight."

"Are you telling me that you will be asking us to sit in on your questioning?" Jonathan was hopeful, but he wasn't surprised at the response.

"Sorry, but we cannot do that. I *would* like to talk some of it over with you later, however, and I'm not telling you to keep to yourselves while we question people further. I only ask that you tell me, Detective Marley, or Officer Milo if you discover anything pertinent to the case. There are refreshments over there." Wilkins pointed towards a picnic table laden with food. "Since it's almost noon, we didn't want to inconvenience anyone. There are cold drinks in the coolers. Dig in."

Coolers littered the ground nearby, but what Jessie wouldn't give for coffee right now! Wilkins must have read her mind, for he turned to Jonathan and said, "Would you mind taking care of the coffee? Everything you need is over there, including a campfire, but we decided to wait for your expertise." Wilkins winked. "It also gives you a chance to lure the suspects into your web."

When Wilkins saw Marley standing a short distance away he said, "Now, we've got to talk to our primary suspect. His guilt is by no means a done deal, though." With that Wilkins turned and joined Marley as they went inside the cabin with Richard Cameron in tow.

"Well, we have our orders," Jonathan said. "That's a first. Mom, would you say that the good detective is not at all convinced of the husband's guilt?"

"So that's Richard Cameron," Jessie said.

"Well, let's get to work." Jonathan approached the lit campfire and began making coffee. "We, too, have people to quiz."

56

The bawdy hand of the dial is now
upon the prick of noon.
—Romeo and Juliet, 2.4.112-113

Richard Cameron was once again being grilled about both his wife's past and her death. "Mr. Cameron, since you followed your wife down the mountain and came out here at Katahdin Stream Campground, we want you on hand while we check your movements. Surely, if you came through here, like you stated, then someone will be able to vouch for you," Wilkins said.

"I swear I don't know where she went. She must have left the trail after the last time I saw her." Cameron gave a chuckle in the hopes of lightening the mood. "She never did have a good sense of direction. I figured she lost her way, so I sat a while and waited for her near that bridge. Then I came here. I'm sure I was here well before noon."

Wilkins was not amused. "Well, sir, we have a witness who saw you arguing with your wife very near that bridge. What do you say to that?" And he did, indeed, have such a witness. When Marley had returned to the Walters house the next day, the teenaged Melissa had told him all about how she'd seen a tall man arguing with Veronica Verne. When he had shown her several photos of people known to be in the park, she had quickly pointed out Cameron.

"That's a lie! I never saw her," Cameron insisted. After the two detectives stared him down for a full minute, he conceded. "Okay, so I did see her. We talked about the divorce papers. I waved them in her face and she laughed at me. She laughed and walked back towards the mountain."

"And you just stood there? You didn't follow her?" Wilkins asked with incredulity.

"No, I didn't follow her. I was afraid of what I would do." Cameron set his jaw and refused to change his story. "That's when I sat down. I crumpled those papers up and fumed for quite a while before I went the rest of the way down the trail."

"I'll have you know that you must have sat there for quite some time, because the witness saw you enter this campground at a time consistent with you having the opportunity to kill your wife."

Cameron sputtered a few times but said nothing further. He clammed up and they couldn't shake him. Wilkins, therefore, took the questioning onto a new track. "What do you know of your wife's past?"

"Nothing to speak of; she was secretive about it. She said it wasn't important, but I did learn later that she had an affair with a man at the television station. His name is Aaron Porter and he works in an executive position, but he never got a promised raise after the scandal came out."

"Scandal?" Wilkins wondered if this could be Barbara Porter's husband.

"By this time I was married to Veronica. One day, when we had a fight, she said that I wasn't the only person who helped her get a job in the industry. She told me all about Aaron getting her on staff as a stand-in for one of our regulars. She said that she'd dumped him because he had promised her more."

"More? What more did he promise her?" Wilkins asked.

"Oh, he said he could make her a TV star." Cameron snorted. "He didn't. All he could get her was a job standing in front of the camera while the lighting was being tested. I guess she thought that would lead somewhere, which it did, but she dumped Porter once she discovered his limitations." He shook his head in disgust. "That's what she said about me during the fight. She said she wanted more. I had gotten her the job as an exercise expert, but she told me it was too much work. She wanted to be an anchor on the nightly news." Cameron fairly hooted at the idea.

"So you didn't have the pull to get her that job? Is that why she was divorcing you?" Wilkins struck close to the bone.

"Yes, I guess that's true, but she'd never find anyone who could get her that job. She just didn't understand. It takes more than beauty to be a news anchor."

"What about before that? Are you saying that you didn't know her real name?" Before Cameron could do more than react with a startled stare, Wilkins said, "Or that she had a baby and gave it up for adoption?"

"What? What?" Richard Cameron was livid with anger. "She told me that she could never have children!"

"So you know nothing about her past life? She never mentioned a man named Barry Rockford?"

"Who's that?" Cameron countered.

"I'm given to understand that he was one of her lovers in high school—one of many." Wilkins was deliberately cruel. He was getting tired of this man.

Richard Cameron was not amused. "I used to laugh at my nickname. Someone gave it to me in high school. I was a football star, you see, so Rocky stuck. You're saying that a man named Rockford was one of Veronica's lovers?"

"Not exactly." Wilkins couldn't believe that this man didn't know his wife's real name. "Bertha Crumm was his lover. That is your wife's real name. And from what we can discover, she never bothered to have it legally changed. She just left Maine and got a new Social Security number under a new name."

Cameron was astounded, but none of these revelations shook him into admitting that he had killed his wife. They didn't have enough evidence to hold him as yet, so they told him to wait outside. Cameron stalked out and sat gloomily in a rocking chair on the ranger's porch. He couldn't believe it.

Janet Morgan

Not only was he now a widower, but it was to a woman named Bertha Crumm!

57

I fear you speak upon the rack,
Where men enforcéd do speak anything.
— The Merchant of Venice, 3.2.32-33

Barry Rockford was next to take his turn on the hot seat. He was angry about having been pulled away from his work, especially since he and his family were only witnesses, and not suspects.

"Have a seat." Wilkins pointed towards a low and comfortable chair that suspects had been given. Keep them comfortable and they tend to give up more than they intend, had always been Wilkins' philosophy.

"What am I doing here? I have a busy schedule and my family has other things to do, too. Kim is going into high school and she needs to shop."

"If you answer my questions, Mr. Rockford, perhaps we will have you out of here soon," Wilkins said in a soft voice. "The thing is, we checked into our victim's background a little more deeply than I'm sure you would care to have us do." He had decided to pull a bluff. If Veronica Verne, aka Bertha Crumm, had given birth before starting her senior year of high school, this man could be the father. "When were you going to tell us about the baby?"

Barry almost choked. And there you have it, Wilkins thought. The poor sap had never guessed they would find out. Did he think they wouldn't connect his former lover with the famous Veronica Verne?

"That's not important. I learned later that she slept with most of the guys on the team. I never did know if I was that

213

kid's father. What does it matter now?" Barry spoke with a note of finality.

"So you just had a high school fling with Veronica...oh, I mean Bertha."

"Yes, no, I mean, I guess that's all it was to her. Okay, so I loved her. I wanted to marry her, but she said she had plans that didn't include sticking around a one-horse town and stagnating. Stagnating; that's what she called spending her life with me. Besides, she told me that it might not even be mine." Barry sighed with resignation. All the life seemed to have drained out of him with that admission.

"So, what happened to the child, then?" Wilkins asked.

"She gave it away. I don't know what she did with it. I guess she just tossed it out as though it was nothing." Barry shrugged.

"What do you mean by that? Where did it go? Surely, you didn't allow her to..."

"No, no, no. I don't mean *that!*" Barry shuddered at the thought of a mother just throwing a baby into a dumpster. "I mean she gave it away. I guess it was adopted. I don't even know if it was a boy or a girl."

"And you were okay with that? I mean, it *could* have been your child, right?"

"I suppose." Barry had no more to say. More important-ly, he didn't seem bitter about the situation.

58

Your fair discourse hath been as sugar,
Making the hard way sweet and delectable.
                                    —Richard II, 2.3.6-7

Jessie and company hadn't wasted any time. If Ben was right, Richard Cameron was not the killer. During the evening before, she had told Jonathan of Ben's theory and he had his own reasons for tending to think Ben was correct.

To that end, the two had split off to question everyone. Willa helped Jonathan make coffee, while Dara and Jessie canvassed the campground. In an effort to not tip their hand, they made the rounds of suspects and witnesses alike.

Jessie and Dara approached Tessa and Roger Rowley, who were sitting on a stump near where they had once camped. They appeared to be relieved to have something to do. "It is nice to see you two again," Jessie said. "We were wondering if you remembered anything new."

"Well, I will admit that it's nicer talking to you," Roger Rowley said, "but we thought that the police were the ones doing the questioning."

"They are, but we've been given permission to talk to people who are here only as witnesses," Jessie said.

"Why is that?" Roger asked. "Are you detectives, too?"

Dara jumped in with, "In a way. At least Jessie's one, of sorts." She smiled at the couple's look of amazement.

"Oh," Tessa said, "I wish we had more to tell you." That did not stop Jessie from trying, but she learned nothing new from this couple. She only hoped that Jonathan and Willa weren't striking out as well.

Unfortunately, Jonathan and Willa got no further along. Wilkins had been wrong. No one came to the campfire for Jonathan's aromatic coffee, so the two decided on a new approach. Each balanced two cups of coffee as they walked up to Marta and Melissa Walters.

Ms. Walters gratefully accepted coffee from Willa while Melissa stepped over to Jonathan. She made sure their hands touched when she took the cup from him.

"I still can't get over your bravery." Melissa simpered all over Jonathan. He was amused when he saw Willa grinding her teeth. He knew Willa didn't care for girls who did that and Jonathan bet she couldn't understand how intelligent men could lap it up.

Jonathan pursued a new line of questioning: "So, you didn't see anything that day? I understand that you hiked to Baxter Peak later than others, but..."

"Oh, Jonathan, we never went to the top. We only started hiking after lunch. We went as far as that rock wall and turned back. It was way too difficult." Until now, Melissa had pointedly ignored Willa. She only looked in Willa's direction when she snorted. "Don't tell me *you* went all the way up there!" Melissa sneered when Willa only nodded.

"Melissa, dear, do not be rude. I'm sure if she says she hiked to the top, then she did," her mother said.

"Actually, everyone in our group went to the top," Jonathan said. All pretense of admiration for the girl dropped from his eyes. He knew Melissa was either all glitter or she was too young to realize her mistake. He decided that this conversation had come to an end. He could see that Willa was not happy and he didn't want to expose her to Melissa's rudeness. "We'd better leave you, then. We're looking for people who saw something important that day."

As Jonathan rose to leave, Melissa sputtered, "But wait; I did see something, or someone, that is. I saw a man fighting with Veronica Verne." Melissa gazed into Jonathan's eyes in an attempt to flirt with the handsome young man.

"Did you?" Jonathan was all business. He was interested in what she knew, until he discovered that the police already had that piece of information *and* were interrogating the husband as they spoke. Jonathan surreptitiously glanced at the feet of mother and daughter before he sighed, politely thanked the women, and escorted a grateful Willa on to the next person.

"Thanks for defending me," Willa took Jonathan's arm as they moved on.

"That girl was just looking for attention. I recognize a phony when I see one."

"After a fashion," Willa gently chided him as they approached Jerome Goodroe.

"Mr. Goodroe, how are you today?" Jonathan asked.

"I've been better. I'll be happier when I have my little piece of heaven back."

"I see you've been kicked out of your home again," Jonathan said. "How about joining us for coffee over at our campfire?"

Goodroe gratefully accepted. He took a cup of coffee from Jonathan and sat by the fire before he said, "Please, I hope we're past last names. You called me Jerome earlier."

"And I'm Jonathan. Do you remember Willa?" When the ranger nodded and gave Willa an admiring smile it was Jonathan's turn to be jealous. *And where did that come from?* Jonathan had always figured he was too old for Willa. She was like a sister. Well, not really, he admitted, but she was still in high school and if he was too old for her, then this man surely was, too.

"Jonathan?" Willa looked quizzically at Jonathan before she sighed at his inattention and took over. "You see, Jerome, we've been given permission to talk to witnesses. I know you can't be a serious suspect, so would you mind answering a few questions?"

Janet Morgan

"Not at all; not for you."

While Jonathan made a fresh pot of coffee, Willa asked, "I know how busy you've been, but did you notice anything that might have seemed unimportant at the time?"

Jerome shrugged. "You're right. I have been busy. I can't recall anything new. Someone did say that the dead woman's husband came through my camp that day. They asked me about it, but I didn't recognize him. We get so many. Is that what you mean?"

"Well, we heard about that man, too. We think he is one of their top suspects. Do you know who saw him?"

"Afraid not, but today I saw him talking to that Barbara Porter. She seemed to know him, so you might ask her."

"Thanks, we'll do that," Jonathan said. Once he had the new pot of coffee percolating, Willa sat back and let him take over the questioning. They should talk to Porter next, but Jonathan guessed they had better be polite and not just dash off. After all, the police had given Jerome a tough time of it. "Are things any better for you here?"

"Yes, luckily for me, the police have left me alone lately so I can do my job properly. We have a new guy in training, which is a mixed blessing. The kid is raw, but he's taken up some of the slack these last few days. I got behind when I was part of the investigations." Goodroe lowered his voice and said, "To be honest, that's one reason the new man got assigned to me today. We're supposed to be making sure no one leaves until the cops tell them they can go." He wiped a warm brow. "I'm just lucky they aren't still thinking of me as a suspect. After all, I told them how difficult these campers can be. That Verne woman was one for the books, but I've dealt with worse, and I've never laid a hand on anyone."

Jonathan laughed at the admission. "Well, if you think of anything else, let us know. And good luck with the new recruit." When he saw Barbara Porter approaching, Jonathan whispered to Goodroe, "We'd better go and talk to that Porter woman."

"Go get her." Goodroe snorted as he walked away.

"Hello, Mrs. Porter. I wonder if you have a minute to chat." Jonathan held up a fresh cup of coffee by way of a lure. She didn't accept the coffee, but approached with a scowl on her face.

"Don't give me that, young man. I heard that you and your bunch think you're amateur detectives." Barbara Porter was angry at being told she must return to the park. She had a new job back home and hadn't appreciated being dragged back to Maine. "What gives you the right? You should be suspects, just like the rest of us. And I read somewhere that the cops should look very closely at the ones who found the body."

"Is that so?" Officer Milo interrupted the interview before it had a chance to begin. "You let us decide that one. As a matter of fact, Detective Wilkins wants to see *you* next, so come along. And I don't want to hear any complaints about *us* wasting *your* time. You *are* a suspect, whether you like it or not." With that, Milo took Barbara Porter by the arm and escorted her over the bridge and towards the cabin.

59

O, when she is angry she is keen and shrewd.
            —A Midsummer Night's Dream, 3.2.323

Barbara Porter was livid: red anger splotches blossomed on her face. "How dare you people treat me this way! I have an important job back in Boston. I know people."

"Oh? And what people do you know?" Wilkins was not impressed.

"Politicians; I know important people in government. I have a new job at the state house and they value my expertise. Do not mess with me!"

"Well, do they know you lied to us?" Wilkins parried.

"Lied? Lied about what?"

"We know all about Aaron Porter's involvement with Veronica Verne," Wilkins said.

"So what! I already told you that. He worked for the TV station that hired that tramp. She played him and he got her a job. What does my ex-husband have to do with me?"

"The fact that he wasn't your ex-husband at the time has a lot to do with it. She broke up your marriage."

"I told you that, too. That nosy woman who illegally searched my tent found that out for you. What's new?"

"It's new that you held back important information," Wilkins said. "Your husband was on the rise when all this happened. Your life did not change for the better after that."

"His didn't either." Barbara snickered. "Not long after that Cameron man married that *Verne* woman, Cameron found out how she got her job. He made sure that Aaron didn't get the promotion he'd been expecting. And Cameron got Aaron fired as soon as he returned to work the other day. Did he tell you that?"

"Interesting," Wilkins said. Cameron hadn't told them that. Wilkins was still contemplating a second interview with the husband, when Barbara Porter shot his theories out of the water.

"It's just too bad he was gone from the park so early."

"What do you mean?"

"I saw him come off the trail early in the afternoon."

"How do you know what time Veronica Verne died?" Wilkins said. It looked as though Porter had just slipped up.

"Well, it was hours before those busybodies found the body."

"As a matter of fact, the woman's time of death was several hours before those 'busybodies' found the body."

"Well, then, maybe Cameron did it after all. And he isn't the only one who could have killed Veronica. Why don't you ask those people who found her? Maybe *they* did it together. A group killing or something; after all, they seem like a suspicious lot to me."

Because Jonathan and Willa had just lost their next prey, they looked around for someone else to quiz. When they overheard Jessie ask Evan Kinderhook a question, they perked up.

"I repeat, why are you so insistent on blaming the husband?"

"If that man had kept his wife in line, I wouldn't be in trouble. She was all over me; I mean, couldn't he satisfy her?" Kinderhook was showing a new face, one that Jessie did not care for. She had only been hoping that the young man could give her a better timeline on who he saw on the mountain that day. Instead, she found him to be belligerent. He apparently had no interest in helping them.

"So you saw no one from the time you deliberately smashed your camera until you returned to the campground hours later. Do I have that correct?"

"How did you know I smashed the camera on purpose?" Kinderhook asked.

"So you *did* break it on purpose. I was only guessing about that." Jessie smiled with a satisfaction that was short-lived.

There stood Officer Milo, waiting to take yet another witness out of their clutches. And she had just been getting started. What happened next shocked her. "You, Kinderhook, and you, Mrs. Tyler," Milo said. "Both of you come inside with me now."

Jonathan just stood gape-jawed as his mother and the young cameraman were both escorted into the cabin of enquiry.

Inside, Milo was greeted with a less than enthusiastic boss. "Milo, what are you doing? I asked for..."

"Hold it, boss; I overheard something you need to hear." Milo pointed to Evan Kinderhook. "This young man admitted to Mrs. Tyler that he smashed his camera on purpose, just like the victim's husband said. And we all thought Cameron was lying to get someone else blamed." Milo shook his head in disgust.

"Well, is that so? Did he tell you that, Jessie?" Wilkins slipped. Both Milo and Marley were surprised at Wilkins' familiarity, but said nothing. They were more interested in what 'Jessie' had to say.

"Yes, he did." Jessie wanted to say more, but Kinderhook turned red in the face and began sputtering.

"I wasn't about to climb to the top of that darned mountain just to suit that woman. She'd pushed me around from the start and made my life a nightmare. She was all over me, and to what end?" Once started, Kinderhook couldn't stop digging the hole deeper. "It wouldn't have gotten me any further along. I have ambitions, too, you know. I heard how she slept her way to the top. If I wanted to do the same, it wouldn't be with her. She was just a user. Anyone with eyes could see that!"

"And before you tell any more lies, let me tell you what we know. You wiped the hard drive in your camera. Just what *was* your plan?" Wilkins calmly inserted his question into the tirade.

"Well, the station had no use for it after the high and mighty Veronica Verne was no longer their big star. And for your information, I didn't have a plan. I just wanted to get out of this thing in one piece. That stupid husband seeing me didn't help." Kinderhook looked around the room. He seemed to sense the danger of his situation. "Say, you don't think I did it, do you? I was going to sneak back into camp and hide in my lean-to, but when I saw those two bickering, I went back and hid in the woods."

"You saw the victim with her husband? And just when did you plan to tell us that?" Marley injected himself into the fray.

"Oh, I knew you'd figure out that he did it, so why should I get involved? If this woman hadn't interfered," Kinderhook pointed an accusing finger at Jessie, "I wouldn't have told you at all."

"Just go outside for now, but do *not* leave the campground under any circumstances." Wilkins dismissed the young man. Once Kinderhook had left the ranger station, Wilkins turned back to Jessie. "Well, you do seem to be my good luck charm. How did you get him to admit to smashing the camera? I'd always wondered how the camera got broken."

Jessie laughed, "I just pretended I knew it all along. It works so well, most people just sputter out their excuses. He never guessed it was a bluff."

The policemen laughed in unison before Wilkins shocked the others with his next statement. "I'm narrowing in on *my* man. How about you? Are you trapping your 'man' so to speak?" Wilkins looked at the other officers and explained, "You see, Jessie thinks the killer is a woman."

"Why?" Officer Milo asked.

"Small footprints," was all Jessie said.

After she dropped that bombshell, Jessie walked outside and into the sunshine. When she was gone, Marley asked, "And just when did she become Jessie?"

60

Piece out our imperfections with your thoughts.
—Henry V, Prologue, 23

The Wyleyville contingent sat at their old campfire discussing the case over fresh coffee. They sipped as Jessie explained why the detective's statement held validity.

"It's actually Jonathan who came up with the idea that the killer might be a woman. I didn't realize it right away, but I told him later that I saw small footprints all around Veronica Verne's dead body. That's when he came up with the idea. Right, Jonathan?"

"Right; Mom told me about the footprints after we got home. Finish what you told me." Jonathan encouraged his mother to continue.

"Until I thought it over, I assumed that the prints were the victim's. You see, those seemed to be the only prints, until the ranger went down there, that is. Besides, the only other option was that she danced around a lot to make the marks in the riverbank before she threw herself into the water and pushed her own head down and held it there."

"Aunt Jessie!" Willa giggled. "Oops, I shouldn't have laughed at someone's death, but you're being silly."

Jonathan smiled at Willa. "Right you are. That's just the point. The only alternative is too silly to believe."

"So we have to rethink our list?" Dara said after successfully controlling her own urge to chuckle. She was not nearly as sorry about it as the others, but they must get serious. "Did you bring the list, Jessie?"

"I copied it into my diary. See, here's my original list, the one I compiled while here." Jessie held it out for everyone to see. "It's changed since then. If we're to eliminate anyone with large feet, we end up with only the women, even ones who were never considered suspects by the police."

While the others talked, Jessie looked around the campground. She wondered if they would ever find the killer. She stared at all the suspects and witnesses in turn, wondering which one was the killer, until Jonathan's comments intruded.

"I think you can take the Walters, mother and daughter, off that list." Willa misinterpreted Jonathan's reasoning and groaned. "No, Willa, I didn't take them off because that teenager flirted with me. I looked at their feet. They're too big."

"That girl flirted with you?" Dara asked.

"So who does that leave?" Jessie didn't want to even *think* about a teenager flirting with her twenty-one-year-old son.

"You have the list, Mom. May I see it?" Jonathan reached out and took the notepad. "Well, we have Barbara Porter. She has small feet, *and* she really hated that woman. How about Tessa Rowley, Mom?"

"Well, she has tiny feet, too, but I can't discover a motive. She seems like a nice lady and I got the impression that she and her husband did all their hiking together. When would she have had time?" Jessie considered as she put down her empty coffee cup.

"Nevertheless, we need to talk to her again. What about the Rockford mother and daughter? I mean, the husband could have been in on it with them. After all, the only reason they aren't being seriously considered is because they alibi one another. Maybe they all did it, with the husband standing back and letting the women do the dirty work." Jonathan beamed with pleasure at his clever theory.

"Really, Jonathan," Jessie said before she took her notebook back and began to write. "We have Barbara Porter,

Tessa Rowley, and the whole Rockford family." She looked up at Jonathan. "If you think the Rockford family could have killed Verne en masse, then how about Roger Rowley being added as Tessa's accomplice?" Jessie was only half serious about this, but she didn't see that there was too much difference between blaming the Rockford family and the Rowley couple.

"You have a point, Mom, but I think both theories are rather dumb. I can't imagine this as anyone's idea of family entertainment. 'Let's all go out and kill together.'" Jonathan was back in his silly mode, to which the women all joined in with a round of laughter.

"Okay, let's get serious. If we blame the Rockford family, then the Rowley couple goes on the list, too," Jessie said. "But seriously, we need a second list to look at. I think the police might have Barbara Porter on their list, but none of these others. So far today, they've questioned Richard Cameron, Evan Kinderhook, Barry Rockford, and Barbara Porter."

"Are those the only people they're looking at?" Dara asked as she looked down at her own feet and was grateful—for the first time—to have average sized feet.

"Well, I think Porter's the most likely from their list," Jessie said after contemplating for a moment. "Of course, I doubt if they're serious about Rockford because his wife and daughter were with him all day." Jessie went on to explain what had happened during her inclusion into the inner circle of police interrogations.

"What did they say when you mentioned the small feet?" Willa asked.

"Oh, Detective Wilkins just told them that we suspect a woman. He laughed, but maybe they're starting to consider our theory."

61

'Twere to consider too curiously to consider so.
                                            —Hamlet, 5.1.206

Detective Wilkins began to understand how Jessie had come to the conclusion that the killer was a woman, but he had procedure to follow. The absence of man-sized footprints had led him to think that perhaps there were two people involved in the murder. He guessed—as Jonathan was now suggesting—that there was a man already in the water, while a female accomplice had lured Veronica Verne to the water's edge. Wilkins, too, had been keeping an eye on the size of everyone's feet as he had interrogated them. He had been surprised—however—when Jessie had mentioned small feet. That woman doesn't miss much, he noted.

Wilkins decided that it was time to talk to everyone one more time. He had begun with Barbara Porter—she of little feet—but he couldn't figure out just who could have been her accomplice. He looked at everyone before he wondered if she had been working with Richard Cameron. The only problem was that she had implicated Cameron with her comment that he had passed through the campground at such a time that kept him in the running. Of course, he argued with himself, Porter had given Cameron an alibi for the time she thought that Veronica Verne might have been still alive. "No, that doesn't work." He didn't realize he'd been talking aloud. Had she been in on it, she would have planned it to give them both an alibi. The killer or killers certainly knew when the woman had died.

"What doesn't work?" Marley had been sitting quietly ever since they had allowed the Porter woman to leave the cabin. He'd said nothing until now because he'd seen Wilkins thinking something through.

"Oh, I've been contemplating on Jessie Tyler's thoughts concerning a female killer with small feet. That's why I wanted to talk to the Porter woman again. The thing is I don't think a woman did this, at least not alone."

"I have two questions. Why couldn't it have been a woman? If it was, why couldn't she have killed Veronica Verne all by herself?"

"Well, I suppose she could have, when it comes to that." Wilkins wanted Jessie Tyler to be wrong. *What a sexist I'm becoming.*

"I have a tendency to think a man did this, so I guess I should have asked a different question," Marley said. "What I mean is, what's wrong with your theory? I take it that you're thinking Porter had the help of a man. I suppose we could go through the lists again. We had the Boston police interview her ex-husband, and not only was he home all weekend, but there is still no love lost between the former married couple."

"Oh? What was his alibi?" Wilkins was curious.

Marley laughed, "Yet another of a long string of beautiful women. But you don't suspect the ex-husband, I take it."

"No, I don't think it was him. I was contemplating Verne's husband and Porter getting together to exact revenge. But in that case, Porter would have known the time of death and not tried to implicate Cameron by saying he was in the campground too early. In truth, Verne had been dead for quite some time before her body was discovered."

"That seems to mean that either Barbara Porter is stupid, or she really didn't know when Verne died," Marley shook his head. "This gets us no further ahead, does it?"

"Actually, it does. I guess I should have told you, but I went to see the local policeman in Wyleyville yesterday and he took me to Killdeer Farm."

"What's Killdeer Farm?" Marley asked.

"Jessie Tyler's place; and before you say anything, I know we don't usually consult potential suspects. You see, this is the third case I have been on where Jessie Tyler and her son have been involved. The first time, we actually thought one or both of them killed the victim. I soon learned I was wrong. Now I realize that their chief of police trusts her and so do I."

That was the longest admission Detective Hank Marley had heard from Wilkins. Marley had come to see that Wilkins was normally a man of few words, but since he was in a talking mood, Marley pressed. "You suspected Jessie Tyler that first time? Why?"

"Well, back in June, the man responsible for her husband's death was found dead inside the locked library where she works. Even though a few other people had access to the building, she was the only one with a motive. And, of course, the son could have borrowed her library key, so it seemed to be an open and shut case." Wilkins shook his head with resignation. "Let me tell you, never assume anything. Those two will push themselves into our business whenever someone they care about is in jeopardy, but they are not murderers. And before you ask, Jessie was trying to defend her son like a mother bear defends her cub, while Jonathan was trying to do the same for his mother. It was Jonathan Tyler who solved that case while we sat on our hands."

"Oh, I thought from the way you talked, it had been Mrs. Tyler who cracked that one," Marley said.

"No, but she and a friend caught the killer last time. They actually had him tied up with a Venetian blind cord before we came to their rescue."

"If you came to their rescue..."

"Don't ask. Just know that we would have had egg on our faces if they hadn't figured out who did it." Wilkins grinned with pleasure.

"So that's why you decided to let them get involved in this case. Be honest. Do you think that they're closer to discovering the killer than we are?" Marley asked, while hoping for a negative reply.

"Well, if Jessie Tyler is correct, then the killer is one of our witnesses, not one of our current suspects."

"Well, that sounds just plain silly." Marley would soon come to regret that remark.

"That's as may be, but I tend to think that she could be on the right track. Let's look at those witnesses and see what we can see." Wilkins produced the list and read:

Tessa and Roger Rowley
Marta and Melissa Walters
Barry, Esther & Kim Rockford

"Well, we already talked to Rockford today. Why don't we start at the top?" In reality, Marley was still leaning towards Verne's husband, despite the 'small feet' theory, but he decided to go along with Wilkins. Since the more they talked to witnesses and suspects alike, the more they seem to learn, who knew what they would uncover with a final round of questioning.

Detective Wilkins agreed with Marley. He knew they had not spoken to Esther Rockford lately, but she could wait. If he had to hear her complain again on how they were wasting her husband's precious time...well, he just wasn't ready for that. "Yes, let's talk to that Rowley couple first."

This line of enquiry produced a dead end. Nothing either Tessa or Roger Rowley had to say led them closer to a solution. The couple seemed totally devoid of interest in Veronica Verne. "Well, thank you again for your time. If all goes well, we'll be breaking up camp within the next few hours." Wilkins consulted his notes on the couple before he said, "We'll probably release everyone by five this afternoon, but if not, we've booked several hotel rooms in town. Do not leave until we give permission."

Just as Tessa and Roger Rowley were leaving the building, Millinocket Detective Walter Briscoe arrived. He had been invited to take part in their interrogations, but had been finishing up other business in town. "Well, how goes it?"

"Sometimes I think we have it almost wrapped up, and then new evidence comes to light. We're questioning all the witnesses that we talked to before. Yesterday, before we returned here, Officer Milo and I called and talked to the ones we didn't think it was necessary to recall to the park. We learned nothing new from any of them."

"In other words, you still don't know who killed Veronica Verne," Briscoe said.

"Ouch! You say it like it is, Walt." Wilkins looked up from his paperwork, "May I call you Walt?"

"Of course you may," Briscoe said.

"I'm Charlie and that's Hank." Wilkins pointed towards Marley. "I have recently discovered that standing on formality puts everyone on edge."

Before Walter Briscoe could reply, Officer Milo returned with Marta and Melissa Walters. "Thank you, Milo." Wilkins invited the young man to sit and take notes. The first thing Walters did was to look down at the feet of both women. He, as Jonathan had done earlier, immediately decided that neither woman had feet little enough to be part of the crime.

"Mrs. Walters, I know that you were out on the trail too late to know much about what happened on the day of Veronica Verne's death, but did you see anything at all out there?" To her negative response, Wilkins continued: "What about that morning? Did you see anything in camp, anything at all? Sometimes the most unimportant bit of information can lead to the solution of a case."

"To be honest, I wasn't even up when that woman headed out on the trail. I did see her come into camp the evening before, but other than bossing the ranger and her cameraman around and being generally mean to everyone, I didn't hear or see anything important."

Up to this point, Marta's teenaged daughter had been

sulky and silent. "Well, I did!" Melissa Walters said with self-importance. "And I was about to tell what I saw to that adorable Jonathan, but the girl he was with was rude to me."

"What did you see?" Wilkins groaned. Jonathan Tyler almost got ahead of him again.

"I heard that woman make a call on her cell phone on the first night they were here. It was late in the evening—after she had been kicked out of her cameraman's lean-to. She was royally pissed off and she was talking way too loud. I'm sure the cameraman heard her. I wonder why he didn't tell you about it." The girl must have gotten a kick out of her story because she sneered as though she had scored a victory.

"Oh? And just who did Veronica Verne call?"

"Well, I have no way of knowing *that* but it must have been someone back where she works because she told someone to fire her cameraman as soon as they got back to Boston." The teenager beamed with pleasure.

"Is that so," Wilkins said.

"Yes, and I bet he was mad enough to kill over it," Melissa said.

The girl would have gone on, but Wilkins had heard enough. As Milo escorted mother and daughter out, Wilkins heard Marta chide her daughter that it wasn't nice to enjoy getting other people into trouble. This revelation made the officers change their order of questioning. Evan Kinderhook was escorted inside once more.

"I had no idea of that telephone call until after I returned to Boston," Kinderhook said after being told what a witness had heard.

"Are you saying that our information is true?" Marley took up the questioning.

"Yes, as a matter of fact, it is, but I had no idea about her call at the time. Your witness is right that I kicked Verne out of my sleeping area. I wasn't going to let her seduce me, but I admit that later on I had a change of heart. That's why I followed her off the mountain. I was going to tell her that I wouldn't object to a little flirtation if it got me a raise." Kinderhook shook his head. "But I didn't see her again, after her encounter with the husband."

"In other words, you lost your job and we're to believe that you wouldn't have killed her," Marley said with a note of disbelief.

"Oh, I didn't get fired. I'd been given another opportunity before I even got back to the station, so I took it. I made more money on Veronica Verne's last days than I would ever make at that miserable station. They treat us cameramen like dirt, so I quit. I called the other place and got a job right then and there."

Marley shook his head with disgust: "You sold the film on Veronica Verne to a competitor? Is that what you're admitting?"

"Yes, and I'm being interviewed for a book on the life and death of a physical fitness star. As an insider, I can ask my price." Evan Kinderhook grinned with delight.

"How did you do that? You told us that the hard drive was wiped clean."

"Well, the camera also has a memory chip. I transferred the footage onto that before I deleted the hard drive. I knew you'd take my camera, so I palmed the chip. Look, you guys are looking in the wrong direction. I think that Porter woman and Richard Cameron are getting altogether too chummy. I heard someone say that she's his alibi."

No one was interested in listening to this young man tell more lies. Wilkins let him go back to his site with a wave of a hand. "So, what do you think? Is he telling the truth, or is he lying again?"

"I think the first part of his story is just evil enough to be true, but the second part? Let's ask our amateur detectives if they've seen Barbara Porter and Richard Cameron together."

"I think we should call Boston and make sure

Kinderhook really did quit his job. You have friends on the Boston Police Department, don't you, Charlie?" Briscoe asked.

"I sure do. Hold on a sec." Charlie Wilkins nodded to Milo and the two of them went into the back office and shut the door. "Milo, call our contact at the Boston PD. We need to find out if Evan Kinderhook was fired or if he quit that television station."

Wilkins returned to the living room, but it wasn't long before Milo came in to tell them that Kinderhook had, indeed, quit minutes before he was to be fired. More interesting, however, was that Verne's producer had received a disturbing telephone call just that day. Milo was informed that the other station has already aired the film.

Milo was sent back into the office to call the station that was now in possession of the Verne footage. Moments later, Milo reported his findings. The station manager admitted that Kinderhook was to be their primary source for a tell-all on Veronica Verne. Kinderhook had also bragged to the studio that he had all the dirt on her because the two had been lovers.

"Well, what do you know," Wilkins said. "Kinderhook pops to the top of our list." He paused to think over the situation. "Okay, perhaps we've put too much credence in the 'small footprints' theory. Perhaps he came in from downstream and somehow lured her into the water. Yes, she would have danced around a bit, maybe to entice him over to her." Wilkins wasn't sure even *he* believed this one, but it was a possibility.

62

Your hand, your tongue;
look like the innocent flower,
But be the serpent under't.
　　　　　　　—Macbeth, 1.5.65-66

The detectives sat together contemplating their next move. Every time they talked to Kinderhook, they got a new story from him. "Okay," Wilkins said. "Let's talk to the Wyleyville contingent about Kinderhook. Let's see if they saw Porter and Cameron getting along too well today. If not, they might have made other observations."

"What about Dara Kane?" Marley wasn't to be deterred. "It doesn't matter that her feet aren't small. She could have an accomplice, like one of those girls that were with them. If we have the whole group from Wyleyville come in, we can hone in on Kane at some point of the interview, just in case."

Detective Wilkins shook his head with resignation. "Okay, let's try it, but do *not* suggest that one of Cassandra Lakewood's girls is an accomplice. That's *all* we need."

"Who?" Marley asked.

After Wilkins reminded him who Gina Day and Willa Royce were, he said, "I hope you're ready for the wrath of Jessie Tyler when she learns that we have more questions for her friend. And, I repeat, do not say anything about one of those girls being part of a plot." Wilkins went outside himself and soon returned with Jessie, Jonathan, Dara, and Willa. "What can we do for you?" Jessie asked.

When they heard what Kinderhook had said, Jonathan snorted. "I liked that fellow, until today. He seemed nice, but after I talked to him, I decided that he was sneaky. Boy, were

236

we ever fooled."

"So you heard what he told your mother?" Wilkins asked.

"Yes, and you should have heard his put-down of the husband just before you arrived to whisk him off inside here," Jonathan said.

"Oh, did I miss something?" Wilkins asked.

"He told my mother that Veronica Verne's husband must not be much of a man, if he couldn't satisfy his wife. He said that the woman was all over him and he had to fight her off."

"Well, he pretty much told us the same thing. He also said that this afternoon the husband was acting very friendly with Barbara Porter. This is one of the reasons why we called you four in to talk to us. Did any of you see something to that effect?"

"Actually, I did," Willa responded. "They were off near the edge of the woods with their heads together. I couldn't hear what they were saying. Did any of you?" When the others shook their heads, Willa finished: "I couldn't hear them, but he put his arm around her when she began crying."

"Well, that seems to agree with one aspect of Kinderhook's statement." Wilkins concluded that the cameraman hadn't lied to them after all. Of course, it still didn't exonerate him.

"Is that all, Detective Wilkins?" Jonathan asked. He had more people to quiz and hoped that they could solve this thing soon.

"Not quite," Detective Marley took the initiative. "We have a few more questions for Ms. Kane, but the rest of you can go now."

"Fat chance," Jessie said. "If you want to talk to Dara, I'm staying." Jessie insisted on acting as Dara's surrogate attorney. Jonathan knew his mother wouldn't let Dara get into trouble, so he and Willa gladly left her to it.

Detective Hank Marley objected to Jessie's presence, but he found himself overruled because Wilkins disagreed: "Marley, if you want to prolong this until Mrs. Tyler calls in an attorney, go for it. I, for one, do not mind having her here."

Marley only shrugged as he began the questioning. He took Dara through the whole day of the murder: from their getting up, to a visit to Grassy Pond, through lunch, and on up to Katahdin Stream Falls. At no time had she been alone. Every time Marley suggested that Dara could have slipped away by herself, Jessie Tyler countered with an alibi. She was not to be budged. If Marley were to believe it, Jessie Tyler must have been fastened to Dara Kane's side with glue.

Marley soon gave up and began questioning Dara on her past. "Are you sure you know nothing more about the victim's past that could help us out?"

"Not exactly, but I hate to suggest anything untoward," Dara said. She was hesitant to speak, but she had seen something today that had shocked her.

"Suggest away." Wilkins couldn't help but interrupt. It was his nature to strike while the iron was hot. He would be darned if yet another person in Jessie Tyler's circle got ahead of him. "Tell me what you're thinking, no matter how strange it might sound."

"Well, do you remember those pages I printed out from Facebook?"

"Yes, yes, but we decided that was just the ravings of jealous people." Wilkins was fast regretting opening this line of questioning.

"Not necessarily," Dara said as she extracted copies of the pages she had turned over to Wilkins a couple of days earlier. She began to read, "'I hate you. You ruined my life and I'll never forgive you. You are such a bitch! I wish you was dead!' were the closing statements of someone named Kimmie."

"So what?" Marley jumped in. "There's no one here named Kimmie."

"But there is a witness named Kim, and well, she's a teenager, so she might call herself Kimmie," Dara said.

Both detectives objected. The child was only fourteen.

"Not a chance. A child couldn't have done this," was out of Marley's mouth before he realized that there was such a thing as children who killed.

"Oh, but I wasn't exactly suggesting the girl. What I meant to tell you was that I think she is Bertie's child, or I should say Veronica Verne's. Do you know if the woman ever gave birth?"

Dara saw the look on Jessie's face, but forestalled her. "Before you ask, Jessie, I saw that girl for the first time today. None of you ever saw Bertie as a child, but that kid is identical to the way Bertie looked when I knew her back in high school, right down to the smirk on her face. I was staggered by the resemblance. When I finally saw Kim, I was instantly suspicious. She or her father—maybe both of them—is in it up to their ears," Dara said with firm resolution.

63

Neither detective wasted time dismissing Jessie and Dara. They needed to check out Dara's suggestion that Kim was not only the Kimmie who wrote of her hatred for Veronica Verne on Facebook, but that she might be the woman's natural child. As they discussed their next move, Milo summoned Barry Rockford.

Detective Briscoe had been entranced with the comings and goings of these people. He had solved his share of cases, but he had never seen so many who figuratively stabbed one another in the back. As Barry Rockford sat on the edge of his chair, Briscoe sat back and listened with growing interest.

"Mr. Rockford, I don't want to hurt your family, but we've learned something new that must be pursued," Wilkins said. "You told us earlier that Veronica Verne—excuse me—Bertha Crumm gave birth to a child and gave it up for adoption. Or should I say *her.*"

"Her? What do you mean her?" Rockford asked.

"Well, was the baby a girl?" Wilkins posed the possibility.

"How should I know?" Rockford demanded a little too forcefully.

"I think you *do* know," Wilkins bluffed as he shuffled through a stack of papers that had nothing to do with Rockford.

"What does it say there? Did you find her birth records?" Barry Rockford was beginning to sweat.

240

"Oh, we found out plenty." Wilkins knew he had the man now.

"Okay, so it was a girl, but what does it matter?"

"Well, we don't think the child was adopted, at least not away from the family. We think you're the father and Bertha Crumm's daughter is Kim." Wilkins looked at a sheet of paper again before he lifted his eyes in accusation. "Shall we test our theory?" He pulled the single sheet away from the others. "Shall I read the birth certificate aloud so we can all hear it?"

"So what if Kim *is* Bertie's daughter? I fail to see what it has to do with Bertie's death. She had a new name and a new life—away from ours—and we had nothing to do with her being murdered."

"Well, I think it has quite a bit to do with Veronica Verne's death. She came into camp, saw her daughter, and planned to cause trouble. Isn't that so?"

"No. No, she never saw my daughter. She left town all those years ago and never tried to see *my* daughter." Barry had been angry, but now he appeared sad. "Look, she didn't want my child, but I did, so I had her sign away all rights before she walked away. And before you throw my earlier statement in my face, I lied about not knowing who the father was for a reason. Bertie was promiscuous, but I had a test run after she put my name on that birth record." Barry pointed towards the blank sheet of paper Wilkins had been holding.

"I wanted to be sure. I wasn't being played for a sucker, but I wanted that child if she was mine. And she was, so I kept her. I even named her. Bertie couldn't even do that. She put 'Baby Rockford' on the birth certificate. Isn't that so, mister detective?"

"Right," Wilkins said with a straight face. "But continue. I want to know why you or your daughter couldn't have killed the woman. After all, you two could have done it together."

"Kimmie? You think Kimmie could have done it? She

doesn't even know that woman was her mother. She thinks her real mother died years ago."

"So she knows that your wife isn't her mother?" Wilkins asked.

"Of course; she thinks she was adopted. Just look at my wife and me. Kimmie doesn't look like either one of us. Esther was another classmate, one who agreed to marry me to give Kimmie a mother. I admit that I married Esther for that reason, but she's a good mother. You leave them alone. I do *not* want Kimmie to know about her birth mother. Leave it alone."

"Yes, I see on one of my documents that you married one Esther Carson a short while after you graduated from high school," Wilkins said. This document was a real one, but he made sure to keep all papers out of Rockford's sight for the time being. "Your wife was willing to marry you, an eighteen-year-old with a child. You expect me to believe that?"

"Well, it happens to be the truth. She always loved me, but I never saw her as being more than the girl next door."

"Until you needed a mother for your child," Wilkins said.

"She didn't mind. And you leave my daughter alone." Rockford seemed willing to do anything for his daughter.

"I'm afraid I cannot do that." The minute Rockford had called his daughter Kimmie, he knew that Dara Kane had been correct. She *had* been the one who said all that awful stuff about Veronica Verne. "You see, Mr. Rockford, I'm afraid that your daughter *does* know about the victim being her mother."

Wilkins pulled the Facebook page concerning Kimmie from his file and handed it to Rockford. Kimmie's father read in silence before he lifted a sad face to the detective. "But, look; Kimmie's all talk; she's just a kid. She couldn't have known. She was too young to realize about Bertie abandoning her. She couldn't have found out." Rockford spoke with less conviction than before. "Besides, she never left my side that day."

Katahdin Drowning

Barry Rockford's life shattered as he realized the truth. He had tried so hard to protect her. He didn't understand how she had found out about her natural mother. It was true that his daughter and Esther had never gotten along as well as he would have liked, but that was none of their business.

64

There's a time for all things.
—The Comedy of Errors, 2.2.65

The minute Barry Rockford was escorted back inside the ranger station, Jessie and Dara went to work. Esther Rockford, who was sitting alone outside one of the free lean-tos, appeared sad and angry all at once. "Hello, Mrs. Rockford," Jessie said. "I'm Jessie Tyler and this is my friend Dara Kane."

The woman seemed ready to kick them out of her small space at first, until she suddenly lashed out: "Say, I know you." She pointed at Dara. "I thought you looked familiar..."

"Yes, I was in school with you, way back when," Dara said.

"I remember you being two years behind us in school. I also remember Bertha harassing you all the time. Do the police know about you?"

"Don't you talk to your husband?" Dara raised a legitimate question.

Jessie knew that Barry had already told the police about Dara so why wouldn't the wife know? "That's a good question, Dara," Jessie said before she turned towards Mrs. Rockford.

"Why are you so surprised?" Jessie waited for a reply, but got none. "Well?" Still no response was elicited. "Look, Dara was upfront with the police. They checked her out. They know that she didn't have much of a reason to want the Verne woman dead. Besides, she has four other people who can alibi her. What about your husband?"

Katahdin Drowning

"Oh, Jessie, I just remembered something," Dara said as she turned to face Esther Rockford. "I never looked at you closely before now. You're Esther Carson. You were in the same class as Barry and Bertie." Dara turned to Jessie. "She was always in the background, mooning over Barry, even though he only had eyes for Bertie."

"That's not true," Esther said. "He married *me*."

"But he had a child with her." Dara zoomed in for the kill.

"Shush!" Esther whispered. "Kimmie's in there. She doesn't know about that woman. And you can't blame her. The three of us were together all day."

Before any of them could react, Kim rolled out of the lean-to with an ear bud dangling from her left ear. "Oh, I knew about my real mother all along. She threw me away like trash. Dad never told me, but I found out." She sneered at her 'mother' and tossed her hair in the same way Dara had seen Bertie do all those years ago. "Just look at me. I'm beautiful, too, just like Veronica Verne."

Meanwhile, Jonathan and Willa were having another talk with Barbara Porter. "Hello, again, Mrs. Porter," Jonathan said. "Would you mind talking to us for a bit?"

"About what?" she asked. "I'm getting sick to death of all these questions."

"Well, would you rather wait for the police to come and get you? If you talk to us, maybe we can convince them that they are mistaken."

"Mistaken about what?" Barbara Porter took the bait.

"Well, they seem to be under the impression that you and Richard Cameron are more than friends. And, of course, that leads to the possibility that you two are in it together."

"What in the world are you talking about? I barely know the man."

"Oh?" Willa chipped in. "Then why was he hugging you a little while ago?"

You go, girl, Jonathan thought. He was proud of Willa for jumping into the fray. Two assailants were better than one.

"He wasn't hugging me," Porter said. "He saw me crying and asked me what was wrong. I decided it was time to get something for myself, so I told him that when he got my husband fired, it meant that my alimony got cut." The woman smiled. "Men are such saps. I knew he'd come to the rescue."

"How did he come to the rescue?" Willa asked.

"Well, I was just cuddling up to him. He said he'd help me out financially after we return to Boston. He thinks I'm beautiful. You see, he didn't know me when my husband fell for that hussy. He doesn't realize that I lost weight and changed my hair color. I mimicked Veronica in an attempt to get even. I had planned to get *her* husband away from her and let her see how she liked it. The problem is that I never got the chance."

"So you never got the opportunity *before* today?" Willa pursued Porter like a lioness who gave its prey no chance to think before reacting.

"Of course not, you dummy! I never met the man before today. Oh, I saw him in the campground on the day the bitch got hers, but I never got a chance to meet him." Porter laughed. "Funnily enough, I gave him an alibi, so now he thinks I'm so nice, I can do no wrong." Porter laughed again, but this time it did not sound at all pleasant.

"So, you're telling us that you're just now moving in for the kill?" Willa asked. "You expect us to believe that?"

"I don't care what you believe. If the police question me, I'll tell them the truth about our little encounter." Porter squinted. "Say, who told you about our meeting?"

"That's something you'll need to ask the police—when they come for you." Jonathan wisely closed the interview. He and Willa smiled at one another as they walked off leaving an upset, conniving woman.

"What do you bet this ruins all her plans, especially if we tell the police and they pass it on to Rockford?" Willa asked.

Katahdin Drowning

Jonathan just smiled at Willa with admiration.

65

Ah, that deceit should steal such gentle shape.
                            —Richard III, 2.2.27

Jessie now realized that Ben had been correct. He had not liked the sound of Evan Kinderhook from the outset, but he had been Ben's second choice. Ben had been correct that the cameraman was not a nice man, but he wasn't the killer, Jessie realized.

"So, Dara, are you convinced?" Jessie asked after the four of them had compared notes. Jonathan, too, had known of Ben's theory, but Willa was still in the dark. She had figured out that the killer was either small footed Barbara Porter or the petite Kimmie. Because those two seemed to be the only ones that Jessie and Jonathan talked about, she misinterpreted the results.

Just as Jessie was about to set Willa straight, Detective Wilkins approached. "So, have you amateur detectives solved this case for me?" To Jessie's nod, his eyes bugged out. "No," he shook his head, "not a chance."

But Wilkins wasn't the only one listening to what Jessie had to say. Just as she expounded on her theory, a loud growl emitted from behind her. A red-faced Esther Rockford flew at Jessie's back and tore at Jessie with a vengeance. "You will *not* take my family away from me!"

Wilkins and Jonathan dashed forward to protect Jessie. They were attempting to pry Mrs. Rockford off Jessie's back when Marley and Briscoe came running. The two detectives had just left the ranger station when they witnessed the

248

attack. Officer Milo still stood on the cabin's porch in rapt silence. He watched, assuming that his boss was about to close the case. What he saw shocked him. He was rooted to the spot, unable to help.

"Kimmie didn't kill that woman! She never left my side. I told you that already." Esther Rockford screamed as Wilkins and Jonathan pulled her away from Jessie. "I hate you! I hate you all! You *won't* do this to my family! *I'm* her real mother in every way that matters, not *her!*"

Marley and Briscoe entered the fray as the woman now tried to claw at the men. Roger Rowley stepped forward to help the officers, but the woman was fierce. Milo, too, had finally dashed to the rescue; he was the one who finally pinned Esther Rockford around the legs and knocked her to the ground.

Once they had Esther Rockford immobilized, Rowley said, "I can't believe it. I saw the resemblance, but are you saying that kid is Veronica Verne's daughter?" To Jessie's gasping nod, Rowley went on: "I never would have believed that a youngster such as that kid would kill her own mother." He was ashamed of himself for holding back vital information, but who would have guessed. "I'm so sorry for not telling you before."

"Tell us what?" Wilkins said through clenched teeth as Mrs. Rockford struggled once more; he grappled with the woman who had twisted from Milo's grasp. Her bid for escape was short-lived, however, when Milo finally managed to handcuff her. Wilkins looked up from the ground and urged Rowley to continue.

"Well..." Rowley still couldn't believe it. And why were they handcuffing this woman? "Well, I saw the girl come into camp alone that day. A short time later, her father arrived and began looking for her, but she'd gone into their tent. By the time she came back out to join him, she'd changed her shirt. It had been wet, you see."

"Are you saying the kid did it?" Wilkins was astounded.

That is not what Jessie had told him. "The kid? Are you sure?"

"Wait a minute." Jessie interrupted this shift of blame. "Listen to what Mr. Rowley is telling us. He said that the kid came into camp, followed by her father." Jessie turned to Rowley. "What about this woman?" She pointed to Esther Rockford, who was still struggling to escape from Milo.

"Oh, I didn't see her until quite a while later. I can't tell you where she was," Rowley said.

"What's going on?" Barry Rockford ran forward. "Kimmie told me that my wife attacked the Tyler woman. What's this all about?"

"There seems to be some confusion concerning where the three of you were on the day Ms. Verne died. Did you or did you not say that you never left your daughter's side?" Wilkins squinted at the man. "Did you lie to us?"

"Not at all," Rockford said. "Kimmie tripped on the way back into camp. She got her hands dirty, so she went to the stream to clean them. She got her sleeves wet in the process and rushed ahead to change her shirt. I was only a couple of minutes behind her, I promise you."

"What about your wife? Where was she?" Wilkins asked with distain. He hated it when witnesses kept changing their stories.

Before Rockford could respond, his wife growled as though she were being killed. Rockford only lowered his head with shame. "She and Kimmie got into an argument on the trail, so she wanted to walk off her anger."

"And you forgot to tell me this?" Wilkins asked.

"No, I didn't forget. I was protecting my family." Barry Rockford sat on the ground with a thump and held both hands over his face. His mumbled speech was barely audible. "I was protecting my family. Esther is family. I never dreamed..."

"Never dreamed what?" Wilkins was relentless. It was all well and good for Rockford to be upset now, but he should have been honest with them from the beginning. He, and then his daughter, had come under suspicion. One of them might have been arrested had his wife not attacked Jessie Tyler.

"I just thought she was walking. Kimmie said something to her that made her mad. I didn't hear it, but I know it was just girl talk."

"No, it wasn't." Kimmie slowly approached. She slid in beside her father and sat on the ground at his side before taking one of his hands into hers. "She's always been mean to me. That's why I told her that I was going to go and live with my real mother—and take you with me."

"Oh, dear; you shouldn't have said that. I would never have gone back to Bertie. She didn't want us, anyway." Rockford now encased his daughter in his arms. "I'm sorry to say it, but Esther is all we had."

"I know, Daddy. I know all about my *mother*. But *she*," Kimmie pointed to Esther, "was never a real mother to me. I only wanted *you!*" Kimmie turned away from the woman who had helped raise her and snuggled deeper into her father's arms.

66

Ambition's debt is paid.
　　　　　　　—Julius Caesar, 3.1.83

Once he saw Esther Rockford led away between the two burly detectives, Charlie Wilkins approached Jessie to make sure she was okay. When she assured him that she would be fine, he said, "You sure do bring out strong feelings in people, Jessie."

"I sure do, Charlie," Jessie responded to the amazement of those around them.

"Jessie? Charlie? When did you two get on a first name basis?" Jonathan asked.

Jessie and Charlie just smiled as they watched Esther Rockford taken into the ranger's station to see what she had to say for herself. It wasn't long before she was driven away by Millinocket Detective Walter Briscoe. State Police Detective Hank Marley escorted Barry and Kim into town in another police cruiser. Wilkins would soon join them to close the case, but first he wanted to talk to some of the witnesses.

"I need to take statements, so I'd appreciate everyone's patience," Wilkins said from the porch. He pointed to Roger Rowley. "You first," he said before turning to his assistant. "Milo, you're with me. This won't take long," he said as they went back inside the ranger station.

A short time passed before Milo came out with Rowley and dismissed everyone but the Tyler party. "We've decided that if we need further statements, we'll contact the rest of you, that is, unless anyone noticed anything that they haven't shared with us yet." When no one spoke, Officer Milo continued. "Detective Wilkins has arranged hotel rooms in Millinocket for anyone who wants to stay overnight." Everyone decided to leave for home right away.

As others packed up to leave, Jessie, Jonathan, Dara, and Willa were escorted into the ranger station one last time. Statements were swiftly taken and the Tyler party was filled in on what Esther Rockford had to say before they were also allowed to leave.

"Well, I hope you keep us in mind if you get stumped again, Charlie," Jessie laughed.

Charlie groaned. It was *all* his fault! He'd started this whole friendship thing, and now Jessie Tyler was pushing it to the limit.

"I guess you should get the last word. After all, you solved the case."

No, Jessie said to herself as she looked over and saw a twinkle in Jonathan's eyes. *Ben solved this case.*

67

And then return and sleep within mine inn.
    —The Comedy of Errors, 1.2.14

The happy foursome celebrated the closing of another case with a hearty meal at Applebee's in Augusta. Huddling around in an oversized booth, they chatted with excitement for what seemed like hours to Jessie. After eating, they once again piled into Jonathan's truck. He drove them to their respective homes.

Dara was greeted by Reesie, whose actions informed her that she'd better stay put for a good long time.

Willa was immediately off to the *Wyleyville Express* to file her report. Unbeknownst to the others, she had snapped off a few shots of Esther Rockford as she sat on the ground in handcuffs. Willa's editor would be delighted.

Jessie and Jonathan did not separate at Killdeer Farm until they had told Ben everything. Once they had congratulated him for unraveling their most difficult case yet, Jonathan asked, "How did you figure it out?"

"Well, when you told me about the small footprints all around the body with no others in sight, I guessed it might be a woman. I never would have figured that a woman was capable of murder, but it just had to be."

"I get that," Jonathan agreed, "but you never did think it was anyone but Esther Rockford. Why?"

"Now, Jonathan, I did think it might have been that Kinderhook lad. The thing is, that created another problem. If he was the killer, then he had a female accomplice, one who lured Veronica Verne close enough to the water for him to grab her." Ben chuckled with pleasure. "You know, Jessie, your son told me how those footprints appeared as though the victim had done a dance before she wound up face-down in the water. I knew he was teasing me, but it did make me realize the importance of those footprints."

"Jonathan, what did I tell you about teasing Ben?" Jessie suppressed a grin.

"Mom! You're one to talk!"

"Yes, she certainly *is* one to talk, but do not let us get off the purpose of this visit. I told your mother to look for someone with small feet, but when she related the dynamics of that Rockford family, I knew something was off about them." Ben shook a finger at Jessie. "For shame, Jessie, you should have guessed the solution of this one. You gave it away when you described them. I know that science had not advanced far in my day, but even then we knew that it is rare, indeed, for two dark haired and brown eyed people to give birth to a blonde child with blue eyes. And their physique was so different from that of the girl."

"That's it? That is all it took?" Jonathan was astounded at Ben's logic.

"Almost, but not quite," Ben said. "I also know the nature of women. I died for one, you know. A woman who is in danger of losing her family will do anything to keep it. Put an average-looking female like Esther Rockford in close proximity to what you called a gorgeous woman, and... well, nature *will* run its course. I am guessing that Mrs. Rockford approached the woman in hopes of having her fears assuaged."

"Yes, yes!" Jonathan was excited to have something to contribute. "Charlie—we get to call Detective Wilkins that now—he told us that Esther went off to confront the woman. Of course, we'll never know now if the Verne woman meant it or not, but she told Esther that she could get her family back any time she chose."

"There you go," Ben said. "Something tells me that is not the end of the story, though."

"You are so wise, Ben. Charlie thinks that Veronica Verne had no interest in saddling herself with a husband and daughter, but she was undoubtedly taunting the wife. That was the victim's mistake, to taunt the other woman. And it was Esther's mistake to believe her; that and the idea that either Barry or Kim even wanted a change." Jonathan looked over at his mother. "What do you think, Mom? You've been awfully silent."

"Oh, I think Barry Rockford never did love Esther and she knew it. But I don't think he still loved Veronica, either, for what it's worth. And I know that Kim hated her real mother, but she wasn't too happy with Esther, either," Jessie said. "I think those two will be better off without either one of them."

Ben and Jonathan nodded in agreement.

What a pleasant change! Jessie awoke from an unusually pleasant dream. Moving day, which had taken place more than twenty years ago, had been one of the most exciting days of Jessie's life. That had been the day when she had come to live at Killdeer Farm. Ever since early childhood, Killdeer Farm had been a constant part of Jessie's life. It had been her second home; she had stayed there with her grandparents at every opportunity. She had tended gardens out of doors with Grandpa and learned to cook and preserve the crops inside the farmhouse with Grandma.

After she had married Jonathan, the couple had rented a cottage on the edge of town. It had been an idyllic time, even after the big move. Grandma and Grandpa were getting too old to take proper care of Killdeer Farm. One evening after they had served Jessie, Jonathan, and their infant son Jonny a hearty dinner, they proposed something fantastic.

"Come live with us," Grandpa had said while Grandma had nodded her approval. Both grandparents beamed with delight when the couple had readily agreed. This was the perfect home. And Jonathan had only to see the farm once before he'd felt the same way. Jessie's dream had recreated it all: the happiest years of her life.

Living here alone was bittersweet, but at least Jessie had fond memories. And waking up in such a pleasant way was a nice change. It made her especially receptive to a new project because today was the day she would do something special for Ben.

The sun nipped the horizon as Jessie sat on the ground looking at the spot between the two apple trees that cradled Ben's bones. She sipped coffee in the bright morning sun and planned the best place to plant her newly purchased plants so as to make Ben's final resting place special. Setting her cup aside, Jessie dug in the dirt and planted several bags of daffodil bulbs around the trees. She would broadcast several packets of forget-me-not seeds over this spot next spring, but today she set out a large tub of mums for fall color.

Jessie gazed up to see Ben looking out the window of his upstairs home. She smiled and waved as she thought how pleased he would be when he watched the daffodils sprout next spring. As she rose from the ground, Jessie wiped dirt from her jeans and set aside her gardening tools. She walked towards the workshop, ready to meet a day filled with new beginnings.

Bibliography

Books:

AMC Maine Mountain Guide. 7th ed. Boston:
    Appalachian Mountain Club Books, 1993.
Austin, Phyllis. *Wilderness Partners: Buzz Caverly and
    Baxter State Park.* Gardiner, Maine:
    Tilbury House, 2008.
Clark, Stephen. *Katahdin: a Guide to Baxter State Park &
    Katahdin,* 5th ed. Shapleigh, Maine:
    Clark Books, 2005.
Fendler, Donn as told to Joseph B. Egan.
    Lost on a Mountain in Maine. Rockport, Maine:
    Picton Press, 1978.
Thoreau, Henry David. *The Maine Woods.* Riverside ed.
    Boston: Houghton Mifflin, 1893.

Information Center:

Baxter State Park Headquarters
64 Balsam Drive
Millinocket, ME 04462

Maps:

Katahdin, Baxter State Park, Maine. Twin Mtn, NH:
    The Wilderness Map Co, 2002.
Maine: Katahdin Baxter State Park Waterproof Trail Map.
    Canada: Map Adventures, LLC, 2011.

Web Sites:

www.baxterstateparkauthority.com

www.DonnFendlerFilm.com

www.maine.gov/dps/msp

Janet Morgan was born and raised in coastal Maine. She received a BA in English from UMA while working full-time as a librarian. She is a member of Sisters in Crime, Maine Writers & Publishers Alliance, and the Wiscasset Public Library Writing Group. Her prior Killdeer Farm mysteries are *Poetic Justice* and *Composted Tyrant*.

CPSIA information can be obtained at www.ICGtesting.com
Printed in the USA
BVOW041700290513

321841BV00001B/2/P